The Comfort of Strangers

by
Peggy J. Herring

Bella
BOOKS

Ferndale, Michigan
2001

Bella Books, Inc.
P.O. Box 201007
Ferndale, MI 48220

Printed in the United States of America on acid-free paper
First Edition

Editor: Lila Empson
Cover designer: Bonnie Liss (Phoenix Graphics)

ISBN 1-931513-09-0

For
Laurie McMillen

You've made a difference in my life.

Acknowledgments

I would like to thank Frankie J. Jones for being my first reader and knowing when and how to tell it like it is. She understands the process and always knows what to say to move me in the right direction.

I want to thank J. M. Davis for her suggestions after an early reading of the first few chapters.

I'd also like to thank Terese Orban and Kelly Smith for giving us Bella Books.

A special thanks goes to Sherrill Morris, a good friend whom I appreciate more than she knows. She helped me keep things flowing with this project by always asking if I had written any "alien sex" lately. I'm giving her full credit for that phrase.

A very special thanks goes to Laurie McMillen for her constant support and insight. I couldn't have done it without her.

About the Author

Peggy J. Herring is a native Texan and a 1953 baby. A very rewarding stint in the Army from 1974 to 1977 deemed her fluent in Morse code for a short period of time.

In the past Peggy has been active in the lesbian community on local, state, and national levels. She was one of two San Antonio representatives for the Texas Lesbian Conference state board.

She lives on seven acres of mesquite in south Texas with her cockatiel and a green-eyed wooden cat. When she isn't writing, Peggy enjoys fishing, camping, and traveling.

She is the author of *Once More with Feeling, Love's Harvest, Hot Check, A Moment's Indiscretion, Those Who Wait,* and *To Have and to Hold* with Naiad Press. In addition, she's contributed short stories to the Naiad anthologies *The First Time Ever, Dancing in the Dark, Lady Be Good, The Touch of Your Hand,* and *The Very Thought of You.*

Her book *Calm Before the Storm* was published by Bella Books in September 2000, and Peggy is currently working on another romance titled *Beyond All Reason.*

Chapter One

K Sector

Kricorian poured more wine in her glass and then gave Lela a generous bowl of steaming soup. With Lela's research keeping her late in the lab, it was the first meal they had shared in several days.

"Are you sure you don't want any?" Kricorian asked as she held up a flask. "This wine is better than the last batch."

"None for me, thanks." Lela slowly stirred the soup before trying any. Cooking had never been one of Kricorian's strong points.

"It's your turn to clean the purifier," Kricorian reminded her. She laughed at the way Lela groaned and rolled her eyes. It had been much too quiet in their cubicle lately since they had both been working extra hours. "I've missed you," Kricorian said, surprising herself with this sudden revelation. "How much longer will this special project of yours take?"

"It's hard to say." With a sigh and an involuntary shudder, Lela said, "I'll try to make time for the purifier tomorrow."

Kricorian chuckled. Her thick, graying hair fell easily into place as she shook her head. "I cleaned it for you this morning." She grinned as she watched Lela blow on a spoonful of soup and then sigh with relief. Kricorian once again offered the flask of wine as she refilled her own glass. "Are you sure you won't try some?"

"Not tonight. I volunteered for border patrol with Colby later."

Kricorian arched an eyebrow. "Border patrol? How did Colby manage to draw border patrol? She's a senior pilot."

"She owes someone a favor." Lela tossed her auburn hair out of her eyes and nudged her bowl away.

"How are things with you and Colby these days?"

They exchanged a serious look before Lela nodded and managed a faint smile. "We'll eventually end up being just friends, but right now we play well together. Those impulsive types can be exciting sometimes."

"Yes indeed," Kricorian agreed, sipping her wine thoughtfully. She pushed up the silver sleeves of her uniform. "Very exciting, in fact. Your mother was like that, you know."

Lela looked up, surprised, and could see the love in Kricorian's eyes at the mere mention of Lela's mother. Meridith and Lela's sister, Romney, had been dead nearly fifteen years now, but Lela's warm childhood memories of the four of them together were still vivid. Lela cherished those memories, and enjoyed sharing them with the only person who treasured them as much as she did. Lela leaned back in her chair, forever grateful to this woman for still loving her mother after all these years. Feeling almost like a child again, Lela said very softly, "Thanks for cleaning the purifier for me."

2

~ ~ ~

The wind began to blow and dropped the temperature just low enough to be uncomfortable for a moment before Lela's uniform made an adequate thermal adjustment. It was late, and the flight deck was deserted except for a few workers in the repair bay. Everywhere she looked there were crates and baskets of goods ready to be sorted and stored. The upcoming trading season promised to be a good one.

Lela saw Colby emerge around the corner at the far end of the loading dock, helmet in hand and short black hair scrambled from the wind. She was tall and angular, and carried herself with confidence. Lela found Colby's spontaneous streak and carefree easiness attractive. They were having sex more frequently, but Lela knew something was missing from the relationship.

"You're early," Colby said. She opened the small door to the mobilecraft. It was the airship of choice for most K Sector pilots while on duty. Mobilecrafts were bigger than the newer, more compact spidercrafts. Border patrol in a spidercraft made the shift seem longer since there was less room inside.

The hum of the mobilizer meant everything was ready. Colby set her helmet down, leaned over, and kissed Lela on the mouth. Lela put her arms around Colby's neck and returned the kiss.

Lela had recently discussed with Colby the difficulties of transitioning from being lovers to just being friends. It was no secret that their relationship was changing, but in the meantime that didn't prevent them from sleeping together. Lela knew that Colby was also interested in someone else, and Lela was surprised at how little that bothered her. They still connected on a sexual level and liked each other's company.

"Border patrol," Lela finally whispered, bringing them back to the present.

"We've got some time still. Get in," Colby said with a wink. "Let's take advantage of it."

3

Lela walked around the mobilecraft and got in on the passenger side. She had never made love in a mobilecraft before.

"Are you early for a reason?" Colby asked as she reached over with her right hand to fondle Lela's breast.

"Maybe. What about you? Why are you early?"

Colby turned to her and smiled. "I'm early because I was hoping you'd be early." She kissed Lela again and pushed the button that slowly reclined their seats. "We have twenty minutes. We always make such good use of our time."

Lela couldn't argue with that. They both lived with other people and seldom had their cubicles to themselves.

Reaching over to open Colby's uniform and touch her breasts, Lela was reminded how much she liked them. Colby's nipples were naturally hard. The only evidence of their arousal was a slight change in color and a puckering that never failed to make Lela smile when she noticed it. Lela knew how much Colby liked having her breasts sucked.

"You are so good at that," Colby whispered as Lela tugged on one of her nipples with her lips. "I could come this way, you know. Just from what you're doing now."

Lela could hear the desire in Colby's voice: She liked making Colby come first. If they worked hard enough afterward, she'd be able to come again when Lela did. She knew that for Colby, the second one was always better and stronger, and twenty minutes was a little more time than they usually had for such things.

"Harder, baby," Colby hissed into Lela's ear. "Please. Suck harder. Yes . . ." She opened her thighs and grasped Lela's right hand and put it between her long legs. Colby's hand was there also, rubbing herself while Lela slipped two fingers inside of her as she continued licking, sucking, and tugging on Colby's nipples.

Colby threw her head back and pumped wildly against Lela's fingers. Lela knew when to stop sucking and when to begin slowly licking. Colby pulled Lela closer, her body demanding pleasure from Lela's fingers. Colby came quickly and then rolled to her back with a drowsy, silly grin on her face.

"You are so *good* at that," she said.

Lela touched Colby's breasts again and wished just once that they didn't have to be in such a hurry all the time. She drew light circles around one of Colby's nipples. The wicked smile she saw when Colby turned back on her side again made Lela chuckle.

"How many times have you done this in a mobilecraft?" Lela asked.

"Too many to count." Colby got Lela's uniform open and her hand eased down Lela's stomach. "You're wet," she whispered before kissing Lela deeply.

It was a relief for Lela that Colby finally remembered what she liked. Kissing was one thing that could send Lela over the edge quickly. A good kiss at the right moment had the potential to make rooms spin and music play in Lela's head. Colby wasn't the best kisser Lela could remember being with, but Colby was beginning to learn when and how to deliver one.

Lela's hand left Colby's breast and worked its way back between Colby's legs. They came together this time, and Lela was once again amazed by their ingenuity. After a brief two-minute rest, they put themselves together again and went to work. Lela knew she would miss this once they became just friends.

Border patrol at night was always dull. At least during the day the scenery had some interesting potential. "I haven't done this in years," Lela said. Despite the monotony, she was enjoying herself. It was a nice change of pace from the lab.

They checked the out-stations and delivered a few supplies. There was a reunion of sorts at the meadow where old friends of Kricorian and Lela's worked and lived. Nooley and Ab were botanists and liked having visitors there at the meadow. Lela wanted to stay longer and talk with them, but Colby was on a strict schedule, so they were off again, through the grass and then over the trees near the lake. Colby set their course for the far boundaries of K Sector, and within minutes they were into the moors and scanning the computer screen for anything out of the ordinary.

A short while later as they were on their way from the moors to the crater section on the south end, Lela noticed a problem with the security signal. There seemed to be a break, which was unusual. *A break in the signal could mean a number of things.* She began to run through a drill in her head. *An electrical storm in the area, a computer malfunction at the remote relay station, someone entering or leaving K Sector in some unauthorized manner ...*

A red light flashed on the panel, and Lela felt a chill rush through her body. Someone or something had just damaged the force field.

"What's going on here?" Colby said as she smartly rapped the panel with a gloved knuckle.

"Alert Command," Lela said as her heart began to race. When Colby didn't respond, Lela said a little louder, "Alert Command."

Colby shot her a puzzled look. "Why? It's only a malfunction." She smacked the panel again with the back of her hand.

"You don't know that. What's the procedure?" Lela hadn't flown border patrol in years. Regulations could have changed since she'd done it last.

"Mobilecraft One, this is Security Command. Acknowledge," came a voice through the headsets in their helmets. Lela's heart was pounding.

Colby touched the mouthpiece to her helmet. "Security Command, this is Mobilecraft One."

"We show a break in the signal due to unauthorized

entry," the voice at Command said. "Restore the signal at this location immediately." Coordinates appeared on the screen as Lela entered them into the mobilecraft's computer.

"What is it?" Colby asked, tilting her head as she touched the mouthpiece.

"We don't know yet," came the reply from Command. "Nothing's showing up on the scanners here."

"Wonderful," Lela mumbled. She peered through her tiny window, searching for the light to the remote. She finally saw something in the distance and pointed in its direction. "At two o'clock."

The glow of the remote wasn't as bright as it should have been. *A surge of power could have damaged the reactor*, Lela thought.

Colby landed the mobilecraft and scrambled out. Lela was right behind her. The terrain was rough, and Lela could feel the sharp edges of the crater's surface through her boots.

Colby touched the mouthpiece in her helmet again. "Command, this is Mobilecraft One. We're at the remote."

Lela heard a low hum coming from the cubed structure and tugged on Colby's arm. "Where's the switch for the reset?"

"I don't know. I've never had to do this before."

"The best I remember, it's different for this station. This one's older than the others," Lela said. She felt along the outside wall of the building and said, "Command, this is Mobilecraft One. We still have a glow on the remote. Tell us where the reset switch is."

"It's inside, Mobilecraft One. Near the solar pack."

"Kricorian!" Lela said, alarmed, recognizing her voice. Her heart raced. "What's happening?" *Kricorian has been alerted and is now the voice of Command? This gives the entire incident a whole new meaning.* The situation was at best serious if not critical.

"Listen to me carefully," Kricorian said, her voice flowing into Lela's helmet. "One of you has to crawl inside the remote to reset the signal. And you have to do it now."

Lela looked at the small building with its eerie, greenish glow. She wasn't eager about going inside. There was no telling what sorts of crater creatures were living there. The only way in was through a tiny window about six feet off the ground.

"Lela," Kricorian said, her voice again flowing into Lela's helmet. "One of you has to go in. *Now*. We are vulnerable as long as the signal's out."

"I'm smaller," Lela said. "I'll go." She grabbed Colby's arm and urged her around the side of the building where they found the window. "Give me a boost." She tapped its corner, and the window popped open. Lela pulled herself up and heard scurrying close by. Wanting to get out of there as quickly as possible, Lela tried not to think about anything but the reset switch on the opposite wall near the solar pack.

"Be careful in there," Colby called from the ground.

Lela could feel her uniform adjusting its temperature again; the remote was close to forty degrees warmer inside.

"Mobilecraft One," Kricorian's crisp, clear voice said. "Several unidentified spacecraft have been located due north heading in your direction."

"Let's get out of here!" Colby yelled from outside.

Lela found the reset switch and pulled the lever, filling the remote with bright green light. She sailed across the floor and jumped for the window ledge, pulled herself up and then out the window. Colby broke her fall just as the first unfriendly spacecraft swooshed over their heads.

"What was that?" Colby sputtered as she ran in the direction Lela was pushing her.

"Mobilecraft One," Kricorian said, "the signal is back and the force field is reactivated. Good work. Now get out of there."

Three more alien spacecraft buzzed over them, sending

lasers slicing through the crater's surface. Sizzling sounds, explosions, and loud thuds surrounded them as flying rock scattered everywhere. Lela scrambled into the mobilecraft and flipped switches to get them on their way.

"Hurry up! Let's go!" she yelled, but Colby was nowhere in sight. Lela climbed back out of the mobilecraft and found her on the ground several feet away. "Colby," she breathed, and rushed over to her. Colby's chest was covered with blood, and the right side of her face had been torn away by a jagged rock. More unidentified spacecraft zoomed by, shooting lasers and spraying more huge chunks of crater rock all around them. With a sudden rush of adrenaline, Lela heaved and pulled Colby's body back to the mobilecraft. After she got Colby in, but before she could get herself safely inside, flying debris caught her in the shoulder, knocking Lela flat on her back.

"Mobilecraft One," Kricorian said urgently, her voice again flowing into Lela's helmet. "Get out of there."

Lela tried to sit up, but the pain in her shoulder brought tears to her eyes. She touched the mouthpiece to her helmet. "Kricorian," she said weakly just as more spacecraft zoomed by overhead. "We're under attack."

"Lela, get out of there!"

Lela struggled to sit up and then get to her knees. "Who are they?" she mumbled, pulling herself up against the mobilecraft. She fell again and grabbed her shoulder. Lela was afraid she would lose consciousness. Trying desperately to get to her feet again, she made her way inside and fell across the seat; the door closed automatically behind her.

"Who are they?" she asked again, breathing heavily and feeling sick to her stomach. She blinked several times to clear her head and saw blood everywhere.

Colby's blood.

"Corlon Star Fighters," came the solemn reply into her helmet.

Queasiness spread through Lela's body. Corlon Star

Fighters. Depending on how many of them had gotten in, everyone in K Sector could be killed within the hour. She remembered how her mother and sister had died so many years ago and how the people of Bravo Sector had nearly been destroyed in a raid.

"You're not *moving*!" Kricorian's voice barked into Lela's helmet. "Why aren't you moving? Get out of there*now*!"

Lela tried to touch her mouthpiece to speak, but her vision was blurry and the control panel in front of her was spinning. She didn't know where she was or why she felt so bad. She closed her eyes and flinched at the pain in her shoulder when she tried to sit up.

"What's happening, Lela?" Kricorian yelled. "Say something!"

"I'm hit," Lela mumbled, feeling very close to passing out. "We're both hit." She reached over and shook Colby's bloody arm. "Wake up," she whispered. "Please wake up." The last thing she heard was someone else from Command issuing further orders to her.

Chapter Two

K Sector

Kricorian checked on Lela again and was glad to see that she was finally beginning to move more as she slept. Kricorian had been up all night, afraid to leave her for even a moment. Icy fear had crept through her veins during the flight to the crater section to get her, and terror had gripped her heart when she saw the blood in the mobilecraft once she had arrived on the scene.

Lela had stirred a few minutes earlier, grimacing. She had a massive bruise where a huge chunk of crater rock had struck her, and a knot on the side of her head. She had no broken bones, but it would be awhile before Lela would be up and around. The healer had recommended that she rest for a few days even though herbal therapy had taken care of a good portion of the pain.

Kricorian converted the cubicle into a work area so she could be closer to Lela. As director of K Sector's Security Command Post, Kricorian would be busy with the investigation into how Star Fighters had penetrated the force field. K Sector had lost one mobilecraft and two pilots in the attack, but they had managed to destroy all six of the invaders. Lela and Colby having restored the signal when they did, prevented scores of other Star Fighters from entering K Sector's perimeter. Kricorian knew how lucky they had been to have so few casualties. Her job now was to find out why the force field had failed and to prevent it from happening again.

She stayed near Lela's bed for hours and watched her sleep. Lela looked so much like her mother at times that it pierced Kricorian's heart just to see her. *Fifteen years*, she thought. *Meridith and Romney have been dead fifteen years.* Losing them had been devastating. At the time, Kricorian thought she would never recover from it. Lela was like Meridith in many ways, and Kricorian had loved Meridith and Romney dearly. After all these years together, Lela seemed like Kricorian's own daughter. Lela had been only seven when her mother and sister died in a raid very similar to the one they had just experienced. Always an emotionally strong child, Lela had comforted Kricorian during her own grief after Meridith's death, and then they had both continued to comfort each other after discovering that the building Romney had been in had exploded, killing everyone inside.

There had never been a question about where Lela would go or with whom she would stay when her mother died. Kricorian and Lela belonged together, and they had taken care of each other off and on during different times in their lives. Kricorian had known very little about children then, but luckily for them both, Lela had been an exceptional child.*And she's grown into an exceptional woman*, Kricorian thought as she watched Lela sleep. She couldn't have asked for a more wonderful daughter.

Kricorian fell asleep in her chair, but woke up the moment she heard Lela stir and groan. She was there beside her when Lela opened her eyes and looked around the tiny room.

"Hi," she said, her voice rough and hoarse.

Kricorian smiled. "Hi. How do you feel?"

"Terrible. My back hurts." Lela looked down at the bandage on her shoulder and arm. "What happened?"

"There was a raid. You were caught in the middle of it. Do you remember anything about that?"

"The remote. Colby and I were at the remote." She looked at her with wide, searching eyes. "Colby was hit. How bad is she? How is she doing?"

Kricorian fussed with the blanket already neatly tucked in. "Get some rest. I'll have the healer give you something more for the pain."

Lela grabbed Kricorian's sleeve with her free hand. "Tell me how she is."

Kricorian closed her eyes and took a slow, deep breath. She would do anything to keep from hurting Lela, but there was no way to make this any easier. "Colby didn't make it. There was nothing anyone could do."

Lela sank back into her pillow and let go of Kricorian's arm.

"I'll leave you alone for a while. Try to rest."

Lela knew she was up sooner than Kricorian wanted, and the mood in the cubicle was somber and strained.

Lela refused to discuss Colby and started having dreams about the raid. Physically Lela was feeling better — her back and her head had stopped hurting even though her shoulder was tender and her right arm was in a sling. But she thought that the healer who had taken care of her hadn't paid enough attention to the details of her injuries, which prolonged her recovery. As the days dragged on, a sense of gloom settled in. At Lela's insistence Kricorian returned to work, and eventually Lela seemed to get better.

"What did you do today?" Kricorian asked one evening a few days later. "Other than prepare this wonderful meal."

"I cleaned the purifier," Lela mumbled.

Kricorian laughed.

"I'm going back to work tomorrow," Lela said. She set her fork down. "I'm beyond bored. I can't stay in this place another day."

"We'll see what the healer says first. It might still be too soon."

"You forget that I'm a healer too," Lela reminded her pointedly. She had gone into her mother's profession and had been formally trained as a healer. Not long after graduating from the academy, Lela had developed an interest in research and spent another two years in training.

Lela got up from the table and went to her room. Her shoulder was feeling better, even though she couldn't go long without the sling. Kricorian followed her and leaned against the doorjamb before sitting down beside Lela on the bed.

"Rest a few more days," she said as Lela put her head on Kricorian's shoulder. "There's no rush to get back to work."

Lela sniffed and rubbed her cheek against Kricorian's uniform. "But you don't understand," she said. "I'm so bored that I cleaned the purifier today."

Kricorian chuckled and kissed her on top of the head. "Yes. I see what you mean."

~ ~ ~

Kricorian stopped by the lab on her way home several days later to question some of Lela's coworkers. Lela had returned to work the day before, but her demeanor suggested that her depression hadn't improved. Kricorian learned that things were even worse than she had expected. Lela had been going for long walks alone. Friends and coworkers urged her to resume her research, but Lela didn't appear to be listening to anyone. For Kricorian, Lela's silence was the most disturbing aspect of her new behavior, and Lela's colleagues at the Research Institute had expressed concern.

When Kricorian arrived at their cubicle later that evening, she sniffed the wonderful smell of Skyler stew. It was Kricorian's favorite, and the aroma alleviated some of her fears about Lela's depression. The table was set, and a flask of wine was already opened.

"I expected you sooner, but it's good that you're late," Lela said. "Come and sit. I made your favorite."

"I know. It smells fabulous." Kricorian pulled their chairs away from the table and poured herself some wine. Indicating the flask, she said, "Are you ready to try some yet?"

"Maybe a little."

After their meal they drank the last of the wine and talked about the harvest and trading season that was quickly approaching. Lela tossed a wisp of hair out of her eyes and took another sip of wine.

"We've filed an official complaint with the Intergalactic Security Council," Kricorian said, referring to the group of women from Alpha Sector, the Amtec Nation, and K Sector who had served as an investigative committee for trespassing or violent acts against all sectors in the galaxy. Kricorian was one of the representatives from K Sector and would be assisting with the investigation.

"Will they do anything?"

"We haven't received an answer yet." She waited, hoping

that Lela would want to talk more. Lela's lack of interest in the lab wasn't surprising, or even unusual under the circumstances, but it had Kricorian worried just the same. She wanted the happy, curious Lela back . . . the Lela who had given up healing in order to pursue her passion for research. It was unsettling to see Lela so distant, but Kricorian was willing to give her more time.

"Are you ready to start working on your research project again?"

"No."

Kricorian studied her for a moment. "Your work has always meant a great deal to you."

"My lover's dead. I can't think of anything else right now."

Lela reached for her glass and stared at it for a long time. She had cried for Colby only once, and had no idea where the tears were now. Tears were important. They were evidence of her loss, the gauge by which she judged her own suffering. Even though tears couldn't relieve her sense of devastation, tears were all she had — and yet even they had failed her.

"I'm flying to the crater section tomorrow," Lela said quietly. "I'd like for you to go with me."

Kricorian set her glass down. "Why? There's nothing there. Nothing but the remote and crater rock."

"I need to go back."

"You're not ready to travel anywhere. Wait a few weeks."

"I'm going tomorrow," Lela said. "I just thought you'd like to go with me."

Kricorian nodded toward their empty bowls. "Is this why we have Skyler stew tonight? My favorite meal?"

"How very suspicious you are," Lela said, and then laughed lightly. "Will you go with me?"

Kricorian shrugged. "If you're going anyway, then you leave me no choice, do you?"

~ ~ ~

They arrived at the crater section, and Kricorian set the spidercraft down where she had found Colby and Lela the night of the raid. After nearly a year of flying one, Kricorian was getting used to how easy it was to maneuver in a spidercraft, and the spidercraft's speed and ballistic range were impressive. The spidercrafts didn't look as ridiculous to her now as they had those first few weeks after their arrival, when they had struck her as huge, four-legged silver tarantulas.

Kricorian jumped to the ground and heard the crunch of the crater's surface under her boots. Helping Lela out of the spidercraft, Kricorian noticed that she still winced in pain whenever she had to use her arm.

Huge pieces of rock were everywhere, along with giant holes in the ground where the lasers had struck and pocked the surface. *Which one hit her?* Kricorian wondered as she glanced around. *Which one killed Colby?*

They peered over at the remote with its green, pulsating hue. It seemed friendlier now than it had that dreadful night.

"What are we looking for?" Kricorian asked gently.

"I don't know. Maybe nothing." Lela went over to the remote and touched the thick smooth wall with her gloved hand. "What would have happened if we had both gotten inside and stayed there?" Lela asked.

"Instead of trying to escape as I urged you to do?" Kricorian replied. She glanced at Lela. "Are you blaming me for Colby's death?"

Lela seemed almost stricken by Kricorian's question. "No, of course not," she said. "If anyone's to blame, it's me."

"How can you say that? There was nothing you could've done."

"I'm a healer, Kricorian. I didn't even try to save her."

"You were hurt too."

"Not until later! I got her in the mobilecraft before I was hit. She was bleeding to death, and I didn't do anything."

17

"Her injuries were fatal, Lela. She died quickly. You couldn't have saved her. Let this be what it is. You were attacked. It's no one's fault." When Lela didn't answer, Kricorian took off her helmet and shook her gray hair away from her forehead. "And to answer your question about the two of you staying in the remote, it was my —"

"I don't need an explanation," Lela said. "I'd trust you with my life, Kricorian. Anytime. Anyplace. Without question. There's no need for an explanation."

They returned to the spidercraft in silence, and before leaving hovered over the crater's surface. From fifty feet above the rocks, the laser burns looked deadly. It was a wonder anyone had survived such an assault.

On the return trip, they stopped at the meadow to see Ab and Nooley and spent time sharing stories and catching up on gossip. Kricorian saw glimpses of the old Lela as the four of them laughed and enjoyed each other's company. Ab fixed Lela a cup of tea made from a plant she had found growing near the pond. The tea helped relieve Lela's shoulder pain. It also piqued a bit of interest in Lela the researcher, Kricorian noticed. Lela would be all right with a little time, she thought.

Kricorian and Lela got up early the next morning; Lela finished making breakfast while Kricorian managed their first cup of tea. The day would be busy. K Sector had received a message requesting clearance for the Intergalactic Security Council's arrival. In addition, there had been talk throughout the corridor about holding a summit that would focus on the recent raids. In the past there had been summits every few years or so where four of the sectors reestablished ties and renewed old agreements. There were two other sectors in the galaxy, Bravo Sector and the Corlon Nation, both with male and female inhabitants. Bravo Sector had nearly been destroyed several years ago and was still rebuilding its space station. Help had been offered early on, but the people of Bravo Sector wanted to do things themselves. Ever since that raid, the people of Bravo Sector had little to do with any of their neighboring sectors.

Tracon, however, served as the hub for trading and recreation in the galaxy, with its permanent inhabitants consisting of vendors and laborers. Males and females lived there, and the people of Tracon worked well together even after having accepted the Rufkin species as a part of the Tracon family. Rufkins were an interesting mix of canine and feline experimentation as well as a generous dose of humanoid intelligence. They were the most intriguing aspect of Tracon's culture. Tracon was an unusual place and because of its overall mission as a trading center, it was considered a neutral entity in the galaxy.

On the other hand, K Sector, the Amtec Nation, and Alpha Sector were composed of only women and shared many common bonds. The three female-orientated sectors were self-reliant, but they exchanged ideas, goods, and other resources to help make the lives of women better. They had shared an interest in reproduction, concentrating on ovum fusion technology, which allowed them to fuse the nuclei of two eggs to create an embryo without fertilization. Genetic research, as well as other areas of science, was high priority.

K Sector and the Corlon Nation were actually small planets. K Sector had an atmosphere conducive to agriculture. Ninety percent of the food produced for the galaxy came from there. Various crops were transported to Tracon where they were then sold to vendors, who in turn traded or sold the goods to anyone with enough credits to purchase them. In addition, herbs grew naturally on K Sector, which also made it a place to train the galaxy's healers.

The Amtecs, however, were the most cohesive of the female societies and lived on the largest of the orbiting space stations. Out of the six sectors, the Amtecs were the most independent and self-sufficient. They had an army of warriors for their own protection and had been governed by a series of rulers for well over three hundred years. The Amtecs kept to themselves and were highly respected. Their warriors could always be counted on for help whenever there was an emergency.

Alpha Sector was the smallest of the space stations and was located in the center of the Intergalactic Corridor. Alpha Sector's interests revolved around engineering, and from their laboratories came the various types of aircraft that were used by all of the sectors. The creation of artificial environments was something they had also been working on for quite some time. This new technology was generating interest everywhere. Alpha Sector was generous with its resources and was always looking for ways to improve things.

Their needs and their enemies drew K Sector, the Amtec Nation, and Alpha Sector to each other. Friendly but separate, they had been united against Corlon for many years. Corlon was the larger of the two planets in the galaxy. There were gender wars within its perimeter, which made it nearly impossible for Corlon's population to increase without turmoil.

A psychopathic, sexist murderer who called himself Exidor had proclaimed himself the Corlon leader many years ago. Exidor had a small army of his own, and even though he claimed them, it was never completely understood how much control Exidor had over that band of unsavory characters. Corlon Star Fighters had a reputation for taking whatever they wanted whenever an opportunity arose. In the process of doing so, women from the other sectors had been killed during Corlon raids. Occasionally women were captured and brought back to Corlon for breeding purposes.

Exidor denied that he had anything to do with the raids, but his Star Fighters were always the culprits responsible. The last few raids, however, had been different from others. Lives had been lost, making the populations on the space stations and in K Sector smaller than they had ever been.

When confronted about the most recent raid on K Sector, Exidor had also complained about being attacked at the same time, his explanation being that pirates had dressed as Star Fighters and had stolen many of his aircraft. No one in the galaxy chose to believe him.

Exidor also encouraged the Star Fighters to steal children from other sectors when possible. The children were used for cheap labor and primitive scientific research. As a result, most sectors took special precautions to protect their children. No one felt completely safe anymore.

Exidor's excuses were lame, and it was easy to conclude that Corlon Star Fighters were responsible for the raid on K Sector.

"If there's a summit, who will host it?" Lela asked as she pulled her chair away from the table.

"The Amtecs have better accommodations," Kricorian said, "and tighter security. Especially after what happened with the Amtec princess. But I've heard that Exidor doesn't like that idea, though."

"So the princess is still missing?"

"As far as I know."

"I can't believe Corlon advisers would agree to participate in a summit anyway."

"A panel of Corlon delegates might attend," Kricorian said. "Exidor doesn't necessarily need to be one of them."

Lela set their breakfast down and took her place on the other side of the table. "Does anyone believe Corlon's explanation for the raids?"

Kricorian shrugged. "You mean the one about pirates stealing their ships? No one that I've talked to."

"Where else other than the Amtec palace could a summit be held?" Lela asked.

"I don't know," Kricorian said. "Tracon, maybe. It's a

neutral sector, but the Amtec palace is the only place that can provide for everyone's safety."

"Do you think the Amtecs will be interested in holding it there?" she asked, popping a morsel of bread in her mouth. "I'd consider going if they did. But it seems to me they should still be concerned about their princess being unaccounted for."

Kricorian nodded. "That's true. Besides, I thought you always hated political gatherings."

"This is important."

"And it'll be just as important if the summit is held at Tracon, don't you think?" Kricorian asked with a smile. "Meega would love to see you again. She's always asking about you."

Lela cringed. "That woman's disgusting. I don't want her anywhere near me. I barely escaped from her lecherous grasp the last time I was there."

Kricorian laughed and reminded her that she didn't answer the question. "You should be concerned about the summit, not where it's held."

"If it's at Tracon and on Meega's turf, then I'll have to think about it some more. How can you trust her?"

"Who said I trusted her? She's a valuable resource."

"And a sexual menace," Lela said. "She keeps you supplied with that wine you like. I don't think you'd be so quick to defend her if it weren't for that."

"You're missing the point here. It's the summit —"

"The summit *is* important to me," Lela said. "As long as it's not held at Tracon."

Chapter Three

K Sector

In the afternoon, the inspection team requested entrance into K Sector's air space. Their arrival was impressive, with two small spidercrafts and two larger mobilecrafts landing smoothly near K Sector's transport bay.

The door to the lead spidercraft opened, and Kricorian saw the white helmet pop out first. Then a tall, slender figure in a white uniform jumped lightly to the ground. Kricorian scanned the four women for weapons and found the team members unarmed.

As Kricorian approached them, she saw blond hair tumble from the white helmet. Incredibly blue eyes suddenly met hers.

"I'm Alaric. Commander of the Amtec Army," the blond said in a cool, clear voice. She held her helmet under her arm and stood boldly with booted feet slightly apart. "This is Lieutenant Jaret, my executive officer," she said, nodding toward a young, dark-headed Amtec warrior in a royal blue uniform. "I believe you already know Keda and Viscar from Alpha Sector. We're here representing the Intergalactic Security Council. I understand you've had problems with your force field."

Kricorian took in the gold brocade on Alaric's shoulders and along the outside seams of her uniform. All four of the women were stately; Kricorian already felt better just having them there.

"I'm Kricorian," she said. "The director of K Sector's Security Command Post. Welcome." As the five women began walking, Kricorian continued. "We were raided ten days ago and suffered two casualties. I'd like to know how invaders got in and why we weren't aware of their presence sooner."

She gave a short tour of the cargo area while they were there. At one point they stopped to watch K Sector's border patrol return; other mobilecrafts left to replace them immediately.

"Lieutenant Jaret is our expert in force-field technology," Alaric said as they began walking again. "She will ask most of our technical questions."

Lieutenant Jaret wasn't quite as tall as Alaric, but she had that same serious military bearing that Kricorian associated with Amtec warriors. Jaret tossed a spray of curls away from her face as the wind rearranged her dark hair. Her blue uniform had only a thin line of gold at the cuffs, collar, and seams, indicating her lower rank. Jaret began asking her about past raids and K Sector's current security features. Kricorian answered her questions and was surprised and intrigued by the young officer's insight and enthusiasm.

At the Command Post, the Security Council met with a panel of K Sector's advisers. An agenda was prepared following a lengthy question-and-answer session. Members of the Intergalactic Security Council appointed Lieutenant Jaret to lead the security inspection project, and she insisted that they begin right away. Alaric and the other three members of the inspection team would tour K Sector's Research Institute.

"Who's the blond?" Lela whispered as Kricorian leaned a little closer to her in the briefing room. Lela had arrived late and was trying to be as inconspicuous as possible.

"Commander of the Amtec Army," Kricorian answered through the side of her mouth. She introduced Lela to the members of the inspection team at the first available moment, and then suggested that Lela show the other three visitors the Research Institute. Kricorian stayed at the Command Post for Lieutenant Jaret's next briefing.

Kricorian watched as Jaret used the computers and asked more questions of K Sector's advisers. They discussed all new ideas thoroughly before any action was taken. During the entire session, Kricorian found herself very aware of Lieutenant Jaret's confidence and candid eloquence. Jaret's blue uniform complemented her dark curly hair, and her piercing brown eyes were serious and penetrating. She was young and attractive, with a well-defined chin and high cheekbones. At one point Kricorian realized that they were looking at each other, and glanced away quickly.

Kricorian excused herself from the meeting and went down the hallway to make a routine check, but before long she was drawn back to the briefing room. Only two of her advisers were still there working. Lieutenant Jaret and the others had already left for the crater section and would be gone several hours.

"Why the crater section?" Kricorian asked.

"Lieutenant Jaret is looking for a particular mineral," one adviser said.

"Which mineral?"

"Lidium. They need lidium to make our force field more effective."

Lidium, Kricorian thought. *Isn't lidium dangerous? Explosive?* She couldn't remember exactly, but she was vaguely familiar with it and knew that K Sector was the only place that had any.

Kricorian located a spidercraft and went to the crater section. A group was gathered at the bottom of a ridge looking up at Jaret and two K Sector geologists on the rocks above. The crater was always cold and dissolute; even the warmest time of the day was miserable there. Kricorian noticed that Jaret stayed on the ridge while the geologists returned below. Kricorian asked an adviser what they had found.

"Lidium," she said. "But they don't think it's enough."

"Now what happens?" Kricorian asked.

"Lieutenant Jaret intends to extract it. Then the real work begins."

Kricorian glanced toward the ridge and started off in that direction. The crater's rough and jagged surface was uncomfortable against the bottoms of her boots. She had never cared much for this part of K Sector. With the recent problem at the remote and Colby's death still fresh in her mind, it seemed as though nothing good ever happened here.

Kricorian was winded by the time she reached the top. Jaret's back was to Kricorian as Jaret looked out across the partially frozen, rocky landscape.

"What do you see out there?" she asked.

Jaret turned. "The Amtecs have nothing like this. It's beautiful in its own way."

"I suppose it is," Kricorian said. She stopped and looked at the terrain. "You've found the lidium."

"Yes." Jaret pointed over the ledge to several rocks below with a yellowish tint to them.

"This could be dangerous," Kricorian said.

"Yes, it could," Jaret agreed. She smiled. "At times like this, experience can be a wonderful thing." She indicated the ledge a few feet below. "I sent the others away. You should leave as well."

The frigid wind blew a dark curl that had escaped from Jaret's helmet. "Amtec warriors aren't expendable, Lieutenant," Kricorian said.

"On the contrary," Jaret said with a hint of a smile. "My commander could have a replacement for me here in a matter of hours." She jumped down on the ledge, landing lightly on her feet.

"Are you sure we know what we're doing?" Kricorian called to her.

"One of us does," Jaret said. She dusted off her gloves and looked up, squinting into the bright light beaming from the sky.

Kricorian chuckled and followed her over the ledge, landing with a loud thud on the rocks below. Jaret reached out and offered a hand to help steady her.

"You don't have to do this," Jaret said. The quiet tone of her voice brought back the seriousness of the situation. "We could both die from this excursion."

"K Sector's security and well-being are my responsibility," Kricorian said.

"All the more reason for you not to be here right now."

Kricorian nodded. "That's a good point, but I'm staying anyway."

"Then let's get on with it." Jaret stepped around the glowing yellow stones. She knelt down and indicated a place beside her with a gloved hand. "I have no intention of dying here."

Kricorian smiled and knelt down beside her with more confidence than seemed appropriate for the occasion. *An*

Amtec warrior can do anything, she thought. *Haven't I heard that all my life?*

Kricorian knew little about geology, the properties of lidium, or the crater section at K Sector, but she knew that all three were to be respected. The lidium deposit that had been located seemed small. It consisted of four egg-shaped stones that were embedded in crater rock. Bending down on one knee and cupping her hands around the stones, Jaret seemed to be taking care not to touch them. She seemed to be totally focused on what she was doing. Kricorian realized that caution in handling the lidium was critical.

"Exactly how dangerous is this?" Kricorian whispered.

"Very dangerous," Jaret said. "Ninety percent of all geologists have artificial limbs due to lidium extraction alone." She pulled a gyro probe and a small blue cube from her pocket. She thumped the cube with her finger, causing it to pop open and expand to nearly ten times its original size.

"Our suits should protect us from the glow," Jaret said. "But if I make a mistake and cause a big enough spark with the probe, we're in serious trouble."

"I see," Kricorian said. Jaret handed Kricorian the gyro probe and then set the cube down beside the glowing rocks. Kricorian peeked inside the box, but didn't notice anything unusual.

Jaret reached for the gyro probe and told Kricorian to hold the box steady. The wind was less fierce on the ledge, but it sent dust and dirt particles swirling around them.

"Are you ready?" Jaret asked.

"I'm ready."

With deliberate, precise movements, Jaret outlined all four rocks with the probe. Tiny whiffs of smoke rose up each time she touched them.

"Alpha and Bravo Sectors have begun using lidium to help power their living quarters and work areas," Jaret said. Her voice was low and soft. "There is a theory that when Bravo

Sector was attacked the last time, the raiders were searching for the technology for adapting lidium for such purposes."

"I remember hearing about that when it happened."

"We all rely on lidium to make our lives easier, but Bravo Sector wanted to free itself from all other sources of energy-producing minerals."

Kricorian watched her loosen one of the rocks and gently place it in the cube Kricorian was steadying. Kricorian felt her suit make a slight thermal adjustment the moment a thin layer of sweat lined her forehead.

"Do the Amtecs use lidium as a power source?" Kricorian asked. Her voice cracked slightly, another indication that she was nervous.

"Yes, but we also have other sources as well. K Sector uses —"

Kricorian saw a small spark from the second rock. Jaret eased the gyro probe back away from that one and started on the rock beside it.

Jaret continued, "K Sector also uses lidium for things other than its force field."

Kricorian raised her eyebrows. "Really?" She was always the first to admit that she knew nothing about geology, healing, or engineering of any kind. Her expertise was security and the politics of intergalactic relations.

"You have no idea how important lidium has become to all of us," Jaret said. "This discovery about its limited life span is a blessing in its own way." She picked up another rock and set it in the cube. Kricorian peeked inside the cube again and noticed that there were now individual sections protecting the stones from each other. She didn't remember the sections being there before.

"You saw the spark earlier?" Jaret asked.

"Yes," Kricorian replied.

"That's what I like to call a hot rock."

She picked up a third stone and placed it in the cube.

Kricorian kept her eye on this one and watched in awe as the cube itself made a snug cocoon for it.

Did you see that? she wanted to shout, but thought better of it.

"What makes a hot rock spark?" Kricorian asked instead.

"Lidium is like a mineral with a root system," Jaret explained. "The other three stones are offshoots of the primary stone. There's no way to tell by looking which one in the rock cluster is the primary. You have to see a spark to know that."

"The bigger the spark," Kricorian said, "the bigger the boom?"

Jaret nodded. "We've been lucky today." She stuck the gyro probe in her pocket and sealed the lidium inside the cube.

Research Institute

Keda rubbed her chin and studied the samples Lela had given them. "As I understand it, K Sector's main functions are food production and research. You also have a healing academy. How many scientists are here?"

"Twenty," Lela replied. "Only six of which are working on synthetic food research and production right now. We also have two geologists out in the field looking for favorable places to grow more crops." Lela had Keda and Viscar's attention and decided to give them the unabridged tour, even though Alaric seemed to be more interested in the facility itself and its security features. "We also have a group of healers doing research in medicine," Lela continued. "All healers in the corridor are trained at K Sector, but not at this particular facility."

Alaric nodded. "Everything seems to be in order."

"That surprises you, Commander," Lela said matter-of-factly. Something about this Alaric made Lela want to challenge her, to provoke some sort of unpredictable reaction or response. Lela decided that the feeling wasn't necessarily unpleasant.

Kricorian closed the door to the cubicle and shuffled toward the table. She was aching everywhere and thought for a moment that even her hair was hurting.

"You look exhausted," Lela said as she came out of the kitchen. "Here. Let me help with that." She slipped around behind her and began messaging the stiffness from Kricorian's neck and shoulders. "Are you hungry?"

"I'm too tired to eat," Kricorian groaned. "I didn't think this day would ever end."

"How much more is left to do?"

"At least another full day. I'm starting to really despise lidium. Really and truly despise it." She moved her head slowly from side to side as knotted muscles began to loosen from Lela's efforts. "Tell me how it went at the lab today."

Lela continued rubbing Kricorian's shoulders. "Security at the lab is excellent. We passed that inspection easily. I even managed to dazzle them with a preview of my research project."

"Bless you," Kricorian said. "Maybe it's not too late to save us from looking like complete idiots for missing this thing with the low lidium levels. We have competent, resourceful women working in force-field technology. K Sector pioneered the system everyone else in the corridor is using! How could something like this happen?"

"Is the force field working properly now?" Lela asked while easing more knotted muscles from Kricorian's body.

Kricorian groaned again. "Yes, but we don't trust it yet. I've doubled the border patrol. The lidium levels on two additional remotes were dangerously low. That's what weakened our force field. Lieutenant Jaret wants to run more tests in the morning."

Lela leaned around to get a better look at her. "How much do you know about these Amtec warriors?" she asked. "I assume they have a purpose."

"They protect the Amtec palace and its people," Kricorian said. "Amtec warriors are an elite group. They are also responsible for protecting the Amtec princess. I can imagine how her disappearance damaged their reputation."

"A princess," Lela said with amusement. "It's hard to believe that these women are ruled by a princess." Her laughter made Kricorian laugh too. "Was there ever a queen?"

"Ah, that was explained to me once," Kricorian said. "If you have a queen, that implies that there should be a king, and the Amtecs don't allow men to live there. So they refer to their royalty as a princess. The one they have now is about the sixth in a row, I think. The Amtecs have been severely rattled ever since she disappeared."

"How long has this princess been missing?" Lela asked.

"About three months from what I understand."

"So how good are these warriors if they can't keep up with one little princess?" Lela asked, making herself laugh.

"The Amtec princess isn't just any 'little princess.' They've had warriors all over the corridor searching for her."

"And what is this princess supposed to do?" Lela asked.

"I'm not sure what role she plays in their leadership," Kricorian said, "but I've heard Meega speak of her many times."

"Meega," Lela said before her body gave another involuntary shudder. "That woman's despicable."

Kricorian chuckled. "You take her much too seriously."

"She tried to drug me to get me in her bed! I'll always take her seriously."

"No harm was done," Kricorian reminded her. "A lot of our trading goes through Meega's cantina. We need her as an ally.

Just don't eat or drink anything she offers you. We've learned our lesson on that, haven't we?"

Lela gave Kricorian's neck a final rub and sat down across the table from her. "How does Meega know the Amtec princess? I can't imagine the Amtecs allowing someone with Meega's reputation to get close to her."

Kricorian moved her neck and shoulders easily; the pain was miraculously gone. "Apparently the princess likes the casino. Meega can be accommodating when she wants to be." Kricorian laughed again as she saw another shudder travel through Lela's body. "We're fortunate to have two warriors on the Intergalactic Security Council. I feel better about this whole thing already."

"I didn't expect the Amtecs to be so civilized," Lela said. "There's a sense of honor about them. Have you noticed that? They reek of intelligence and courage. On the surface it's easy to trust them."

"I sense that cynical side of you rearing its head."

Lela shrugged. "I'm leery of anything that looks that good."

"Are you saying that attractive women can't be honorable?" Kricorian asked in a teasing tone.

Lela looked at her, but didn't answer.

"The number of K Sector women who are tripping all over each other just to get a look at the two Amtecs would surprise you."

"I'm sure," Lela said dryly.

"Everything I've heard about them tells me that they can be trusted and relied upon in an emergency. We would do well to keep our relationship with them friendly."

"So you're saying that we should just accept the fact that the packaging is appealing?"

Kricorian laughed. "To those not familiar with the Amtecs, their appearance can be deceiving. I've seen a few warriors use that to their advantage."

"It's possible that I've misjudged them," Lela admitted.

After a moment Kricorian said, "You seem to be more like your old self again.

"I'm feeling better," Lela said. "Work was interesting today. I enjoyed showing the inspection team around. They asked several good questions, and it made me realize that what I'm doing is important to many people."

They got up from the table at the same time. "A princess," Lela mumbled. "How quaint. Maybe the Amtecs aren't as civilized as I thought." She put her arm around Kricorian's shoulder and gave her a hug. "Let's eat something and then get some sleep. We've got another big day tomorrow."

Lieutenant Jaret was working diligently at the Command Post when Kricorian arrived the next morning. Aeronautical graphics and mathematical computations cluttered the immediate work area. Jaret seemed to be engrossed in what she was doing. Her mane of black, curly hair against the dark blue uniform was such a nice combination, Kricorian thought as she once again took in the thin line of gold braid along Jaret's collar, shoulders, and down along the sleeves of her uniform. As Kricorian watched her working, she thought how attractive Jaret was. For Kricorian, just admitting such a thing was unsettling. She could feel herself getting restless and impatient. The emotional whirlwind blowing through her life had kept her awake the night before, and in the morning she found herself with little appetite. Kricorian had caught herself daydreaming about this young, impressive warrior off and on. After having met Lieutenant Jaret, Kricorian questioned her ability to focus on anything.

Jaret looked up from the map that was spread out in front of her.

"You're at it early this morning," Kricorian said briskly. "Or have you been working through the night?"

Jaret smiled. "Amtec warriors need little sleep," she said

as she moved the map to another stack in front of her. "My concentration hasn't been what it should be. I find it easier to focus here."

"How much longer will this take?" Kricorian asked.

"I'm certain we'll finish today. Atmospheric conditions are favorable for the tests we need. Your panel of advisers can do the other things that should be taken care of." She ran her fingers through her hair and tilted her head. Their eyes met again and Jaret said, "Lela isn't your lover."

Kricorian blinked several times, shocked, and didn't recognize her own voice as she muttered, "Lela is my daughter."

Jaret tossed the cloud of raven curls away from her forehead again. "Please accept my apology for asking such a personal question."

"There's no need to apologize." Kricorian watched as Jaret cleared her things from the work area.

"You're not receptive to the idea of having a young lover?" Jaret asked with a slight grin.

"I've never thought about it."

"Never?"

Kricorian smiled sadly. "Not in a long time."

Jaret activated the scanner beside her and entered in several coordinates. "I have this uncontrollable urge to ask you questions."

Kricorian was surprised at how much she liked Jaret's attention, but found herself wanting to withdraw from her nonetheless. "Most questions are harmless," she said.

"Then I'll ask them as they come to me."

Other panel members began to arrive, and Kricorian left to begin work of her own. As she ambled down the hallway to her office, she wondered if the lieutenant was this inquisitive with everyone. "Of course, she is," Kricorian mumbled to herself. "Of course."

Chapter Four

K Sector

Several hours later there was a knock on the door to Kricorian's office. Lela breezed in and closed it behind her.

"What are you doing in here?" Lela asked. "We've got guests who've been asking about you."

"We can't all have the luxury of entertaining dignitaries," Kricorian replied.

Lela took her usual seat on the corner of Kricorian's desk, but seemed a bit pensive.

"Since the dignitaries have been doing all the work," Lela reminded her, "you can't possibly have that much to do here."

She turned a little and made eye contact. "The young one. Lieutenant Jaret," Lela said. "You know what she told me?"

Kricorian's pulse quickened at the mere mention of Jaret's name.

"She suggested," Lela said, "that Colby's death saved thousands of lives throughout the corridor. Jaret said that without the raid on K Sector, the low lidium levels wouldn't have been found in time to do anyone any good. Alpha Sector and the Amtecs are making proper lidium adjustments to their own systems now because of it." She lowered her voice. "It was a nice thing for her to say," she whispered. "How true do you think it is?"

"It's good to find something positive come out of such a tragic situation," Kricorian said. "You're right. It was a nice thing to say."

Lela leaned her head back. "Can I ask you something?"

Kricorian looked over at her and saw the uneasiness in her expression. "You can ask me anything."

Lela closed her eyes. "Was I in love with Colby?" she asked quietly.

Kricorian waited for her to say something else; to ask the real question she had come to ask, but nothing further happened. Finally Kricorian said, "Were you? You're asking *me*? You're the only one who knows the answer to that, Lela."

"Oh."

Kricorian reached over and squeezed her hand. "If you have to ask, then I'd say you probably weren't."

"Is it that easy?"

Kricorian leaned back in her chair. "How many women have you been with?"

"Four."

"Did you feel the same way about all of them?"

"I don't know." Lela shrugged. "Maybe."

"You told me once that you and Colby would just be friends some day. You even mentioned that she was interested in someone else."

Lela nodded. "I'd forgotten about that."

"Why all these questions? It's easy to confuse good sex with love," Kricorian said. "You can certainly have one without the other."

Lela sighed and pushed herself up into a sitting position. "I'm not sure I've ever had either. I haven't missed her enough yet. Maybe I'm feeling guilty."

"Guilt is a wasted emotion," Kricorian said. "Tell me what's really going on with you right now."

Lela jumped down from Kricorian's desk, keeping her back to her. "I feel so shallow sometimes. So superficial." She turned around with searching eyes. "It's been fifteen years for you, Kricorian. You've never so much as looked at another woman."

A small ray of guilt touched Kricorian's heart, but she nudged it away quickly. "Are you comparing what I had with your mother with what you had with Colby?"

Lela shook her head. "I guess I just need for you to tell me it's all right to feel this way. To be aware of other women. That it's okay to stop having the horrible dreams." She lowered her voice to a whisper. "To forget what Colby looked like. Sometimes all I can remember is the blood . . . and . . . and torn flesh where I used to . . ."

Kricorian squirmed in her chair. She knew exactly what Lela was talking about. Kricorian still had terrible dreams about the raid that had killed Meridith and Romney, and she could still describe Meridith in such remarkable detail that it always brought a smile and then tears to them both. Kricorian sighed and chose her words carefully.

"Don't punish yourself for not being in love with Colby when she died. You couldn't have saved her no matter how much you loved her." Kricorian went around the desk to give Lela a hug. "Try to get on with your life as fast as you can, little one. If you can find a way to heal your heart, then do it."

Lela hugged her fiercely. "I realized this morning that I

held my mother while she was dying and that I ended up doing the same thing with my lover."

Kricorian kissed the top of her head. "I'm so sorry," she whispered.

"It makes me leery of getting too close to anyone again. It's like I need to protect myself."

"All of that will pass with time."

Lela picked up her helmet from the desk. "Alaric received word that the Amtecs have agreed to host the summit," she said. "I'd like to go with you to represent K Sector. Can you arrange that?"

"I'm sure I can," Kricorian said.

"She also wanted me to tell you that they would be at the remote closest to the meadow. I think the Security Council wants you to be there too." Lela stopped at the door and turned. "Thanks for listening. I'll see you later."

Kricorian watched Lela leave and felt her sadness.

Lela had lost all track of time; her coworkers had left hours ago. Locking up the lab and walking down the dim hallway, she took comfort in the quiet hum of the Research Institute. During the day there were always too many other things going on to hear it, but at night the hum was soothing and peaceful.

She entered the access code to the main entrance, and the door swooshed open just long enough to let her out. It was dark, and the wind was starting to blow. Lela noticed how unusually empty the streets were as she pulled on her helmet. There was a hovercraft that someone had left near the entrance, but she decided against taking it home. The walk would do her good. She wanted to check and see if Kricorian and the Security Council were back from inspecting the other two remotes.

Halfway between the Research Institute and the Command Post she heard an explosion. Lela froze. Several seconds later, she saw Star Fighters running through the streets with weapons drawn and ready. The sound of their boots, heavy and intense, slapping against the cobblestone as they ran, was frightening. Star Fighters were heartless and brutal, and Lela knew what her fate would be if they found her.

With her heart pounding, she stepped back against the dark building. As her survival instincts kicked in, she knew she had to find somewhere to hide. Going back to the Research Institute was out of the question. She was too far away from the entrance, and getting there would require being out in the open.

She slipped into an alley, staying pressed against the building. Lela could hear them running and shouting. At the far end of the narrow street, she saw several Star Fighters chasing something. Lela inched her way down the alley, fighting panic with each step, and rounded the corner to another street. The Star Fighters didn't seem to be looking for anything in particular. It was impossible for them to get inside any buildings without an access code, but so far that didn't seem to be their purpose.

Lela felt warm air blowing up from the cobblestone as she moved against the wall. The air was coming up from a grate in the street. She knelt down and yanked on it, and to her surprise the grate came up easily. Lela squeezed down into the hole and dropped almost eight feet into complete darkness. There was an unpleasant, musty smell and about an inch of stagnant water where she landed. She was in a drainage tunnel, designed specifically for the monsoon season.

She heard dripping all around her and saw a faint beam of light nearly forty yards ahead. Lela ignored the little scurrying noises near her boots, and, just as she had during her brief time in the remote at the crater section, she tried not to think about what might be causing such a sound. She crept through the darkness, inching her way along the damp, sweaty walls. Other tunnels branched off into new directions.

She stayed in the main one. The dripping was the only constant sound she could hear, other than the Star Fighters running and shouting in the streets above her. From the noise, Lela could tell that many more had arrived. She kept going, diligently inching her way along the wall, listening for anything new or familiar.

The tunnel seemed to be getting lighter, and occasionally Lela thought she could hear other voices fading in and out. Before long she realized that some Star Fighters were underground too. It occurred to her that she was trapped, and she had no idea what to do next. She heard the sound of footsteps moving toward her. Her heart began to race. Suddenly a gloved hand clamped around her mouth from behind, and an arm across Lela's chest jerked her up against the wall even farther into darkness. She froze. Fear consumed her.

"Don't even breathe," came the slow whisper in Lela's ear.

Two Star Fighters, shrouded in dingy, smelly uniforms, walked past them, close enough to touch. She tasted fear, heavy and thick on her tongue, and fought down the screams struggling in her throat. As the Star Fighters continued on, Lela wasn't sure if she would be sick or not.

"Follow me," the voice whispered. The gloved hand eased from Lela's mouth, and the steel grip of Alaric's arm dropped from across her chest. Lela turned, then wilted against her, amazed at how totally exhausted she had suddenly become. Alaric pulled her closer, keeping them both firmly against the wall. "Don't be afraid," she whispered, her voice low and calm. "Follow me."

They stayed in the tunnel and moved quickly and quietly through the darkness. Alaric led the way and held Lela's hand so they wouldn't get separated. Star Fighters were everywhere, and several times Lela and Alaric came across well-lit areas that revealed dead Star Fighters with necks broken and twisted at unnatural angles. Lela gingerly stepped over the bodies and continued on in silence.

The farther they went, the cooler the temperature seemed

to become; Lela could feel her suit making thermal adjustments to keep her comfortable. They found another open grate to the street above, and Alaric pulled herself up and crawled out. She offered a helping hand down to Lela and pulled her up as well.

"Where's Kricorian?" Lela whispered.

"At the meadow with the others. You have to trust me if we're going to make it there."

Lela nodded. It was amazing how much better she felt already. She watched Alaric check a scanner on her wrist and then point toward a ridge.

"I've got a spidercraft hidden close by," Alaric said, "but Star Fighters are looking for it. We can't go there yet."

They started off, climbing over rocks and boulders, fighting the wind that battered at them. Alaric stopped to check her scanner again and motioned to the right quickly. Lela noticed a slight indentation in the rock that she saw was a small cave as they drew nearer. The howling wind was deafening, but once they were safely inside, it was no more than a whisper. Alaric pulled a small light from her pocket and adjusted the beam enough so they could see better. There were no signs of previous inhabitants, and the cave was large enough to accommodate several people. Alaric minimized the light, softening the glow, and then gave it to Lela.

"Stay here," Alaric said from the cave's entrance.

"Where are you going?" Lela demanded. The thought of being left alone again frightened her.

"I won't be long."

"You're not leaving me here."

Alaric checked the scanner again before tugging at her gloves. "I asked you to trust me."

"I do trust you."

"Then stay here. I don't have time to argue with you."

Lela watched as Alaric took the scanner from her wrist and then also handed over a thin, five-inch-long tube that Lela recognized as a stun gun.

"I'll be the red dot on the scanner," Alaric said. "Star Fighters will be green." She nodded toward the stun gun and said simply, "So please don't shoot me when I come back."

She was out of the cave and quickly into the monstrous wind, leaving Lela too scared to be angry and too upset to do anything but tremble. Lela turned down the light and huddled against a wall in the cave to wait.

Chapter Five

The Meadow

In Nooley and Ab's cabin, Kricorian watched Lieutenant Jaret from across the room as Jaret studied her charts and occasionally stared at the screen in front of her. Jaret had taken full responsibility for allowing Star Fighters through the force field again even though nothing more than bad luck had actually been the cause.

Star Fighters had been in the area when lidium levels had become dangerously low on the last two remotes and the signal finally failed again. K Sector had been more vulnerable than anyone realized, and with Jaret dispatching K Sector's border patrol earlier in the day — an order that probably saved scores of lives — all reasonable precautions had been taken. They had been lucky, but the significance of what had happened had a sobering effect. Kricorian hadn't been able to do anything but pace until they finally received word from Alaric that Lela was safe.

Kricorian watched as Keda, one of the Security Council representatives from Alpha Sector, spoke to Lieutenant Jaret briefly. From where Kricorian was sitting, she could tell that Jaret's answers were curt. The young officer still managed to maintain that dignified briskness that all Amtec warriors had, but Kricorian could see the struggle on Jaret's face and the weariness in her eyes.

"She says the Amtecs are here," Keda whispered as she sat next to Kricorian at the table. "If that's true, it won't be long now."

Kricorian looked again at Jaret and couldn't believe how much better she felt having her there.

After what seemed like hours, the crunch of boots on gravel outside the cave's entrance made Lela's heart race again. She'd been following the red dot on the scanner, but she wasn't totally convinced that it was Alaric coming back.

Someone in a white uniform stumbled inside and took off her helmet. Alaric's thick blond hair tumbled down to her shoulders. "I'm sorry I was gone so long."

Lela snapped the light brighter as tears of relief stung her eyes. Alaric set her helmet down and dropped a supply pack next to it.

"How did you get that bruise on your cheek?" Lela asked as she led Alaric away from the entrance.

"There were six of them," Alaric said, as if that were explanation enough. She eased down and leaned back against the cave wall. Her white uniform and blond hair made the bruise look even worse than it probably was. Alaric closed her eyes the moment Lela touched her chin for a better look.

"Be still. I'm a healer. I can fix this." She took Alaric's face in her hands, trailing her fingers along the fine cheekbone. Lela could feel Alaric's warm silky hair and the pulse beating steadily at her throat. "You said there were six of them. Six what?" she asked.

"Six Star Fighters," Alaric said.

Lela moved her fingertips along Alaric's jaw in a light, circular motion. "Anyone foolish enough to tangle with six Star Fighters deserves a bruise like this."

Alaric opened her eyes. *Intoxicating pools of blue.* Lela nearly lost her concentration.

"Weren't you afraid?" Lela asked. She continued to work on Alaric's cheek. "Fear would be healthy under the circumstances, don't you think?" She put her fingers under Alaric's chin and tilted her head back with determination. She took Alaric's face in her hands and moved her fingers slowly, deliberately into the silky hair and then down to the back of her ears. Lela resumed another gentle caress on Alaric's cheek and then moved her hand around to the back of her head. "Do all warriors talk as much as you?"

Alaric raised her piercing blue eyes again and looked steadily at Lela.

"Do they?" Lela repeated boldly. She could see the discoloration of the bruise beginning to fade under her touch. She seldom got a chance to heal anymore since research now took up so much of her time. "Where's the spidercraft you mentioned earlier?" Lela asked.

"Hidden not far from here," Alaric said. "They're still looking for it." She pulled away and reached for her helmet. "Thank you. It's much better."

"I'm not finished," Lela said, reclaiming Alaric's chin and turning her head back around. "I can keep it from swelling. Be still. This won't take long."

Alaric reluctantly let her continue.

"We're stuck here, aren't we?" Lela asked, already knowing the answer.

"Momentarily. Safety's my main concern right now. There're still too many of them out there for us to do anything but wait."

Lela finished with the bruise and checked her work; all discoloration was gone. She sat down next to Alaric and leaned back against the wall. "How did you know I was in the tunnel earlier? I don't think I've ever been so scared," she admitted with a shiver. Lela rubbed her arms and then felt her suit make another adjustment. She looked over at Alaric and momentarily felt lost in her cool, blue eyes. "You saved my life."

There was silence as they looked at each another. Lela pulled her knees up and wrapped her arms around them. "You saved my life," she said again.

The gaze was steady but not uncomfortable. Lela waited a moment, holding the look and taking great pleasure in what she saw. She remembered how Alaric's blond hair had felt against her fingers a few minutes before and how it always seemed to be in place no mater what the circumstances — a fierce wind or a helmet. Lela's gaze settled on Alaric's mouth. *Oh my. She's got nice lips.* She looked away.

"Do warriors take lovers, Commander?" she asked after a moment.

Alaric leaned her head back against the wall and said, "Some do."

"And you? Do you have a lover?" Lela stretched out her legs and set her helmet on her lap. "I imagine it wouldn't be a good idea to sleep with anyone in your command, would it?" She shrugged. "Might boost morale a bit, though."

"Morale is fine," Alaric said. She picked up her gloves and stuffed them in her helmet.

"You didn't answer my question," Lela said, resorting to childishness. She sensed that Alaric was in no mood for it, but that only seemed to urge Lela on. "So do you, Commander? Do you have a lover?"

Alaric's blue eyes were reigning in a flicker of impatience.

"Maybe I'm being too presumptuous," Lela said. "I'm assuming that you like women."

"Why is my sexuality of so much interest to you?" Alaric asked. "I imagine your curiosity is what makes you so good at research."

"Perhaps." Lela had to look away and focus somewhere other than Alaric's mouth. "Do you ever answer a question, Commander?"

"A relevant question would have my undivided attention."

Hours later Kricorian was outside the cabin, being happily crushed by Lela's hug. "Oh, little one," Kricorian whispered. "How you scared me." Unexpected tears clouded her vision as she held her.

"It was frightening," Lela admitted. She let go of her and began walking away from the others with her arm around Kricorian's waist. "Alaric saved my life."

Kricorian gave her another squeeze and whispered, "More about that later."

A Star Fighter's laser had badly damaged the communications system, but the force field was now performing better than it ever had. Kricorian monitored the Amtec reports that trickled in with news that the Star Fighters had left almost as quickly as they had arrived.

Kricorian and Lela watched the Amtecs return to the meadow, each with a spidercraft lined up in perfect formation. There was little talking as they waited for everyone to arrive.

Lieutenant Jaret called them to attention and ordered each squad leader to report the status of her squad. Jaret spoke briefly about what the group had accomplished and what was still left to do. She then turned the command over to Alaric.

"She insisted on going after you," Kricorian said quietly. Lela was beside her in the doorway of Ab and Nooley's cabin watching the Amtec formation. "As soon as I realized that I couldn't reach you at the Institute, Alaric was asking questions and getting a layout of the area." Kricorian looked down at her and raised her eyebrows. "She *insisted* on going."

Lela felt a little flutter of excitement as her eyes left Kricorian's and drifted over to Alaric standing so regally in front of her troops. "Insisted?" Lela repeated.

"Insisted," Kricorian affirmed. "After Alaric left in a spidercraft, Jaret told me that the commander would be able to find you and that she would bring you back safely. Jaret said she couldn't explain how Alaric always knew where to go or where to look, but that this wasn't the first time she had seen such a thing happen. It gave me hope," Kricorian said. She gave Lela a hug. "And here you are."

The Security Council gathered around the table in Ab and Nooley's cabin to discuss the events leading up to the raid and to form a plan of action to prevent future problems. Kricorian had overheard a brief, angry exchange between Alaric and Jaret just before the meeting started. She hadn't heard enough to know what exactly had been discussed, but Lieutenant Jaret didn't seem happy about it, whatever the issue had been.

"Thirty Star Fighters were killed and two were captured," Alaric said. "Neither K Sector nor the Amtecs suffered any casualties."

"This time," Keda interjected, and everyone nodded solemnly.

"The Security Council has discussed the possibility of

stationing a squad of warriors here to help you with border patrol," Alaric said. "More lidium tests need to be run on your force field, and there are several unanswered questions about why your communications system failed at such an unfortunate time. The two are not known to be related, and that concerns us greatly. Lieutenant Jaret has suggested we assemble an intergalactic group of engineers with specialties in these areas to help find answers as quickly as possible. The presence of Amtec warriors here might be a psychological boost as well as a deterrent to any future raids." Alaric nodded toward Kricorian. "Your thoughts on this?"

"Are you suggesting that sabotage might be the cause of our communication problem, Commander?" Kricorian asked.

"We've ruled out nothing."

Kricorian's mind was reeling. *Sabotage? Who?* She studied each face at the table. She felt a sinking sensation in the pit of her stomach.

"It seems to be an interesting coincidence that Star Fighters have been in the area each time your signal has failed," Alaric said. "It's as if they knew there would be a problem."

"That would give more credence to the sabotage theory," Viscar said. "Someone on K Sector taking advantage of a weak lidium connection."

"I don't believe that," Kricorian said. "We haven't had any visitors in months, and those who live here wouldn't jeopardize anyone's safety."

"Another possibility could be," Jaret said, "that wherever these Star Fighters are coming from, they've already experienced problems with lidium."

"Are Star Fighters smart enough for that?" Viscar asked. A light chuckle went around the table.

"They're smart enough to know where to be when our signal is out," Kricorian noted.

"We may never know why this has happened," Jaret said. "Our job now is to make sure it never happens again."

Everyone agreed on that.

"Some of the tests that need to be conducted involve lidium and its possible effects on communication links," Jaret said. Her voice was low, but she had everyone's attention. Kricorian could see and hear how tired she was. "Everything that happens at K Sector needs to be studied and documented," Jaret continued. "We still have a lot to learn about lidium. The security of our own communications system could be in jeopardy if we don't take the time to study what's happening here."

"So," Kricorian said, letting out the deep breath she'd been holding. "You're suggesting we keep a squad of warriors for protection while a group of scientists and engineers try to find out what's wrong here?"

"Correct," Alaric said.

"How long will all of this take?"

All eyes moved to Lieutenant Jaret for an answer. She shook her head and ran her hand through a spray of dark curls. "I have no idea. It could be days or it could be months."

Kricorian and Alaric briefed the squad of ten warriors that were to remain at K Sector. Each member of the squad was young and eager, and Kricorian was impressed with them. Alaric, Keda, and Viscar would be leaving the next day to transport the two captured prisoners to Tracon for questioning and disciplinary action. Lieutenant Jaret would be staying at K Sector to oversee the lidium testing and supervise the remaining squad of warriors. Kricorian was more than ready to have the whole thing over with.

Kricorian also solved the mystery about the heated argument between Alaric and Jaret that had taken place at the meadow. Jaret was unhappy about having to stay behind and had been vocalizing her discontent with the situation. According to Ab, who had overheard the entire exchange,

Jaret thought the geologists at K Sector could handle the testing. She didn't feel as though she was needed there. Alaric had a different opinion.

"I'm assuming we'll see all of you at the summit," Kricorian said as she and Lela escorted the Security Council to the transport bay before their departure. Keda and Viscar confirmed that they would be attending the summit, while Alaric announced that she would be deeply involved in maintaining the security of the Amtec palace while the summit was taking place.

Lela clasped her hands behind her back as she met Alaric's gaze one more time. "I hope you'll be taking better care of us than you did the Amtec princess," she said. The biting remark was meant to goad Alaric into some type of reaction, but Lela was disappointed. Instead, she heard Kricorian sputter in disbelief at the comment, and Lela knew that she would receive a verbal lashing for it later.

Alaric, on the other hand, never so much as blinked. She did, however, return Lela's steady look and said with a slight smirk, "Now I'm trying to remember why I went to so much trouble to save you from Star Fighters."

Several days later, Kricorian, Lela, and the rest of K Sector were still adjusting to having warriors there with them, but there were no more signs of hostile activity anywhere in the corridor. The Amtecs were making their presence known everywhere, and it seemed to be helping. Lela looked up as she heard someone come into the lab. She smiled at Kricorian. "I thought you'd be gone by now."

Kricorian slid onto a stool beside her. "You've been pretty quiet since the invasion," she noted. "Are you sure you're all right?"

"I'm fine," Lela said. She switched the screen off and put

the specimen that she was working on away. "Why haven't you left yet?"

Kricorian offered a greeting to one of Lela's coworkers and was amazed at how young the working force was these days.

"I'm on my way to the loading dock now," she said. "I thought I'd see if you'd changed your mind about going with me. A shopping trip doesn't come along everyday, you know."

Lela laughed and shook her head. "No, thanks." With a twinkle of mischief in her eyes she said, "I'd rather stay home and clean the purifier."

Kricorian's laughter filled the room. Lela walked with her, arm in arm, to the door.

"If all goes well I'll be back late tomorrow night," Kricorian said. "If trading is slow I might stay longer. Are you sure you won't come with me? Getting away might do you some good."

Lela kissed her on the cheek and gave her a hug. "I'm fine. Bring me something interesting."

Kricorian laughed. "Like what?"

"I don't care. You'll know it when you see it." Lela hugged her again on impulse. "And be careful. Keep company with a few warriors if you see any while you're gone."

Chapter Six

Tracon Trade Center

Kricorian cruised into the Tracon Trade Center and logged in her arrival time. She found several Rufkins in the cargo bay looking for work, and spent over an hour helping them inventory her merchandise. Kricorian liked using the Rufkins; they were such interesting little creatures, with their calico fur and squeaky voices. They were always full of market gossip and a tip on good buys. Most traders brought their own help for the occasion, choosing to unload and inventory their goods through scanners, but Kricorian always insisted on using local resources whenever she could.

"Sporae has been looking for you," the Rufkin leader said.

His eyelids were heavy with sleep, and sprigs of white fur sprang from his floppy ears. "He's had us watching for you."

"We expected you last week," another one called from outside the cargo area of Kricorian's air transport.

"K Sector has had a few problems lately," she said. "I couldn't get away sooner." She could hear the music from the cantina in the market on the other side of the cargo bay. The trade center was busy; Kricorian had a feeling she would have no trouble getting anything she wanted this trip.

"Corlon Star Fighters get you?" the Rufkin leader asked. "We've heard reports of raids all over. Sporae has news for you."

"Then I suppose Sporae should be my first stop," Kricorian said good-naturedly. Their eager nods made her laugh. Sporae paid them well for each customer they were able to send his way.

"Did you bring any lidium?" the Rufkin leader asked. "It's in big demand right now. We can get you a good price."

"Who's looking for lidium?"

"Everyone! Stealing it is too dangerous. Did you bring any?"

"No. Do you have the facilities to store it?"

"Facilities?" he said. "This is Tracon! We're one big happy facility!"

Kricorian left the trade center once her credits were safely logged and her routine purchases entered into the computer. The Rufkins would ensure that her usual order was delivered and loaded quickly.

She could hear the tinkling music from the cantina the closer she got to the marketplace. The streets were bulging with peddlers and shoppers. A pack of juvenile Rufkins scurried underfoot, causing merchants and customers to scatter. As Kricorian neared the cantina she heard shouting and hearty laughter. She let herself be swallowed up in a rib-crunching hug from Meega, the cantina's owner, who had already received word of her arrival. Kricorian disengaged herself from Meega's embrace and stepped back and smiled at her friend's outrageous new hairdo with its bright pink curls springing in every direction.

"Nice color," Kricorian said. Meega looped her arm through Kricorian's and pushed the cantina's batwing doors open. She led the way to her personal table, which was located in a secluded area away from the bar and casino. An attractive young woman who had been sitting at the table got up and disappeared toward the back.

"You like?" Meega asked Kricorian with a nod of her head and a nudge with an elbow.

Kricorian laughed and pulled out a chair. "That's a different one from the last time."

"This one's moody, but she'll do," Meega said. "Could I interest you in something?" Her voice took on a tone that Kricorian recognized immediately. An offer was undoubtedly on its way. "Maybe the three of us?"

Kricorian smiled politely and gave Meega's hand a friendly pat. "Not this trip."

"This trip?" Meega threw her head back and belted out a laugh. "Not *any* trip, as far as I can tell!" She squirmed in her chair and crossed her legs, lowering her voice again. "Maybe just the two of you then. Would you like that?"

"I'm here on business," Kricorian said, "but I appreciate the offer. Maybe some other time."

"You're no fun, Kricorian. When did you stop being fun?"

"I've never been any fun. At least by your standards."

Meega's friend came back to the table with three drinks and pulled her chair closer to Meega's. It was time to get on with business.

"Do you have any more of that wine I got from you last time?" she asked.

"No," Meega said, "but I've got a new batch that's almost as good." She sipped her drink and winked. "I know what you like. I'll save you some of the other if I get any in."

Kricorian nodded. Their business was concluded and she had other stops to make. She tried to get up to leave but Meega gave her a little shove back down in her chair. "What's your hurry? You haven't finished your drink."

"I'm here on business," Kricorian reminded her again.

"No women or drink?"

Kricorian wasn't interested in drinking or eating anything Meega had. Visions of waking up naked in some sleazy room upstairs flashed in her head. She pushed her chair back and was relieved when Meega didn't insist that she stay.

Meega followed her to the swinging doors and held them open. "Did you bring any lidium?"

Kricorian was surprised by the question. "No."

"Everyone's asking for it, and you're the only one who has any. I'll give you a good price."

This is getting out of hand, Kricorian thought. *We've never sold lidium before. It's always been harvested by anyone who needed it.*

"I'll have to get back with you on that."

"Plan to stay longer next time," Meega said. She reached over and ran her fingers through Kricorian's hair and whispered, "I bet you could be lots of fun."

Sporae swept back the curtains to his entranceway and offered a delighted smile. Kricorian towered over him by nearly two feet, but his sharp mind and keen, uncanny perceptions outweighed whatever physical attributes he lacked. Sporae looked up at her with bright liquid eyes and nodded toward a table in the back. He had been expecting her.

"Meega found you first," he said. "I wasn't sure you would have time for me."

"I always have time for you," Kricorian said. She followed him into the other room. "The Rufkins recommended that I make time."

"The Rufkins," he said fondly. Sporae scratched his bald head with one of his three-inch-long fingernails. "It's good of you to use them. You're one of the few they don't cheat." He sat down slowly, as if bending or moving his thin, frail body pained him greatly.

"They don't cheat me *now*." She relaxed in a chair across from him and pushed her cup closer so he could more easily fill it with the steeping tea. "The Rufkins and I have had our share of misunderstandings."

"They were only testing you."

"It's been one of my more interesting relationships." She sipped her tea and nodded approval. "They mentioned something about the raids," Kricorian said. "What have you heard?"

"Tracon is one of the few sectors that the Star Fighters haven't raided," Sporae said. "Anything of value that they've acquired is brought here and sold."

"What are the reports from the other sectors?" Kricorian asked.

Sporae smacked his lips. "The corridor has been busy with more traffic than usual. Failed attempts to enter perimeters. The reports are all virtually the same. They were lucky with their attack on K Sector. Those Star Fighters were probably just as surprised as you were when they realized they were inside your perimeter."

"Do you think they are Corlon Star Fighters? Some of our people seem to think they are pirates. Robbing, stealing, and maiming for the fun of it."

"They all appear to be from Corlon, but Corlon is denying it, of course. Exidor has his usual story. He claims that several of his airships have been stolen and that pirates have taken them over. And that could possibly be true," Sporae said with a shrug. "These raids aren't being done by terrorists. These people have no political agenda that anyone is aware of. This is a band of greedy thieves, who I think can be much more dangerous," he said. "They have no loyalty. Their best friend is anyone who can give them the highest price for whatever it is they are selling." Sporae took a sip of his tea. "There is even evidence that Exidor and Corlon have been raided."

"Solid or manufactured evidence?"

Sporae smiled, and Kricorian snorted.

"Exidor is delusional again," she said. "Does he really expect us to believe that he's been attacked too? We're not the fools we once were."

"I understand your suspicions, but I've also heard that Corlon is on the brink of civil unrest and that a revolution there is closer than any of us realize."

"Exidor has had this coming for years."

"I agree with you on that. Did K Sector suffer heavy losses during the raid?" he asked.

"One mobilecraft and two pilots. Lela was injured, but she's better now."

"Darling Lela," he said with a warm smile. "Will you ever bring her back here with you?"

Kricorian laughed. "She's busy with her work."

Sporae refilled their cups with steady hands. "Our Meega gave her a scare last time. Lela seemed annoyed by all the attention."

"Lela can take care of herself in that area," Kricorian assured him. "I have a question for you," she said. "There's been a lot of interest in lidium recently. Has Tracon ever had a vendor for it? Or has my memory failed me again?"

Sporae smiled. "There have been several customers here looking for lidium during the last few months. K Sector is the only place that has it. We've never sold it here. Isn't it free where you live?"

Kricorian laughed. "Very free! I need to do more research on this."

Sporae set the teapot down and looked up at her with amusement in his eyes. "Come with me. I have something you might be interested in." He pulled himself up from the chair and shuffled farther back into his shop. Thin, colorful curtains separating the rooms flowed past him as he went. He held the curtains open for her and motioned to a bright gold coffin-size tube.

Kricorian was speechless as she drew closer. Tiny, intricate carvings were etched in gold all along the cylinder's top and sides. The ornamental majesty of the huge case was breathtaking.

"What is it?" Kricorian whispered. She moved closer and felt an overwhelming urge to touch it.

"I don't know what it is," Sporae said. "I've never before seen anything like it."

"Neither have I." Kricorian let her fingers caress the golden side. A seam running along the tube's entire length had several deep scratches where someone had tried to pry it open. Kricorian got down on one knee and inspected the seam and the scratches closely.

"It's for sale," Sporae said into her ear. "I'll sell it to you for what I paid for it."

"What is it? Where did it come from?"

Sporae shrugged. "I don't know where it came from, but four unsavory characters delivered it and sold it to me."

Kricorian stood up, but kept her hand on the cylinder. "It's interesting. Very interesting." Lela's parting words popped into her head just then. *Bring me something interesting*, Lela had said. Interesting indeed. "How much did you pay for it?"

"Two hundred credits."

"I'm sure it's worth much more," Kricorian said. "The case alone is worth that. And there's no telling what's inside." She smiled. "Could be treasure!"

"Then we have a deal?"

Kricorian laughed. "I'm not using two hundred credits for something I can't even identify. I don't care *how* good of a deal it is." Even as she spoke, her gaze drifted back to it. *You'll know it when you see it*, Lela had said. Kricorian gave the case a last lingering rub and then stepped back away from it. "Absolutely no idea what it is?"

"It takes up too much room here. One hundred and seventy-five credits." Sporae said. "I'm feeling generous."

"But we don't know what it is."

"One hundred and fifty. That's my final offer."

Kricorian studied the decorative object with a pensive look and crossed her arms. *Bring me something interesting. You'll know it when you see it.*

"Can the Rufkins have it on my transport within the hour?" she asked.

"I'm sure they can." Sporae smiled up at her. "I'll make the arrangements, and we'll finish our tea. I have a good feeling about this, Kricorian."

"What if it's filled with deadly bacteria or something?"

"Your Lela is a researcher," he said reasonably. "Have her discover a cure!"

Kricorian laughed heartily and followed him through the curtains and back to their tea, feeling comfortable in her knowledge that Lela would have something interesting to occupy her time for a while.

K Sector

Several days later, Kricorian received a message from Lela to meet her at the lab. Lela had been spending nearly all her time there working with the computer and the new cylinder. She hadn't eaten much and had slept little, and she hadn't been home in two days. Kricorian had gone to the lab late one night and had found Lela asleep on a mound of opened journals, the cylinder behind her.

Kricorian marched down the dark empty hallway of the Research Institute and opened the door to Lela's lab. Lela looked tired and haggard, and her shoulders were slumped. Kricorian stood there against the door, waiting. After a moment the sigh of relief she had been unconsciously holding eased itself out.

"You look so tired," Kricorian said. "Let's go home."

Lela stretched and rubbed her back and then her neck. She shook her head and pushed her hair away from her eyes.

"It's alive, Kricorian. There's something inside that's alive."

"Inside what?"

"The capsule. It's a life capsule. There's a slow sluggish heartbeat, and from all the tests I've run there's every indication that it's human."

Kricorian didn't let Lela's calm delivery keep her from feeling uneasy about this news. Ruthless Star Fighters were human. Exidor was human. Just because there wasn't a dreadful virus or a ravaging animal inside didn't mean the contents weren't to be feared.

"Male or female?" Kricorian asked. "We can't have any males here."

"The tests aren't conclusive yet, but I'd say it's female. I don't sense any negative energy." Lela continued rubbing her neck as she talked. "I'm ready to open it. I thought maybe you'd like to be here when I do."

"Now? You're ready *now*?"

Lela smiled tiredly. "I'm ready now."

"I think we should wait," Kricorian said. "You're exhausted. What if it needs extra attention once we've got it open?" Kricorian slipped up behind her and began to gently massage Lela's shoulders. She could feel the knotted tension in them. "Let's go home," Kricorian said. "A few more hours won't make any difference. You need some rest."

"I don't want the others here when I open it."

"Then we'll come back early in the morning or stay late tomorrow." Kricorian could feel Lela relaxing as she continued the massage. Lela would be asleep in a matter of minutes if they kept this up. "Let's go home, little one," Kricorian whispered. "We'll be back early. I promise."

~ ~ ~

The next morning Lela was up and ready to go, but much too excited to eat anything. Kricorian, however, insisted that they have breakfast together before leaving for the lab. For Kricorian it was a relief to see her in such an animated mood.

"So you think it's human inside?" Kricorian asked once they arrived at the Research Institute. "Where did it come from?"

Lela opened the door to the lab; the life capsule's golden presence seemed to almost glow in the darkness. "Yes, it's human inside," Lela said. "I'm certain about that. Something nonhuman wouldn't sound this way." She put her hands lovingly on the capsule. "It's fascinating, isn't it? The capsule itself is actually alive."

Kricorian nodded and thought she finally understood what had been driving Lela these last few days. Encountering the unknown and trying to explain the unexplainable had always been such an important part of Lela's personality.

"Are you ready?" Lela asked. "What we find in there may not be pleasant."

"I'm ready." Kricorian suddenly thought of what they might have to do if something truly powerful and unworldly should be inside. As if Lela had read her mind, she handed Kricorian a laser rod.

"If it's ugly, zap it," she said. "Don't be afraid to use this thing. It's the capsule itself that I want to study further." Lela reached over on the table behind her and dipped a thin, six-inch gyro probe into a bubbling solution. She took the probe and inserted it halfway into the carvings in the center of the capsule. When the probe was in place, the capsule began to glow and become brighter. A green mist seeped from the seam, and the smell of lilac suddenly filled the room.

"Look!" Lela whispered excitedly. "I knew it! Look! It's opening!"

The top of the cylinder slowly opened up as if on invisible hinges. The green mist was thick one moment and then virtually gone the next, but the glow inside the capsule was even brighter than it had been on the outside.

Kricorian was ready with the laser rod, her heart pounding and hands slightly trembling, and for the first time since the capsule's arrival, she was actually glad about letting Sporae talk her into purchasing it. The thrill Kricorian heard in Lela's voice helped her remember that she had done the right thing in buying the capsule.

"Look!" Lela said again.

Kricorian moved in closer and lowered the laser rod. They heard coughing and gasping coming from inside. "She's choking," Kricorian said. "Help her up."

Lela was around the front of the capsule quickly, and a few moments later the young woman inside the cylinder was sitting up, clutching her throat. "Hand me the vial," Lela said. "It's there behind you. Be careful with it."

Kricorian gave her the small container, and Lela forced the liquid into the woman's mouth. The gasping stopped almost immediately, and the sporadic coughing ceased soon afterward. Lela checked for a pulse and was satisfied that the crisis was over. She and Kricorian stepped back as the glow from the cylinder faded.

The woman shook her head and blinked several times. She was young, beautiful, and had shiny light brown hair. Her skin was pale, and when she saw Kricorian and Lela she seemed confused. She raised her hand in a gesture asking assistance out of the capsule.

With Lela and Kricorian on either side of her, the young woman was able to stand on her own. She wore a lavender tunic that came to her knees and black pants and boots. Kricorian, still amazed at everything she had just witnessed, helped her take a few steps before asking who she was and where she was from.

Acting as though she hadn't heard what Kricorian had said, the woman looked at the capsule and then at both of them again. Nodding toward the cylinder she said, "This means I've been in danger."

"Who sealed you inside?" Kricorian asked.

"I did," the woman said.

"You did? How?"

"I don't know how it works."

She became quiet, and Kricorian asked her again who she was and where she had come from.

"My name is Tavia." That confused look came over the woman's face again as she studied her surroundings.

"Tavia," Kricorian said. Her eyes widened, and she led the young woman back the way they had come and helped her sit on a stool. Kricorian glanced over at Lela, who was once more engrossed in the capsule. It was then that Kricorian noticed the gold brocade on Tavia's lavender tunic — the same pattern that had outlined Alaric's and Lieutenant Jaret's uniforms.

Kricorian leaned over toward Lela and whispered, "Do you have any idea who this is?"

"No," Lela said as she gave the young woman a quick visual inspection. "But she looks harmless enough."

"I think we've found the Amtec princess," Kricorian whispered.

Kricorian immediately called the Command Post and requested that someone find Lieutenant Jaret and get her to the Research Institute as soon as possible.

Chapter Seven

K Sector

Kricorian watched Jaret's expression change from annoyance at having been called away from her work to joy and reverence at finding the Amtec princess alive and unharmed. Jaret held the princess at arm's length and then hugged her fiercely as if to convince herself that what she was seeing was actually real. When Jaret finally let go of her, she knelt on one knee in front of the princess and bowed her head.

Tavia placed a hand on Jaret's shoulder, touched Jaret's chin, and tilted her head up so she could look into her eyes.

"I knew my warriors would find me."

"Your warriors can't take credit for this," Jaret said.

"But you're here, and that's what matters."

Jaret stood and asked Kricorian how long the princess had been there and why they hadn't said anything sooner.

Lela smiled at their two guests. "She hasn't been here that long. We didn't even know that we had her. We were as surprised as you are. Actually, Kricorian bought your princess at the Tracon marketplace just the other day."

"*Bought* me?" Tavia said, horrified.

"You were a real bargain from what I hear," Lela said.

Kricorian imagined that the look on Jaret's face matched her own. *No, no, no,* Kricorian thought. *This isn't going well at all.*

"Who are you?" Tavia asked in an amused voice as she gave Lela a once-over.

Jaret introduced them and explained that they were from K Sector. "That's where we are right now."

"K Sector," Tavia repeated. "The land of scientists, healers, and herb farmers?" She added with a nod, "All noteworthy professions."

"What do you remember about being captured?" Jaret asked. "And when and where did it happen?"

"I don't remember much of anything," Tavia said, embarrassed. "I was in the transport bay at the Amtec palace on my way to Tracon when someone grabbed me from behind. That's all I remember." She glanced at Lela. "Actually, the last thing I really remember is coughing and seeing you. Nothing in between." Her gaze returned to Jaret, and in a low voice she said, "Where is Alaric?"

"I'll send for her immediately," Jaret said.

Kricorian volunteered to relay a message to the Amtec palace and motioned for Lela to follow her. "I'll also arrange for your quarters," Kricorian said over her shoulder.

"You've been very helpful," the princess said.

Lela held the door open for Kricorian and whispered, "She's been sleeping in a giant test tube for the past few months. Even K Sector's accommodations have to be better than that."

"Kricorian," Jaret called.

Kricorian stopped at the door and turned.

"Thank you," Jaret said, her voice brimming with emotion.

Kricorian nodded. "You know where to find us if you need anything. Someone will be here shortly to help you get settled."

Kricorian and Lela met the Amtecs as they arrived. Kricorian thought that Alaric and her entourage were even more impressive now than the first time she had seen them. Amtec women were striking and had such poise and confidence in everything they did.

A total of five spidercrafts were lined up perfectly in front of the cargo bay. Seven Amtec warriors, wearing the dark blue uniform of junior officers, and one healer, dressed in a ceremonial Amtec robe with blue and gold markings on the sleeves, stayed close to the spidercraft formation. Alaric, standing out from among them with her white uniform and blond hair, gave them instructions while the warriors stood at attention.

"Kricorian," Alaric said when they met on the runway a few minutes later. "I don't know how to thank you for finding her."

"It was a nice bit of luck, actually."

"I'd like to speak to both of you privately before I see the princess."

"Certainly. Our cubicle is close by."

"Lieutenant Jaret is with the princess now?"

"She hasn't left her side," Kricorian said. "I've arranged for the rest of your group to be taken to the Command Post until you're ready for them."

Once at the cubicle, Alaric wasted no time getting to the point. She wanted a detailed account of how the princess ended up at K Sector. "I'm particularly interested in anything the princess said once she was released from the capsule," Alaric said. "So please start at the beginning."

Kricorian related the series of events, stopping occasionally to answer a question. When Kricorian described purchasing the cylinder, Alaric's eyes widened.

"And then Lela took over and conducted some experiments on the capsule," Kricorian said finally.

Alaric sat back in her chair. "You *purchased* the Amtec princess," she repeated.

"A hundred and fifty credits," Lela said. Her smirk had returned.

My Lela is enjoying this, Kricorian thought with a shake of her head.

Lela then explained her part in opening the capsule and how it eventually became obvious who was inside.

"I see," Alaric said. "I'm sure I'll have more questions later." She started to stand, and then Kricorian informed her that the princess didn't remember anything. Alaric sat back down again.

"Nothing?"

"Nothing," Lela said. "Other than being grabbed from behind in the Amtec transport bay the day she was abducted."

"So she never made it to Tracon," Alaric said.

"Not according to what little the princess does remember," Kricorian replied.

Alaric was quiet for a moment before asking if K Sector had a healer trained in hypnosis. Lela acknowledged that they did. "And all our resources are at your disposal," she added.

"Thank you. I'm ready to see the princess now, and I'd like your best hypnotist with me when I do."

As they left the cubicle Alaric added, "Please have two of my warriors sent over to where the princess is staying. I'll put Lieutenant Jaret in charge of the others."

Lela volunteered to locate the hypnotist and to find Lieutenant Jaret. On their way out the door Lela whispered to Kricorian, "She even *sounds* like she knows what she's doing."

Alaric was relieved to see the princess looking so well. Her hopes of finding Tavia alive had been nearly dashed only weeks ago. The Amtecs now had new security measures in place at the palace to prevent anything like this from ever happening again.

Alaric liked the psychologist that Lela had chosen to do the hypnosis. She was in her late fifties and had a soothing voice.

The princess was lying on her back on the bed, and the psychologist was in a chair beside her. Alaric was seated at a desk across the room, writing questions that she wanted the psychologist to ask.

Once the princess was sufficiently relaxed, the psychologist nodded toward Alaric, who handed the list of questions to her. Alaric waited and listened carefully to the exchange.

"Do you remember the last time you wanted to go to Tracon?" the psychologist asked once the princess was completely under.

"Yes," came Tavia's reply.

"Why did you try to leave without an escort?"

"I have more fun at Tracon without my warriors."

"But you understand that it's dangerous for you?"

"Yes."

"You're in the transport bay at the Amtec palace," the psychologist said as she read from what Alaric had written. "You're on your way to Tracon without an escort. What happened next?"

"Someone grabbed me."

"Do you know who it is?"

"Yes."

"Are you frightened?"

70

"No. I'm angry."

"Why are you angry?"

"I think she wants to stop me from going to Tracon alone."

"Is that why she grabbed you?"

"No."

"Who is the person who grabbed you?"

"Zigrid."

At hearing Zigrid's name, Alaric's breathing changed and anger bubbled up inside of her.

"Were you frightened?" the psychologist continued. She was now using a good mix of her own questions as well as Alaric's.

"Not at first."

"When did you become frightened?"

"When I saw the others."

"What others?"

"The two Star Fighters."

"Then what happened?"

"We struggle, and I am able to fight them off for a moment, but they are too much for me. I'm out of practice."

"What do you remember after that?"

"Waking up in the laboratory. Coughing."

The psychologist glanced over at Alaric, who nodded.

"I will count to three and you will wake up," the psychologist said. "You will not remember anything that we have discussed. One, two, three."

The princess woke up and stretched sleepily. Then she searched the room for Alaric.

"How did I do?"

The psychologist smiled and moved the chair out of the way. "Very well."

"Thank you," Alaric said to her and opened the door.

As the psychologist left the room, Tavia reached for Alaric's hand. "Come here and tell me what happened."

Alaric moved the chair closer and sat down beside the bed. Tavia took her hand and squeezed it.

"We have a traitor," Alaric said quietly. "As of right now, we know of only one."

Tavia made a fist with her other hand and slammed it on the bed beside her. "Who is it?" she asked through clenched teeth.

"I'll tell you when we get back to the palace. In the meantime, be suspicious of everyone."

Tavia gave her a sharp look.

With a weak smile Alaric added, "Including me, of course."

"Never you," Tavia said. She moved over on the bed and pulled Alaric down beside her. Reluctantly, Alaric got on the bed and held her. Tavia rubbed her cheek against Alaric's uniform.

"It's been a long time since we were together this way," Tavia whispered.

"I'm sorry about the circumstances." Alaric gave her a hug. "I'll take care of this. I'll find out why it happened and how many are involved." With a sigh of relief she added, "I'm just glad you're safe now. I intend to keep you that way."

"How can I go back to the palace and not be able to trust anyone? It's my home. Those are my people!"

"We'll know more soon. Just trust me for now."

Tavia nestled further into the comfort and safety of Alaric's arms. "I do trust you. Please tell me it's not one of my warriors."

"No. It's not one of your warriors."

"Because if it is, just do away with them and never tell me about it. I couldn't handle that."

"I know," Alaric said.

Tavia rubbed her cheek against Alaric's uniform again. "How long have I been gone?"

"Three months."

"Three *months*?" she said, sitting up and looking down at her. "I haven't had sex in three months?" She returned to Alaric's arms again and teased her by saying, "No wonder you feel so good."

Kricorian gave adequate personal space to the two warriors guarding the room where Alaric and the princess were. It had been less than an hour since the psychologist had left, and then another twenty minutes passed before Alaric came out. Alaric gave instructions to the two warriors and then motioned for Kricorian to follow her.

"We'll be leaving in the morning after the princess has rested, if that's all right."

"Of course."

"I can't thank you enough for finding her," Alaric said. "This has been an incredible ordeal for our people, and we know how lucky we are that you found her instead of some . . . some . . ."

"I know exactly what you mean," Kricorian said. "We're glad everything is working out."

"I'd like to see Lela again before it gets much later. I also need to get in touch with one of my warriors back at the palace. There are still several questions I want answers to."

Kricorian took Alaric to her office at Command Post so she could reach the ranking warrior who was currently in charge of the palace. Alaric gave an order to send three warriors to Tracon to ask Meega about gambling debts owed by any of the Amtecs. Alaric stated that she wanted the information by the time she arrived at the palace the next day.

Just as Alaric and Kricorian left the office, Lela rounded the corner, and the three of them went to find Zigrid. She was already waiting for them in a room at the end of the hall.

Zigrid stood up from the table, furious at having been detained. She had an air of superiority about her that Kricorian didn't care for, but other than that she looked like most other master healers.

"How is she?" the healer demanded. "When can I see her?"

"She's fine," Alaric said. "Resting now."

To Kricorian, the healer said, "Take me to her."

"We have other business to tend to," Alaric said in a commanding voice. "The princess is fine."

Lela's presence helped relieve some of the tension. Alaric introduced them. "Kricorian and Lela, this is Zigrid. She's the master healer for the Amtec people."

It seemed to Kricorian that Alaric disliked Zigrid. They found an empty conference room and took their seats. Lela sat down at the end of the table and Kricorian sat beside her. The other two were across the table from them. Alaric got right to the point. She addressed Zigrid first.

"Our good friends have found the Amtec princess," Alaric said, "and they only have one request of us in return for that. Lela is interested in the capsule that the princess was in and has asked that we leave it behind so that more research can be done on it."

"That's out of the question," Zigrid said without hesitation.

"I've discussed this with the princess already," Alaric continued, "and if it's at all possible for us to grant the request, then the princess and I think it should happen."

Zigrid's mouth was set in a permanent scowl. Her graying hair was pulled back severely away from her face, making her look older than she probably was.

"I have concerns about the capsule now," Zigrid said. "We need to do our own research on it. The fact that someone opened it at all needs to be clinically investigated. There are obviously flaws in its development."

Lela said, "Then we both have things we can learn from each other."

Ignoring Lela's remark, Zigrid stated again that the capsule had to return with them to the Amtec palace for further analysis.

"We're allies," Lela said. "Sharing such technology can only benefit all of us."

"It's possible that you could have killed her with your tampering."

"Tampering?" Lela repeated.

"This is getting us nowhere," Alaric said. "The princess and I agree that Lela's request is a reasonable one."

"Why are you so willing to compromise years of Amtec research and technology?" Zigrid demanded.

"We have the princess back because of these people," Alaric said. "We owe them a great deal, and they obviously have beneficial information for us. This can work to our advantage as well."

"Maybe something can be arranged in the near future," Zigrid said. "But right now the capsule must return to the Amtec laboratories to be studied. As I stated before, there are obvious flaws in its construction if an herbologist can open it. Amtec healers are the only ones with that ability." Zigrid shrugged and continued. "I'm not opposed to having K Sector help us find out what the problem is, but that has to be done at the Amtec labs. Not here or anywhere else independently."

"First of all, let me remind you of something," Lela said. "As a master healer, you were once trained here at K Sector. Is that not true?"

Zigrid glared at her and didn't answer.

"We have similar backgrounds in education," Lela said. "You've been doing it longer, perhaps. So when you attempt to insult me by calling me an *herbologist*, you're also insulting yourself. Let's stop the name calling and get on with this." She lowered her voice. "As a scientist I understand your position. However, I see this as something that could immediately benefit the entire Intergalactic Corridor if enough of us work together."

"In what way?" Alaric asked.

"The capsule kept the princess alive for several months," Lela said. "My guess is that she didn't age during that time. For example, her fingernails were a reasonable length when she was released."

"Your point?" Zigrid asked.

"I'm interested in testing the capsule for its effects on

mineral properties," Lela said. "A mineral such as lidium." She knew that she had their attention now. "Suppose the capsule could be reproduced to make the shell of a remote or even the casing where the lidium is actually stored at a relay station. Or where our power supplies are kept. If lidium has a limited life span, maybe we can make it last longer with the technology that gave you the capsule. Lidium is one of three minerals that reproduces, but it's done at such a slow rate that we need to conserve it whenever we possibly can."

Alaric looked at Lela, then turned her attention on Zigrid. "That sounds like something that could benefit all of us and is worthy of our immediate attention."

"I can discuss it with the head of the Amtec lab," Zigrid said. "In the meantime, the capsule will return with us."

To Lela, Alaric said, "I'll see to it that research begins immediately."

"Thanks."

To Kricorian, Alaric said, "And I'll see to it that your one hundred fifty credits are restored."

Chapter Eight

Intergalactic Corridor

For the safety of the princess, Alaric and Tavia were in the middle of the formation as they flew back to the Amtec palace. Once they were on their way, Alaric made an adjustment to the communications in their spidercraft so that no one else could hear what they were saying. She wanted to be aware of what the others were talking about, but didn't want anyone else to hear what she and the princess were discussing.

"When will all this be over?" Tavia asked.

"As soon as we get back," Alaric assured her.

"How can you be certain you've arrested them all?"

"I'll know when I find out what her motives were."

Tavia adjusted her helmet and sighed. "How do you plan to protect me while you're taking care of things?"

"Warriors can be trusted explicitly," Alaric said with confidence, "but there are some who are in love with you, of course. I know who they are, and I'll assign them to protect you right away."

Tavia threw her head back and laughed. "There you go, pumping up my ego again."

With a smile Alaric said, "As I recall, your ego has never needed any nurturing."

"How many are in love with me?" Tavia asked coyly.

"Eight, that I know of."

"Only eight?" Tavia teased.

"Every Amtec warrior would die for you," Alaric said. "Without question. But some would do it with more passion than others."

"Just be careful who you assign to protect me. I haven't had sex in three months, you know." When Alaric didn't respond, Tavia asked, "Why can't you protect me? Why can't I stay with you until this is over?"

"Certain unpleasant things will be happening," Alaric said. "Things that you will not want to know about."

"But I'll feel safer with you."

"I'll always be close by."

"That's not the same."

"You'll be safe," Alaric said. "Mistakes were made before. Those have been corrected now. Security is tighter, and fewer people are involved in the decision-making process."

Amtec Palace Reception Bay

With clever maneuvering and expert landing skills, the five spidercrafts set down without incident in the crowded reception bay at the Amtec palace. Their Princess had returned, and hundreds of Amtec women were excited to see her again.

"Look," Tavia said as she took off her helmet. "They've brought the children!"

On the right side of the reception bay stood fifty or more little girls, each holding something they had made for the princess. Tavia was delighted to see them. She loved spending time with them and often visited the Amtec village of Ambrose where they lived. Located not far from the palace, Ambrose was specially designed to accommodate the children's needs from infancy through the age of twelve.

The children began to sing for her the moment Tavia got out of the spidercraft. While they were singing, a warrior whispered in Alaric's ear. Alaric turned and gave instructions to several other warriors in the immediate area. Four warriors then carried the capsule to the Amtec lab, while two others escorted a disgruntled Zigrid to Alaric's office inside the palace. Alaric and another warrior stayed by Tavia's side until the children finished singing.

The reception bay burst into thunderous applause when the song was over.

"Thank you, my darlings," Tavia said. "Are those gifts for me?"

"Yes!" they all cried. The children giggled and waved the gifts they held.

While the princess addressed the crowd, more warriors slipped into the assembly. Tavia told her people that she was glad to be back and that she wanted to see the children in the atrium right away.

Amtec Communications Center

The two warriors who had escorted Zigrid to the communications center stood at attention outside the door of Alaric's office. Alaric went in and sat down across from Zigrid. The tiny lines in Zigrid's eyes crinkled and twitched.

Keeping her contempt for this woman in check, Alaric waited for Zigrid to speak first, but Zigrid only glared at her. As Alaric continued to watch, she sensed a hunger for power in Zigrid's expression, a struggle for dominance, and a need for control.

"Well?" Zigrid said finally as she plucked at the sleeve of her robe. "When can I see the princess? She needs a thorough examination."

"The healers at K Sector examined her. She's fine."

"You can't be serious."

Tired of this nonsense, Alaric quietly asked, "Did you actually think I wouldn't find out? That I wouldn't be able to locate the person who caused all of this?"

Zigrid laughed nervously. "Caused what? I have no idea what you're talking about."

"We're beyond playing games, Zigrid. You've betrayed the Amtec people, and now you have to pay for it."

"I have —"

"I will do the talking," Alaric said calmly. "I know what happened the night the princess disappeared. You let them in and had her taken. That's now a matter of record."

Zigrid's breathing changed, and her eyes hardened into cold, dark marbles.

"You've betrayed us," Alaric said simply, "and now I expect you to do the right thing."

"And what do you consider the right thing?"

Alaric took the vial sitting near the scanner on her desk and moved it closer to her. "I'm giving you the chance to die with honor, Zigrid. It's certainly much more than you deserve, and much more than you would have given the princess."

Zigrid's jaw was set, but her chin quivered as her eyes moved to the vial and lingered there before moving back to Alaric.

"And if I refuse?" Zigrid asked through clenched teeth.

"If you refuse?" Alaric slowly fought to control her rage. "I'll kill you right here," she said simply. "With these hands. In this very room. Without blinking an eye. Without so much as a moment of regret or a flicker of compassion for your limp, dead body." She stood up and slowly went around the desk. "You arranged to have the princess abducted and let at least two Star Fighters into our perimeter. You put the palace in danger and betrayed the Amtec people. That's treason and will not go unpunished."

"How did you find out?"

Alaric picked up the vial. "That doesn't matter."

"I won't do it," Zigrid said. "You'll have to kill me yourself."

Alaric's face showed no emotion. "Why would you want to give me such pleasure?" Alaric leaned closer to her. "Such a delightful pleasure it'll be," she said. "When I think about you being responsible for those filthy Star Fighters touching her, it's all I can do to keep from killing you right now . . . this very instant."

"You've always had an unhealthy relationship with the princess." With a new sense of confidence, Zigrid met Alaric's gaze. "You'll have to keep me alive for a while longer. Others were involved in this. I couldn't have done it on my own."

"I've already taken care of that, Zigrid. I know that you worked alone and that you did it to pay off your gambling debts. I have all that information already."

"How could you possibly know that?"

"Everyone associated with the palace has been accounted for during that time. Everyone but you. Also, our friend Meega, who owns the cantina at Tracon, was very generous with information about your mounting gambling debts."

Alaric picked up the vial. "You allowed her to be taken from us by murderers and thieves. We could have lost her forever."

Alaric reached and gathered a handful of Zigrid's robe, pulling her up from the chair. Their faces were only inches apart, and Alaric could smell the fear on her. "I have a few questions to ask before you die," she said. "I want to know why. Tell me why you would gamble with Star Fighters."

"I'm telling you nothing."

Alaric let go of her and dropped her back down in the chair with a thud. "Then do the right thing. Drink it." She set the vial on the edge of the desk. "Don't make me kill you. That will be far less pleasant for you."

When Zigrid didn't move, Alaric leaned over and hissed, "*Drink* it!"

With a steady hand Zigrid reached for the vial and picked it up. She opened it and stopped inches from her lips before closing her eyes. She hesitated only a moment, and then drank the potion, draining the last drop from the small container. There were no more words. The waiting was over. Moments later, Zigrid slumped in the chair. She was dead.

Alaric had two warriors take care of Zigrid's body. She would personally tell the princess what had happened and then explain the new security procedures that had been in place for the last three months since Tavia had been gone. Alaric found her in the atrium with the children and stayed toward the back until the princess was finished with them. Each child received a hug and a thank-you for the present she had made. Several healers were there to take the children back to Ambrose.

"Help me carry these," Tavia said, indicating the paper flowers, hand-carved figurines, and finger paintings that the children had given her. "We're decorating the dining hall with them."

"Right now?" Alaric asked.

Tavia laughed. "Yes, right now."

"Don't you think the command suite would be a better place for them? A more personal touch?"

"I want to show them off to everyone. I can't do that if I keep them in my room."

Alaric carefully stacked the paintings by size. "They weren't made for everyone. They were made for you."

Tavia nodded. "I see. It would mean more to them if they knew their presents were in a personal place rather than a community place." She nodded again. "Yes, that's a much better idea. Thank you, Alaric. Help me carry them to the command suite."

They made it in one trip, and as Alaric helped the princess decorate her room with the children's gifts, she told her about Zigrid's betrayal. Tavia stopped the decorating and sat down in the closest chair. She was shocked and frightened.

"She was the only one involved from here," Alaric assured her.

"How can you be certain of that?" Tavia was pale and trembling.

"It's my job to be certain," Alaric said softly.

"Please hold me," Tavia said. "Please." She held out her hand and stood up. Even though she was safe in Alaric's arms, Tavia continued to tremble. "Did she say why?"

Alaric explained about the gambling debts that were uncovered and Zigrid's friendship with a few Star Fighters.

"We've learned a lot from this," Alaric said. "You have a responsibility to your people. I can't stress enough how important it is for you to stay safe."

Tavia hugged her fiercely. "I know it was careless of me to want to get away, but I've done it before and nothing ever happened to me."

"If you won't take a few warriors with you when you have to get away, then maybe we can bring the diversions here to you instead."

Tavia put her head on Alaric's shoulder. "I want to see her."

"Zigrid? That's not possible. She's been taken away." Alaric felt the princess sinking into her body and heard her sigh with relief. "There's something that might help take your mind off of this," Alaric said.

Tavia let go of her and absentmindedly stared at the new decorations in the room. "Something like what?" she asked as she resumed hanging the children's pictures.

"There's been talk of holding an Intergalactic summit again. Representatives from all the sectors will meet and discuss mutual problems and form policies that we can all live with."

Tavia shrugged. "That sounds like a wonderful idea. We've had similar meetings before, but not nearly that inclusive."

"It was also suggested that the Amtecs host such a gathering."

Tavia stopped what she was doing and gave Alaric her full attention. "I like that idea even better." With a smile she asked how soon they could have it.

"That's totally up to you," Alaric said. "We've tightened our security since you were abducted, and we have the resources available to make this a safe place for dignitaries to meet."

"Then I'll get started on it right away." She gave Alaric an impulsive hug. "Thank you. I'm always amazed at how you know exactly what I need."

"That's part of my job."

Chapter Nine

K Sector

Kricorian found it both a relief and a disappointment to see Lieutenant Jaret leave. K Sector's force field was once again strong and dependable as a result of Jaret's hard work, so it was nice knowing that her services were no longer needed. There was a mutual attraction between them, and Kricorian didn't want to admit that she would miss seeing the young officer every day. It was just as well that Jaret's time at K Sector had come to an end. Kricorian could get her emotions in order and carry on with everyday life. At least that was the plan before Kricorian and Lela received the invitation to visit the Amtec palace.

"So the summit is on," Lela said as she brought steaming bowls of stew to the table for their dinner.

"So it seems," Kricorian said. "Ten representatives, two from each sector."

"Who will represent Corlon? If they send two Star Fighters, that'll certainly be interesting."

"So far there's been no word from Corlon. An invitation has been extended, but they haven't agreed to come yet." Kricorian poured herself some wine and offered the flask to Lela, who declined. "Keda and Viscar from Alpha Sector will be there, and Sporae and Meega from Tracon."

"Meega," Lela said with a shudder.

"I've also heard some grumbling from Tracon about only being able to send two representatives," Kricorian said. "The Rufkins are requesting voting privileges, stating that Tracon has many diverse groups."

"Sporae can speak for them," Lela said. "Tracon needs to work that out among themselves. I'd rather have a Rufkin at the summit than Meega. At least a Rufkin never tried to drug me."

"Meega can be quite persuasive in her own right," Kricorian noted. "She usually doesn't need to resort to those tactics to get what she wants."

"So have you ever dabbled in Meega's —"

"Me?" Kricorian said. "Goodness no! But every time I've seen her she's been in the company of some very nice women." Kricorian added, "And she didn't have to drug them. They were happy to be there."

"Some drugs make women stupid," Lela said.

Kricorian laughed. "Maybe. Are you sure you want to be a K Sector representative? You might end up being on a committee with Meega. I have no idea how this thing is going to be set up."

Without hesitation Lela said, "Yes, I want to be a part of

the summit. I'll do whatever is expected of me while I'm there."

"Good. Then we're leaving in two days. The Amtecs want us there early for some sort of celebration. Can you put your projects on hold for a while?"

"What kind of celebration?"

Kricorian shook her head and rolled her eyes. "We found the Amtec princess, Lela. They want to thank us for that."

"Alaric thanked us already," Lela said.

"They want to thank us again," Kricorian said simply. "So can you be ready to leave in two days?"

"Yes. I can be ready."

Amtec Air Space

Kricorian was granted clearance into the Amtec perimeter and set the spidercraft down in the transport bay a few minutes later. The princess and four warriors were there to greet them.

"Welcome to the Amtec palace," Tavia said. "We're glad you could come."

"It's an honor to be here," Kricorian said. She had been to the Amtec palace many years ago on a supply run after Star Fighters had briefly invaded Tracon and upset the entire trading mechanism for the corridor. The raid had left K Sector no other way to market their goods other than personal delivery. The Amtecs paid well and at the time had appreciated the extra effort that K Sector had made. Kricorian's visit back then had been strictly business related, but she'd never forgotten the luxurious surroundings she had seen.

"Would you like a tour of the palace?" Tavia asked. "Or we can wait until later if you prefer."

They elected to have a tour then. Kricorian liked the way

the princess insisted on taking care of them personally, when another Amtec dignitary could have just as easily handled things. Kricorian also noticed how the princess kept Lela's attention by touching her arm to explain various points of interest.

"We're having a banquet in your honor this evening," Tavia said. "The Amtec people want to show their appreciation." To Lela she said, "And several of our researchers are interested in how you managed to open the capsule without killing me."

Lela grinned. "It's an old herbology trick."

They had seen the Amtec atrium where real trees and flowers grew and Tavia showed them the theater where the summit might possibly be held. The halls of the palace were huge and impressive with forty-foot ceilings trimmed in gold. Lela had heard about the Amtec palace her whole life, but the rumors had in no way done it justice.

Kricorian saw Lieutenant Jaret giving instructions to a cluster of warriors at the end of the long hallway. At the sight, Kricorian's heart began a tango in her chest. She realized that she had unconsciously been looking for Jaret ever since her arrival. Now that she'd seen her, she was having difficulty staying focused on what the princess and Alaric, who had left the group to meet the princess halfway, were saying.

"My apologies for not meeting you earlier," Alaric said to Lela and Kricorian.

"It's good to see you again," Kricorian said. "I know this is a busy time for you."

"I want you and Lieutenant Jaret to sit with us at our table this evening," the princess said to Alaric. "Walk with us to their rooms."

As they drew nearer to where Jaret and the other warriors were standing, Jaret stopped talking when she saw Kricorian. Their eyes met and Kricorian was helpless in her attempt to look away. A tingle of excitement spread through Kricorian's body, and a touch of fear made her weak with anticipation.

Jaret, her smile warm and friendly, left the group to meet them.

"It's good to see you both again," Jaret said. "We have some wonderful things planned for you."

Tavia told Jaret that she wanted her to sit with them at their table later that evening. Jaret looked at Kricorian and nodded slightly.

"Carry on with what you were doing," Tavia said to Jaret. Then to Kricorian and Lela she said, "This is close to where you'll be staying while you're here."

They went down another elaborate wing of the palace that had several private suites. Lela and Kricorian would have their own rooms with a warrior posted at each end of the hallway.

"Ample security is merely a precaution," the princess noted.

Tavia showed them their rooms, and Kricorian was quick to notice that the accommodations in each room were better than the cubicle she and Lela shared at K Sector. The princess asked if Kricorian would like to see the communications center, where the Amtec security section was located. Alaric offered to take her there.

"And if Lela is up to it, I'd like to show her the Amtec research labs," Tavia said.

Kricorian and Lela were supposed to rest before the banquet, but they were too excited. They were in Kricorian's room enjoying the comfort of reclining chairs.

"What are the research labs like?" Kricorian asked.

"Incredible. Huge. Everything imaginable was right there. The possibilities for serious research are endless."

"Have they done anything with your idea about the capsule and the lidium for future remotes?"

"I met two of the four women working on it," Lela said.

"They seemed glad to see me. They're making great progress and should have something ready in about two weeks."

"It's good to see that you're not upset about that project being located here."

"It makes a difference to me that those who are doing the work are interested in results. I like their enthusiasm." Lela laughed. "I did the easy part."

"Did you get to see any other projects that are being done here?"

"I mostly saw the facilities," Lela said. "Although I did talk to one researcher who was interested in the synthetic food project I'm working on. And there was one area where I wasn't allowed into, but that's understandable. K Sector also has projects that are sensitive in nature. So what about you? How was your tour? Was Alaric her usual charming, chatty self?" Lela asked dryly.

Kricorian laughed. "She was open about what their mission is and how they accomplish it. I liked what I saw. I feel safe here." Kricorian took a deep breath and remembered how she felt when Jaret had entered the communications center earlier. Kricorian had immediately become a babbling fool. She had finally stopped trying to talk and let Alaric and Jaret carry the conversation.

"So Alaric will be there at our table tonight," Lela said.

"And Lieutenant Jaret," Kricorian added. That's all she had been able to think about that afternoon. Where would Jaret sit? Would they talk? Would other warriors be there to dominate Jaret's time? Kricorian wondered briefly if there was a way to get out of going to the banquet at all. Maybe she could tell them she was ill or tired from her journey. That way no one could see her confusion and uncertainty. Kricorian was sure that her emotions were etched in every expression on her face and in every word she uttered.

"Did Alaric say anything about me?" Lela asked.

"No. Why would she?"

"Oh."

Kricorian chuckled. "You like her type. Those quiet strong ones."

"Don't be ridiculous."

"Admit it, little one. You agreed to come to the summit so you could see her again."

"I'm here to represent my —"

"Sure you are," Kricorian said with a laugh.

"Well," Lela said after a moment. "Do you think she's noticed me anyway?"

"Not the way you're hoping she would. She's a warrior. Even worse, she's the *commander* of the warriors. You don't get that position any other way than by hard work and determination. She's not interested in a relationship of any kind." Kricorian stretched and got even more comfortable in the chair. "But I wouldn't be surprised to hear that she and the princess have been lovers in the past. It's common knowledge that Amtec warriors make the best lovers."

"So I've heard."

The banquet hall, decorated in blue and gold, was capable of accommodating at least six hundred people. Eight musicians were playing near the entrance, and banners welcoming Kricorian and Lela to the Amtec palace had been hung at the main door.

Tavia introduced them to the Amtec Council, whose members were advisers to the princess. The council consisted of four women close to Kricorian's age. They were dressed in long blue-and-gold robes that matched the decor of the hall. As Kricorian and Lela made their way to the table in the back, they greeted everyone they passed.

Before they sat down, Lela leaned over toward Kricorian and whispered, "How many people live in this place?"

"I have no idea."

Their table was on a raised platform, which gave them a

different view of the hall. Women of all ages were in attendance, and a mixture of laughter, female voices, and chamber music filled the air. When Kricorian saw Lieutenant Jaret and Alaric come in, she realized that they were the only two warriors there.

Tavia told everyone where she wanted them to sit, and Kricorian was relieved yet anxious to have Jaret sitting on her right and Alaric on her left. Lela was between Alaric and the princess, and the Amtec Council was seated by seniority on the other side of Tavia.

"How is your room?" Tavia asked Lela. "Do you need anything that isn't there?"

"My room is unlike anything I've ever seen before."

Tavia poured wine into Lela's goblet and then her own. "Am I to take that to mean everything is fine?"

"Yes, everything is fine. Thank you." Lela turned to her right and asked Alaric if she was having wine with them or if she was still working.

"I'm always working."

"I see," Lela said as she took a tiny sip. "Saved any helpless women lately?"

Alaric shook her head. "No. Not lately."

"That's too bad. You're very good at it." Lela saw the faint trace of a smile at the corner of Alaric's mouth.

"Has anyone officially thanked you for saving the princess?" Alaric asked.

"About eight hundred of them," Lela said with a nod toward the sea of Amtec women at the tables below.

"You did a great thing. You'll never know how much it means to us to have her back."

"I know what it's like to lose someone you love."

Alaric nodded. "And the Amtec people love their Princess."

Lela took another sip of wine. "What are you doing later tonight? After this little party is over?"

"I have work to do. We're still preparing for the summit."

"Is there anything I can help with?"

Alaric offered another faint smile. "No. We have it all under control. You're a guest. But thank you anyway."

Lela was surprised when the princess leaned around Lela to say, "Alaric, I'd like to see you in my office later this evening. Now let's formally welcome our guests to the Amtec palace."

Chapter Ten

Amtec Banquet Hall

Kricorian began to relax while drinking her first glass of wine, which seemed to stay full. Then she realized that Jaret was continuously refilling it. Jaret was also doing a large majority of the talking.

"What have you seen at the palace so far?" Jaret asked.

Like all the other Amtecs, she was wearing a more ceremonial version of her usual uniform, and Kricorian thought how nice she looked in it. The gold brocade on the collar and sleeves was the same pattern that had been carved into the capsule the princess had been in. Kricorian had seen the pattern everywhere in the palace. The pattern was an elaborate part of archways, floor tiles, and handrails. It seemed to unite all areas and bring everything together into some sort of Amtec theme. Kricorian realized that K Sector had nothing that represented them in such a unified way. K Sector had simple utility uniforms, and little hierarchy among its people.

"Besides the command suite," Jaret said. "Alaric gave you a tour of that earlier. And I know the princess likes spending time in the atrium, so you've probably seen that as well."

"Yes," Kricorian said. "Tavia showed us the atrium and the area that's being prepared for the summit."

"You should see the observatory before you leave," Jaret said. "It's one of my favorite places."

Kricorian was feeling a warm buzz from the wine, but she placed her hand over her glass when Jaret tried to fill it again. Jaret poured a bit more into her own glass and smiled.

"I'm usually on duty," Jaret said. "I never get to do this."

"I have a little wine with dinner occasionally."

"Would you like to see the observatory later? After the celebration is over?" Jaret asked. "It's quite impressive at night."

Before Kricorian had a chance to answer, Tavia began making an announcement at the other end of the table.

"Let me have everyone's attention," the princess said. Her voice carried easily, and a hush fell over the banquet hall.

"I'd like to formally introduce our two guests from K Sector, Kricorian and Lela." With an air of amusement in her voice she said, "Kricorian purchased me for one hundred and fifty credits at the Tracon marketplace." The gasp from the audience was followed by laughter when the princess added, "I always thought that I would bring at least a hundred and seventy-five."

To the sound of thunderous applause, Kricorian found it amusing that Tavia could make light of what could have been a tragic situation had the capsule fallen into the hands of the wrong people. Tavia's willingness to trivialize things made the festivities that much more enjoyable and Kricorian's and

Lela's involvement less of an act of heroism and more of the string of good luck that it actually was.

"The commander of the Amtec Army has seen to it that I've been paid for in full," Tavia added.

Kricorian couldn't be sure, but she thought she heard Alaric chuckle as the laughter from the hall swelled again. Lela and Kricorian rose and acknowledged the applause, and not long afterward the food was served.

"Have you given any more thought to how K Sector wants the lidium harvested?" Jaret asked Kricorian. "It would be an economic boost if you did it yourself."

Kricorian nodded, a bit amused at Jaret's inability to simply relax and have fun. *This one always thinks of business.* "We're considering that," Kricorian said. "Even more so now since my security advisers don't like the idea of having a lot of unnecessary traffic coming in and out of our perimeter."

"You could mine it and then transport the lidium to Tracon for it to be sold," Jaret suggested. "There are merchants who already have the facilities to handle and store it." She shrugged. "As long as it's available in whatever quantities are needed, there should be no problem."

"You make it sound so easy," Kricorian said with a light laugh. "No one on K Sector wants any part of harvesting or transporting lidium. It may be something I end up doing on my own."

"I'd be happy to help you with that," Jaret said seriously.

"You have duties here."

"Arrangements can be made. You forget that you found the Amtec princess and returned her safely to us. We have much to thank you for, and helping to harvest and transport lidium would be an easy thing for the Amtecs to do for you."

"Then I might take you up on that offer."

Jaret raised her glass and clinked it against Kricorian's. "To the first of many promising arrangements."

~ ~ ~

"Tomorrow you will see Ambrose," Tavia said as she poured Lela more wine. "It's where the Amtec children live."

"Why don't they live in the palace?" Lela asked.

Tavia smiled. "The palace is boring for them. They come here for visits, but Ambrose was made especially for them. It has everything they could possibly want or need. Trips to the palace are special for them. And for us, too. It's a little treat for everyone when they are here."

"Who cares for them there?"

"We have a trained staff of teachers, child psychologists, and healers that take care of them. The facility they live in is exceptional, and Ambrose itself is quite an amazing place. Once you've seen it, I want to discuss something with you."

"Something like what?" Lela asked with sudden interest.

"I'll wait until after you've been given a tour. What did you think of our research facilities here?"

Lela nodded. "Impressive. K Sector has the same things basically, but on a much smaller scale."

"Research can mean the difference in survival these days," Tavia said. "My mother drilled that into me at an early age. She wanted to make sure I never took anything for granted. We can't move forward without it, so research has become an intrinsic part of what we do and who we are."

"I understand that completely," Lela said. "K Sector feels the same way."

Tavia smiled again. "That's something else I'd like to discuss with you later."

The evening passed with light conversation and more wine-induced laughter. Lela was tired from traveling, touring, and smiling so much. And since she had spent most of the evening trying to keep Alaric's attention, she was tired from that, too. There was something about her that Lela found incredibly attractive, whether it was Alaric's aloofness or her sense of honor and duty, Lela didn't know. But she was drawn to it and couldn't stop herself from flirting shamelessly with her. Alaric, on the other hand, seemed to be immune.

"You must be tired," Tavia said as she stood up from the table. "I'll take you back to your room when you're ready."

"Thanks," Lela said. "I'm ready now, and yes, I'm very tired." She turned to Alaric and said, "It was nice seeing you again, Commander."

Alaric nodded slightly. "On behalf of the Amtec people, let me say once again how grateful we are that you found the princess and returned her to us safely."

"Think nothing of it, Commander. We had no intention of keeping her."

Tavia motioned toward the platform stairs and let Lela go first. To Alaric, the princess said, "Don't forget that I need to see you later."

"I'm not in the habit of forgetting such things," Alaric reminded her. "I'll be waiting for you."

The hallways were busy with Amtec women who were lingering and chattering on and on about the banquet; some had stayed behind to continue dancing. On their way out of the banquet hall, the princess had encouraged everyone to stay and continue celebrating as long as they wanted. She and Lela waved to Kricorian, who was still seated at the table and deep in conversation with Jaret. Kricorian smiled and waved back at them once they got her attention.

"Lieutenant Jaret will make sure she gets to her room," Tavia said as they made their way through the crowded hall. The closer they got to Lela's room, the emptier the hallways became. They were finally at the part of the palace where the visitors' quarters were. They approached the hallway where a young warrior was posted. Tavia introduced them and explained that if Lela needed anything, all she had to do was ask and there would be a warrior close by.

"I'll be around to collect you and Kricorian for breakfast," Tavia said. "Sleep well."

Tavia knew that Alaric would be standing by the scanner checking the surveillance cameras throughout the palace before she even entered the command suite.

"How do you think it went?" Tavia asked.

"The banquet? It was a nice touch, and very successful." Alaric switched the scanner off. "You were quite charming, as usual."

With hands on her hips, Tavia took a deep breath. "But not quite charming enough."

"What makes you say that? Your people love you."

"My people, yes. But this Lela person." Tavia made a little growling noise as she waved her hand in the air as if to dismiss the entire subject.

"What about Lela?"

"She's interested in *you*!" Tavia snapped. "Not me! Nothing I said tonight made any difference. She couldn't wait for me to shut up so that she could ask *you* something else."

"That's a bit of an exaggeration. I didn't see that at all."

"Of course you didn't! You never do."

Alaric waited for the princess to stop pacing. This was not a new conversation for them.

"So this is what I want you to do," Tavia said as she moved closer to the console that Alaric was leaning against. "I'll meet them for breakfast in the morning, and just before it's over I want you to arrive. You'll be Lela's escort to Ambrose for the day. I want her to see the entire facility, but spend a lot of time where the children are kept and cared for. Then I want you to take her to the lake." Tavia stopped in front of her and looked Alaric squarely in the eye.

"Then what should I do with her?" Alaric asked.

"You'll figure it out." Tavia turned away from her. "Afterward, I want you to bring her back and be as available to her as your schedule will allow." She looked up again, and Alaric met her penetrating gaze. "Do you understand what I'm saying?"

"Yes, I understand what you're saying. I'm just not sure why you're saying it."

"I have my reasons. I'll see you in the morning."

Kricorian and Jaret talked for hours on the platform while the celebration continued down below them. Kricorian had stopped drinking wine earlier and had no idea where she was getting her energy; she should have been tired hours ago. Jaret again mentioned the observatory and asked her if she wanted to see it.

"Or maybe another time," Jaret said suddenly. "You've had a long day already."

"I think I'm up to it." Kricorian was stiff from having sat for so long, and her knee creaked as she stood. Instead of embarrassing her, the popping sound made her laugh. She limped down the steps that led to the platform; it felt good to move around again.

Once they were mingling with the masses on the main floor of the banquet hall, scores of happy Amtec women hugged and thanked Kricorian as she and Jaret tried to leave. After they were away from the music in the banquet hall, the crowd began to thin out. Kricorian felt content and happy as she walked alongside Jaret.

"We've received official word from Alpha Sector and Tracon about the summit," Jaret said, "but nothing from Corlon yet. Bravo Sector can't send anyone, but they appreciated the invitation. They might be ready for the next one."

"I'm glad to see there's so much interest in this," Kricorian said.

"I agree, but if Corlon refuses to participate, we run the risk of aligning ourselves against them even more than we already have." Jaret opened a huge door and took them into a part of the palace that Kricorian hadn't seen yet. "And I'd like to see a more inclusive, diverse group than what we have so far," Jaret said. "Without Corlon's participation, we won't get as much accomplished as we should. This is a great opportunity for everyone."

"We can't force them to participate."

"No, but we can go out of our way to encourage their involvement and extend a more positive and personal invitation."

They turned down a narrower hallway where Jaret entered a code into a panel outside the nearest door. Kricorian was awestruck by what she saw once they went inside. In front of her was a window looking out into space, out and beyond the Intergalactic Corridor she traveled through so often. Kricorian had never witnessed this view from anywhere other than a porthole in a spidercraft.

There were reclining chairs identical to the ones back in Kricorian's room, and Jaret motioned toward them in an invitation to sit and enjoy the spectacular view.

"I've never seen anything so magnificent," Kricorian murmured as she eased into the chaise. Billions of specks of light stood out against the crisp backdrop of deep space, and her eyes fixed on the huge window that looked as though she could reach out and touch the stars.

"This is my favorite place in the palace," Jaret said. She turned her head and looked over at her. "I've been wanting to share it with you."

Kricorian felt the warmth of Jaret's arm against hers as they sat in the chairs. She found herself enjoying their closeness.

"Thank you for bringing me here. You knew I would like

it." She was so relaxed and comfortable that it occurred to her that having a chaise longue in her own cubicle back at K Sector was a wonderful idea. *Must be the wine*, she thought. *I don't need my own room. Just leave me here and nudge me when I have to be somewhere else.*

Then, Kricorian felt something touching the back of her hand as it lay on the armrest. She looked down to see Jaret's index finger making a light trail on her skin. A swirl of delightful emotion swooshed through Kricorian's body, almost making her dizzy. A chill ran over her skin. After a moment she loosened her grip on her portion of the armrest and let herself enjoy being touched. She turned her head and saw that Jaret was fixated on what she was doing, as if looking somewhere other than Kricorian's hand would break the magic that was happening between them.

Kricorian felt paralyzed and absolutely speechless, and the power of what Jaret was doing made her feel weak all over. Jaret covered Kricorian's hand with her own; Kricorian's, in return, squeezed back.

They sat in silence, gazing out into space and holding hands. Kricorian didn't know how long she had been asleep when she finally woke up, and she was initially embarrassed at having done so, but when she looked over at Jaret and found her asleep as well, she smiled. *She looks so young,* Kricorian thought. *What am I saying? She* is *young.*

Jaret stirred. She squeezed Kricorian's hand again and then let go.

"I should get you back to your room," she said as they both stood up.

"How long did we sleep?" Kricorian asked.

"Not long." Jaret reached for her hand again, and their eyes met. Jaret leaned closer and kissed her.

The first kiss was as light as Jaret's initial touch had been, and Kricorian was too surprised at the suddenness of it all to feel anything other than fluttering in her stomach. Their lips touched as if to say hello, and Jaret kept the soft, steady introduction alive for them with her own obvious desire. But the second kiss, which was a more intense continuation of the first, opened a flood of emotion that raced through Kricorian's body. The moment Jaret's tongue touched hers it was as if liquid heat were oozing through each of Kricorian's veins.

It had been fifteen years since someone had kissed her this way.

"I can't," Kricorian said weakly against Jaret's lips. "Please."

But the kissing didn't stop, and Kricorian's body didn't want it to stop. Her body was taking control even though her heart had a different idea about what should be happening. *Your heart or your conscience,* she thought as the kisses became deeper.

"I can't do this," Kricorian said as she pulled away.

"I'm sorry," Jaret whispered.

"No," Kricorian managed to say. She was full of emotion and brimming with guilt from having betrayed Meridith this way. "Please don't apologize. It's me. I can't . . . I haven't . . . I —"

"I'll take you to your room."

Kricorian noticed that Jaret seemed to be just as shaken. They left the observatory in silence and walked down the hallway the same way they had come. When Jaret quietly pointed out other areas of interest in the palace, Kricorian relaxed a little. She needed someone to talk to about all these feelings that were running through her head and her heart, but she wasn't sure this was something that she could discuss with Lela.

Chapter Eleven

Kricorian frowned when she saw the two warriors posted in the hallway leading to where she and Lela were staying. Earlier, Kricorian had taken it in stride, but now she found it irritating.

"No one is in any danger," Jaret said, noticing her expression. "We want to make sure that someone will be readily available to help you if you need anything during the night."

What a little diplomat you are, Lieutenant, Kricorian thought with a smile.

"How thoughtful," Kricorian said. "K Sector's hospitality must have seemed quite unfriendly and foreign to you."

"Not at all," Jaret said. "The princess simply has a certain way she wants things done." They stopped in front of Kricorian's door. "We don't get many visitors here. We want your stay to be a memorable one."

Kricorian forgot the guards posted in the hallway and caught herself falling into the blue of Jaret's eyes. She wanted to taste the sweetness of Jaret's mouth again and feel those strong arms around her. But instead of picking up on that telepathic thought, Jaret reached over and opened the door to Kricorian's room.

"If I don't see you tomorrow," Jaret said, "enjoy your day. I'm sure the princess has many things planned for you already."

Suddenly Kricorian felt tired. The long trip, the palace tour, the banquet, the wine . . . all of it was catching up with her. She wanted to lie down and go to sleep, and she also wanted to forget the way Jaret's hand had felt in hers earlier, the way Jaret's arms had given her such comfort.

"If you need anything —"

"I'll be fine," Kricorian said. "Thank you."

"Kricorian."

Jaret came into the room, and Kricorian felt an array of contradictory emotions. She wanted to be alone, but at the same time she also wanted Jaret to stay. Kricorian knew that whatever feelings she was having right then were making no sense to her, and she was willing to blame everything on fatigue and wine.

"I think I've upset you," Jaret said, "and I didn't mean to do that."

"I'm just tired."

Jaret nodded but seemed reluctant to leave. She made the motions to do so anyway, and just inside the door she turned and said, "If my actions earlier offended you, I'm sorry. Believe me, that wasn't my intention."

"Jaret, I —"

"Don't forget breakfast with the princess in the morning. Good night." She closed the door and was gone.

Kricorian sighed and closed her eyes. She willed herself to stop thinking so much and just get in bed and go to sleep. Tomorrow would be busy, and there had been indications that she would be helping with some of the security features to be implemented for the summit.

She removed her uniform and slipped into bed; it felt good to relax and unwind. The linen on the bed was cool against her warm skin, and within seconds Kricorian drifted off to sleep to the sounds of the faraway music and laughter in the banquet hall. She slipped into a dream about being back home at K Sector. In the dream she was a much younger version of herself, standing outside of the Command Post and talking with two of her friends.

Kricorian heard the warning alarm only seconds before she saw the first Star Fighter zoom by shooting all around them. It had been almost a year since K Sector had been raided, but during that time they had been planning and preparing for the next one.

Kricorian ran toward the cargo bay where Meridith and Lela were helping load a shipment destined for Tracon. Another series of explosions sent Kricorian racing toward the destruction that had once been the loading dock. With adrenaline and terror rushing through every cell of her body, she rounded the corner to the cargo bay and found only two people there among the rubble.

Lela's tiny arms held her mother's broken, mangled body. Romney was at another location. Screaming hysterically and covered with blood, Lela clutched her mother to her chest and held on to her. Kricorian pried Meridith out of Lela's grasp, picked up her lover, and carried her inside the cargo bay. In shock and at the mercy of her breaking heart, Kricorian gathered Meridith into her arms and cried as she held her.

Seven-year-old Lela tugged on Kricorian's arm a while later. They were in danger. Kricorian was in a daze, but allowed herself to be led away from her dead lover and to a hiding place in the cargo bay. Star Fighters were still in the area where she and Lela were hiding, and Kricorian cried when she thought about Meridith's lifeless body.

"This can't be happening," she mumbled through her tears. "It can't be."

Lela slipped her hand into Kricorian's.

"No, no, no!" Kricorian cried.

Someone was shaking her, and she was roused from the image of Meridith's blood and her unnaturally limp body.

"Kricorian," a voice said urgently. Someone continued to shake her. "Wake up. You're dreaming."

Kricorian startled awake.

"I heard you cry out and was concerned." Jaret sat on the edge of the bed; her hand was still on Kricorian's shoulder.

"Jaret," Kricorian said, confused. Then she realized that she had been dreaming about Meridith and the raid; the sadness once again overwhelmed her. "I'm sorry," she said in a voice laced with sorrow. The dream was always so vivid that each time she had it, she would look at her hands, expecting to find Meridith's blood there. The dream image of Meridith in the arms of her child continued to haunt her.

It was usually Lela who heard her crying out into the night, Lela who would come into her room to make sure she was all right, Lela who would relive that day with her and help her get through it just as she had done as a child. On that terrifying day it had been Lela who had sensed the danger they were in and had gotten them away safely. And it was always Lela who held her as they cried together over their loss.

Kricorian began to tremble and wanted to rip that vision from her mind. A thousand times over during the last fifteen years she had wanted to obliterate her memory of Meridith's torn, bloody face and of Lela holding her dead mother. So when Jaret slipped into bed and took Kricorian into her arms without saying a word, it was the most natural, soothing thing that had happened to Kricorian in a long time. Kricorian didn't feel alone any longer. It was easy for her to nestle into Jaret's arms and let the tears flow without shame or reason. She felt a sense of freedom from the past that had been haunting her for so long. Kricorian admitted to herself how much she liked having Jaret there with her.

They fell asleep that way, with Kricorian safe in Jaret's arms and the comforting texture of Jaret's warrior's uniform soft against Kricorian's skin. Kricorian's head fit neatly under Jaret's chin, and it was calming the way Jaret rubbed Kricorian's bare arm as they drifted off to sleep. When she woke up several hours later, it was with a peacefulness that she hadn't felt before.

Her stirring woke Jaret, and Kricorian eased away from her a little. Even though she was aware of being naked in another woman's arms, it seemed strangely natural to her right then. Having a sudden overwhelming need to touch her, Kricorian reached over and ran her fingers through the dark curls in Jaret's hair. When Kricorian heard Jaret sigh and then close her eyes and tremble, it was as if the door to Kricorian's heart had opened. Kricorian could see the effect she had on this strong, handsome woman, and she waited until Jaret opened her eyes again before leaning closer and kissing her lightly on the lips.

Jaret responded without hesitation, and Kricorian was driven with desire and a sharp hunger for more. The thrill of having Jaret's tongue touching hers made Kricorian's body smolder with anticipation. Jaret slipped her boots off, while Kricorian worked steadily in between feverish kisses to rid her of her uniform.

It was an incredible rush to feel a woman's body next to hers again. Kricorian had forgotten how wonderful it was to be so close to someone; she felt delirious with sensation.

The intensity of Kricorian's desire surprised her; she hadn't expected to ever feel that way again. She needed to touch Jaret. She needed to have someone say her name while making love. She needed to smell and to taste a woman. She needed to experience the very essence of life. Kricorian felt alive and young and at peace.

Oh, how I've missed this, Kricorian thought. *How could I think I would never want it again?*

A light caress of Kricorian's breast made her weak with pleasure, and a more intense fondling over her hip and down her thigh immediately followed it. Just as Kricorian's body ached with desire, Jaret broke away from the kiss and covered one of Kricorian's nipples with her mouth. The gentle sucking that followed sent an exquisite surge of pleasure scampering through Kricorian's body. She filled her hands with Jaret's hair and reveled in the texture of her hair against her cheek.

Jaret seemed to touch her everywhere with light, feathery caresses; Kricorian was ravenous for more. Jaret's kisses made Kricorian arch into Jaret's body as a continuous stroking between her thighs caused her to gasp with delight and anticipation. Jaret touched her in the most intimate way, as if she had always known what Kricorian's body wanted and needed. Again and again Jaret's lips sought deep kisses. Kricorian felt the rush of heat stirring between her legs, and her body moved in search of that hot, magic connection, that exquisite rush of warmth.

Kricorian wrapped her arms around Jaret tightly as she came with sweet, wild release. Her body shook from the intensity of it all as she held Jaret close to her. Kricorian let herself enjoy the small aftershocks that continued to bring her little quivering tremors of pleasure. Jaret kept her fingers inside as Kricorian's warm, velvety flesh tingled from exertion and delight. Jaret buried her face in the crook of Kricorian's neck.

"Thank you," Jaret whispered.

Kricorian held her tightly and kissed the side of her head. "I'm the one who should be —"

"No," Jaret whispered. "I know how lucky I am to be here."

Chapter Twelve

Lela woke up and stretched sleepily. It irritated her that her first thoughts were of Alaric. Her attraction to Alaric was purely physical, and Lela didn't like thinking of herself as superficial, but she had to admit that Colby had made her feel the same way. *But that blond hair and that white uniform sure have my attention,* she reminded herself as she got out of bed and prepared for the day. *Maybe I am superficial,* she admitted grudgingly. Lela wanted to talk to Kricorian first thing to see how the rest of the celebration had gone. It had been unusual for Kricorian to want to stay so late since they had been up all day. Kricorian was usually the first to retire from such an event.

After getting dressed Lela left her room and found a

warrior posted outside of Kricorian's door. When Lela tried to enter, the warrior stepped in front of her.

"What's the problem here?" Lela asked, annoyed.

"The princess is expecting you," another warrior said pleasantly from behind her.

Lela whirled around and wondered where this one had come from. "Where's Kricorian?"

"She'll be along shortly." Making a motion with her hand, the second warrior indicated that Lela was to follow her. And with that Lela was escorted to the command suite where the princess was waiting for her.

Lela had no idea what was going on, but she felt better once Kricorian joined her at the princess's table for breakfast a few minutes later. All the secrecy surrounding her whereabouts that morning had made Lela nervous. She gave Kricorian a questioning look as she sat down at the table; Kricorian apologized for being late.

"Too much wine last night?" Lela asked, hoping to get some insight into where Kricorian had been. Lela had never known her to indulge in excessive alcohol before, so she was hoping that the question would serve another purpose.

"I certainly had more than I'm used to," the princess admitted. "Did you both enjoy the celebration?"

"I did," Kricorian said without hesitation. "How about you, Lela?"

Studying Kricorian a bit more closely, Lela noted that she looked different for some reason. *Younger maybe,* she thought.

"Well?" Kricorian prompted.

"I had a nice time last night," Lela said finally. "But I still don't understand what all the fuss is about." She placed a few small pieces of cheese on her plate. "It's not like we wouldn't have given you back the moment we figured out who you were," she said to the princess.

Tavia laughed. "Apparently I had been missing for quite some time. I feel fortunate to have been returned safely."

"We had no intention of keeping you, if that was ever a concern."

"You're about to hurt my feelings," Tavia said with a crooked smile.

Just then Alaric came in, and Lela tried to be nonchalant about looking at her. But she still couldn't stop staring, and she knew that she was being obvious about it. *Without a doubt, it's the white uniform*, Lela thought again. *It has to be the uniform.*

"Have a seat, Commander," the princess said. "Have you had breakfast?"

"Yes, thank you."

Tavia broke a biscuit apart. "I want you to take Lela to Ambrose today and show her the facilities there." The princess turned to Lela and asked if that was agreeable to her.

"Sure. Where is this place?" Lela asked.

"It's on the Amtec compound and not far from here. It'll be a nice change of pace," Tavia said. "Kricorian, I was wondering if you'd be interested in helping me with a few details left for the summit. Some politics are involved in all this, and I'd appreciate your opinion on a few things."

"I'd be glad to help in any way."

Lela forced herself to take her time finishing breakfast. She didn't like the fact that she was anxious to get started on her excursion with Alaric, so in order to convince herself that she wasn't quite so taken with her, Lela nibbled more cheese and helped herself to a muffin.

"What sort of political issues are we talking about?" Lela asked.

Tavia shrugged. "I'm concerned that Corlon won't agree to participate in the summit, when we need their cooperation the most. Then again, I'm concerned that they *will* participate and possibly be disruptive. I want things to go smoothly. What type of delegates will Corlon send? Star Fighters? Murderers?

Slave traders?" Tavia lowered her voice. "If they send some-one, no matter who it is, we have to provide for their safety and do it in such a way that it isn't obvious that they might be in danger while they're here. It just seems so natural to want to kill Star Fighters, so it's all complicated. There isn't a person in the galaxy who hasn't been affected in the most negative way by Corlon's actions, but the safety of their delegation needs to be a high priority. We all have our own reasons for doing away with them, but it's my responsibility to prevent that from happening here at the summit."

"I agree," Kricorian said, "and I would feel the same if the summit were being held at K Sector."

Lela nodded. "If we aren't certain that we can keep a Corlon delegation safe, or that we can keep the rest of the delegates safe from them, then maybe we should discourage Corlon delegates from attending at all."

"That's the main reason I'm asking for help," Tavia said. "This is a sensitive issue, and I don't want to make such a decision alone."

Alaric said evenly, "We can guarantee everyone's safety, even breeders and murderers. It doesn't matter."

Lela looked at her and nibbled at the muffin. "Such confi-dence coming from someone who let Star Fighters snatch a princess." For some reason she couldn't stop herself from needling Alaric. Being obnoxious made Lela feel less intimi-dated by her, and in return it made Alaric seem more normal, if such a thing were possible.

Tavia laughed and shook her head. Lela noticed the astonished look on Kricorian's face.

"I'm the one responsible for what happened to me," Tavia said. "Alaric and my warriors trusted me to behave in a mature manner and not put myself in danger. I did a foolish thing, and I'm much wiser now because of it."

The fun is over, Lela thought. *We're just sitting around patting each other on the back now.* Lela folded her napkin and set it on the table beside her plate. To Alaric she said, "I'm ready when you are."

Lela was informed that the flight to Ambrose would only take three minutes. She was once again distracted by the closeness she and Alaric shared in the spidercraft. *Stop thinking about her so much,* Lela mused. *She's conceited and pretentious. I have more important things to do.*

"Did the princess tell you anything about Ambrose?" Alaric asked as she put on her helmet.

"A little."

"Ambrose is where the Amtec children are. They go to school and live there."

"K Sector doesn't keep its children separate," Lela said. They had so few children there now anyway. A society of mostly young scientists, K Sector's priorities had changed over the years.

They flew through a tunnel that was a part of the palace. There was dim lighting on both sides, but from what Lela could see, a spidercraft was the only means of transportation available to get them there. Lela also noticed the lack of any specific security features along the way, and decided that everything was probably controlled from a central location at the palace.

The spidercraft eventually shot out of the other end of the tunnel to a burst of color that made Lela smile. The sky was clear and blue, and as far as she could see there were fields of green grass on both sides. Off to the right, Lela noticed several buildings; the spidercraft headed in that direction. Alaric landed close to the front entrance. Within seconds young girls, ranging in age from four to twelve and all dressed alike in bright red jumpsuits and black boots, surrounded them. Their excitement was contagious as the squealing and chattering got louder. Lela took off her helmet and smiled at them.

"Welcome to Ambrose, Commander!" they all said in unison.

"Commander!" a small voice called from the back. "You didn't bring the princess!"

Alaric set her helmet inside the spidercraft. "The princess will be here for her regular visit tomorrow, but right now I want to introduce a friend from K Sector."

"Are you the one who saved our Princess?" someone asked. There was a hush over the group as all eyes focused on Lela.

Suddenly unsure about what was expected of her, Lela glanced at Alaric for help with an answer.

"She was lost and you found her," one of them prompted.

"That's exactly right," Alaric said. "Without our friends from K Sector, the princess would still be lost."

The chattering began again with questions about how the princess had been found. Several girls were vying for Alaric's attention while the others continued getting information from Lela. Lela's arrival piqued their curiosity. Lela could see the admiration and awe in the children's eyes, and it was obvious that Alaric was one of their favorites. As everyone began walking toward the entrance, Alaric leaned closer to Lela and whispered, "It's best that we not mention how the princess was acquired at Tracon."

Lela chuckled. "You mean the bargain we struck for her? I understand."

A pleasant, middle-aged woman, who was also wearing a red jumpsuit and black boots, met them at the door.

"Welcome to Ambrose," she said with a warm smile. "My name is Medio and I'm the director of child development. You must be Lela."

Lela noticed that her voice was calm and soothing. To the

children Medio said, "The commander will be here for a while. Everyone will have a chance to ask her questions." She seemed as amused by Alaric's popularity as Lela was.

"Can we have a ride in the spidercraft, Commander?" a small voice asked over the buzz.

Alaric's laughter set the mood for the rest of the day.

For Lela, Ambrose was a fascinating place, and she quickly became caught up in the dynamics of its operation. When the children weren't involved with their studies, the older ones helped to care for the younger ones. The children were bright and inquisitive. Lela could guess which ones wanted to become warriors — the ones who were poised and confident and who had a bold and self-assured ambiance about them. Those same girls seemed to be the ones with an obvious crush on Alaric.

Lela learned that having visitors from the palace was common at Ambrose, but that having a visitor from another sector was unusual. The children were curious about Lela and asked many questions about where she lived. Lela enjoyed watching Alaric's interactions with the younger ones who seemed to adore her. Alaric took them on spidercraft rides and let the older ones actually fly it for a few minutes. It was also apparent to Lela how much the children loved their Princess. Everything they did was in the name of the princess. Over and over the children asked to hear Lela's tale of finding Tavia and of finally discovering who she was and where she had come from.

Much later, while on their way to the nursery, Alaric asked Lela what she thought of Ambrose.

"You have wonderful, well-adjusted children here," Lela said. "Several of them want to grow up and be just like you."

Alaric didn't say anything, but her face turned a light shade of pink, which made Lela laugh.

"After we spend a few minutes with the infants and the toddlers, I'll show you the warrior camp. Then we've been invited to dine with the four-year-olds."

"Warrior camp and lunch with four-year-olds," Lela said. "Leave it to you to know how to show a girl a good time."

The few occasions where Lela had been around babies, she had liked them immensely. The bald, drooling ones were her favorites, and she found herself cooing and gurgling right along with them.

"They always smell so good," Lela said as she hugged the squirmy infant and kissed her fuzzy head. "Holding her makes me want one."

"Swords used to do something similar to me," Alaric said. "I would hold one and have to have it right away."

"Only a warrior would compare a baby to a sword."

The baby Alaric was holding began to cry, so she handed her over to Medio. Alaric said to Lela, "You make that sound like such a bad thing."

Chapter Thirteen

Ambrose

After lunch with the four-year-olds, Lela and Alaric left the main compound and took the spidercraft to the other side of Ambrose. The landscape reminded Lela of the meadow at K Sector with its green fields and tall trees. Ambrose was much bigger, but K Sector's meadow served the same recreational purpose and Lela had always loved it there.

"One of the reasons the children wear red is so we can find them easily from the air," Alaric said. "Occasionally they wander off or try to practice their escape-and-evasion skills."

"I can see why they would want to explore a little," Lela said as she spotted a lake through the trees. "This is a beautiful place."

Alaric set the spidercraft down near a small beach, and they got out and walked along the water's edge. Lela felt a breeze on her face and enjoyed listening to the water lapping against the shore. She asked questions about the children and the opportunities available to them once they were too old to stay at Ambrose.

Walking slowly with her hands clasped behind her back, Alaric said, "About eighty percent choose to become warriors."

Lela liked the way the breeze brought Alaric's hair to life, rearranging it softly around her face.

"The warrior academy is at another location at the palace," Alaric continued, "but cadets have to be at least sixteen in order to be accepted." They stopped walking and sat down under a tree in a grassy area near the water. "As you know, the teenagers who have the talent for healing are usually sent to K Sector for further training," Alaric said, "and those who have engineering interests are encouraged to train at Alpha Sector."

Lela leaned back on her elbows and took a deep breath of fresh air. "How much of this place is real?"

Alaric smiled. "Real? It's all real."

Lela nodded. "Then how much of it is natural?"

"Absolutely none of it is natural." Alaric pulled a blade of grass, and they both looked at it carefully. "Alpha Sector has outstanding engineers who developed the technology to reinvent parts of our environment."

"Whoever created this place did an excellent job." Lela leaned back on the grass and rested her head on her arms. The blue sky and the rippling water close by threatened to lull her to sleep. "Ambrose seems to agree with you, too, Commander. You've been pleasant this afternoon." Lela chuckled. "At lunch when the children all wanted to sit next to you I saw you blush for the second time today. I thought by now you'd be used to all the attention."

"I visit them as often as my schedule allows." Alaric shook

her head. "The princess enjoys teasing me about the reception I always get here."

"It must be nice to have such an effect on people." Lela closed her eyes and let the sound of the water relax her.

Stretching out beside her, Alaric asked Lela what her favorite part of the day had been.

"The nursery, I think," Lela said with her eyes closed. "I didn't realize how much I missed being around babies. I also liked having lunch with the four-year-olds. It was much more entertaining than I thought it would be. Some of those questions they asked you were embarrassing. That was certainly fun."

"I'm not surprised you found that so amusing," Alaric said dryly.

"They had a lot of energy," Lela said, "and they were inquisitive and playful. It was easy to see which ones would grow up to be warriors."

Lela felt a flutter against her cheek, and she opened her eyes to find Alaric tickling her with a blade of grass. To Lela it would have appeared to be such a simple thing had it been anyone but Alaric touching her this way. But she suddenly remembered the silkiness of Alaric's hair and what it had felt like to be close to her the night they had been trapped in the cave together.

Lela held her breath as Alaric leaned down to kiss her. Before this moment Lela would have denied wanting this, but right then a kiss was the only thing that seemed to matter to her. A rush of warmth traveled the entire length of Lela's body as their lips met. The kiss was light and tentative. Lela, however, didn't want this to end. When Alaric leaned over to kiss her again, Lela met her halfway.

She didn't expect such tenderness and attention to detail, since warriors were considered to be trained killers and obstinate protectors of the Amtec people, but Alaric seemed to know exactly what Lela wanted and precisely when she wanted it. The second kiss was slow and steamy, with a tiny break in between where Alaric traced the tip of her tongue along the very edge of Lela's ear. Lela trembled, and she briefly took Alaric's lower lip between her teeth and sighed when Alaric's tongue took its sweet time mingling with hers. Lela felt as though Alaric knew intimate things about her that even Lela herself didn't quite know yet, the way she liked having her breasts touched through her clothing, having her nipples rubbed until they strained the fabric of her uniform.

As deep, probing kisses continued, Lela sucked Alaric's tongue into her mouth as if it belonged there. And just when she needed more direct and focused stimulation, more of Alaric's mouth and tongue, her eagerness and passion, Alaric's talented hands opened Lela's uniform, exposing her to a desire that she had never known.

Alaric teased Lela's breasts with slow, broad strokes and then tasted her left nipple with her mouth. She began rubbing Lela between the legs, cupping her there and causing complete chaos to scamper through her body. Lela wanted to touch Alaric the same way, which led them to help each other out of their clothing. The grass provided a cushioned surface for what Lela had in mind, and when Alaric was finally out of her uniform, Lela gazed down at the perfect body waiting for her. She was sleek and slender with well-defined muscles in her arms and legs, and Lela had never seen such a magnificent woman. She urged Alaric down on her back while Lela took in every inch of her smooth, flat stomach and firm breasts. Lela's eyes set everything to memory.

Alaric pulled Lela on top of her, and Lela straddled her body, sinking her knees into the lush grass. Alaric raised up and flicked her tongue over Lela's nipples and ran her fingernails lightly along her back. Lela arched into her, wanting Alaric to take more of her breast into her mouth. Alaric did so eagerly, and their lovemaking became a mutually satisfying exchange of passion.

Tilting her head back, Alaric nuzzled Lela's breasts. Lela

liked taking her time while making love. With Colby they had always been so rushed, snatching minutes here and there to be alone together. Colby had never been a patient lover; getting right to the point was part of what had been so exciting about her at first. But right now, with Alaric continuing to rub Lela's back, their soft moans mingling with the sounds of the water lapping at the shore, Lela was getting a glimpse of how incredible sex with Alaric could be.

Alaric slipped two fingers inside, and Lela ached with her touch. Alaric's mouth moved up Lela's body and lingered at the soft hollow at her throat. Alaric kissed her hungrily while slowly working her slim fingers in and out. Each time their lips met, Lela felt a new rush of excitement as Alaric's tongue matched the steady rhythm of her fingers. Lela's left hand went to the back of Alaric's head and pulled her closer, deepening their kiss and strengthening their connection. Lela's other hand found Alaric's left breast and a hard nipple that was ready for her. Touching her this way and hearing Alaric respond made Lela squirm. She gently pushed her into the grass, and they were once again side by side and absorbed in each other. But it was the constant nibbling, kissing, sucking, and nipping that had Lela on the edge. She liked being kissed on the throat and along her shoulder, and Alaric was adept at granting her unspoken wishes.

No words were exchanged between them. None had to be.

Lela woke up in Alaric's arms and snuggled closer to her. She kissed Alaric's bare shoulder, and sensed that something wasn't quite right. Alaric seemed distant as they awkwardly disentangled themselves and gathered their clothing.

"You're a good lover," Alaric said quietly, as if she were preparing Lela for some sort of inevitable truth that was about to follow.

You're a good lover, but, Lela thought as she dreaded what was coming next. Alaric slipped into her uniform and reached for her boots.

"You sound surprised," Lela said. She was annoyed at Alaric's sudden aloofness. When Alaric looked over at her Lela asked, "Why is that?"

They had made love and it had been remarkably passionate and tender, or at least it had been that way for Lela. Alaric's disinterest now made her question exactly what had just happened between them.

Alaric stood up; she offered Lela a hand. Lela extended her hand and let Alaric pull her up. Standing only inches apart, their eyes met. Lela was confused by what she saw in Alaric's expression.

"I didn't want you to be," Alaric whispered.

Immersed in the hypnotic blue of her eyes, Lela suddenly lost her train of thought. She felt the fluttering in her stomach, but she managed to ask, "What is it that you didn't want me to be?"

"A good lover," Alaric answered. She leaned forward to kiss her again. The passion had returned for them and was even more overwhelming than before. Lela melted into her arms and wanted Alaric's mouth on her throat, wanted her hands in her hair.

"We can't do this again," Alaric said, her voice low and husky with desire. She kissed Lela's neck and then sucked on her earlobe.

Without knowing how they got there, Lela was delighted to find herself on the grass again with Alaric, struggling to get clothes off once more. This time when they made love it was even slower than before, but Lela had doubts about the depth of her own desire. She didn't want to think of this as just sex, but something about Alaric was leading Lela to believe that there was little else going on for Alaric. She didn't seem to be the kind of woman who was interested in or capable of loving. But even with that in mind, Lela wanted her desperately at that moment.

~ ~ ~

A while later when they were ready to return to the palace, Lela sensed Alaric's lack of interest in what had happened between them. It was as if in order to function, Alaric had to separate her feelings and her actions from everything else going on in her life. Lela couldn't just turn it off and on that way, however. Things had changed, and Lela was ready to move on to another level.

They climbed into the spidercraft and, before Alaric could put on her helmet, Lela reached for her hand and gave it a squeeze. Alaric lightly returned the gesture, but sat still and looked straight ahead.

"Explain to me what's happening," Lela said. Her confusion at being so easily dismissed had resurfaced. "We make love and then you shut me out. You say we can't do it again, and then the next thing I know we're rolling around in the grass. Now all of a sudden I'm getting this uncomfortable silence from you again." Lela lowered her voice. "What just happened between us?"

"I'm sorry," Alaric said, finally giving Lela's hand the firm squeeze it deserved. "You're making it hard for me to keep my mind on work."

Lela had to admit that she liked that answer. Some of the tension eased from her body.

125

Chapter Fourteen

Amtec Palace

Lela hoped that Alaric would want to at least kiss her again, but there was no further kissing. They hardly spoke on the way back. When they landed at the palace, Alaric mentioned needing to be at a security briefing.

"So that's it?"

"I'll come and find you later."

"Don't bother."

"Lela, I —"

"I'll make sure I'm busy."

~ ~ ~

Feeling angry about what had happened and needing to talk to someone about it, Lela looked for Kricorian. When she arrived at Kricorian's room Lela noticed that there was another warrior posted outside the door. Still uncertain why a guard was needed there, Lela decided to push for an answer, but just as she approached, the door opened and Lieutenant Jaret came out.

"Lela," Jaret said, surprised.

"Is everything all right? Having all these guards lurking around makes me nervous."

Jaret smiled. "Warriors never lurk. We're finely tuned fighting machines here for your convenience and safety."

Lela rolled her eyes. "Then tell me how I've managed to survive for twenty-three years without one."

Jaret smiled but didn't answer. She knocked on Kricorian's door and then opened it to admit Lela. To Lela she said with a grin, "If you need anything, there should be a warrior close by."

Command Suite

Tavia was pacing when Alaric arrived. "Well?" she said impatiently.

"I did what you asked," Alaric said.

The princess looked over at her and glared for a moment. "I'm sure you were as accommodating as usual."

Alaric held the look and quietly repeated, "I did what you asked."

"Then I'll assume that everything is as it should be," Tavia said. "Delegates from Alpha Sector will be arriving within the next few hours, and the Tracon delegation will be here later this evening." She resumed pacing as she collected her thoughts. "Have Jaret give me an update on how ready we are. In the meantime, I want you to spend more time with Lela today." Tavia turned away from her and walked to the scanner on the other side of the room. She activated it and brought up a visual of the clearing by the lake at Ambrose.

"You were watching us," Alaric said.

"No," Tavia answered. "Not really. I couldn't after a while." Switching off the scanner, Tavia turned around. "She's falling in love with you."

Alaric laughed. "I don't think so."

"She is."

Alaric didn't say anything else; there was an awkward silence between them. Finally, Tavia looked at her and said, "Spend as much time with her as you need to. It's important that we keep her happy."

Kricorian was sitting in one of the chaise longues when Lela went into her room.

"Were you sleeping?" Lela asked.

"No, just resting."

Kricorian was exhausted and tried to pay attention to what Lela was saying, but all she could think about was the way Jaret had just made love to her. She visited the scene over and over in her head, and it made her smile each time she thought about it.

"Has anyone ever undressed you before?" Jaret asked. "I mean completely," Jaret said in a near whisper. "Slowly removing an article of clothing and then kissing you there before moving on." As she spoke, Jaret did exactly as she described. She kissed Kricorian everywhere. Kricorian tried to explain again that her body was old, but Jaret silenced her with another kiss.

Kricorian was amused and relaxed, but just when she thought Jaret was finished with her, Jaret asked if anyone had ever dressed her after making love to her. A low chuckle rumbled in Kricorian's throat just thinking about someone else trying to put boots on her feet. Jaret then put Kricorian's clothes back on her in the reverse order that each article had been removed. It wasn't long before another round of love-making began.

"Are you listening to me?" Kricorian heard Lela say.

Kricorian opened her eyes wider and then snapped her head around to look at her. Had she been asleep or just day-dreaming, she wondered. "I'm sorry, little one."

"Are you all right?" Lela asked. "You're all flushed."

"I'm fine. Just tired, I think." Kricorian offered a weak smile and then got more comfortable in her chair. "I haven't been sleeping that much lately," she said. *I haven't been sleeping. I've been having sex!*

Lela kicked back in the chaise she was sitting in and got comfortable. "It's not home, but I slept well last night."

"Tell me about Ambrose," Kricorian said. "What was it like? You two weren't gone long."

"Imagine a place about fifty times bigger than the meadow, with five adults and sixty or so children living there. It was more organized than I thought it would be, and I had a lot more fun than I expected to have."

"Hmm. What were the children like?"

"Amazing kids. Inquisitive kids. Curious and smart. And there were babies, too! I saw toddlers and newborns and the gurgling, drooling ones I like so much."

Kricorian smiled. "You've always liked babies."

"And then Alaric took me to a lake not far from where the children live." She stopped suddenly and thought about Colby. She missed Colby more at that moment than she ever had before. Colby would have enjoyed hearing Lela describe what had happened at the lake that day.

"We made love there under a tree," Lela said quietly. She turned her head to catch Kricorian's reaction.

"Really?" Kricorian said.

"Really." Lela suddenly felt tired. "You know that rumor we've always heard about Amtec warriors?" she asked. "That rumor that used to make us laugh so much?"

Kricorian nodded. "The rumor about Amtec warriors being such good lovers?"

"That's the one. I think in a technical sense it's true," Lela admitted, "but on a personal level, I'm not so sure. Don't get me wrong. It was all good, but I also like the other things that go with it. There was something missing today, but I can't figure out what it was." *It had also been missing with Colby,* she thought. Lela turned her head and looked at Kricorian. "Maybe I was expecting too much."

"Maybe," Kricorian said with a shrug.

After napping a bit in the chaise, Lela decided to go to her room and get some real sleep. Kricorian could be a noisy sleeper. Stepping into the hall, Lela noticed that a warrior was posted at the end of the hallway instead of outside Kricorian's door. Lela attributed that to her conversation with Jaret earlier and the way she had poked a little fun at them.

"There you are," Alaric said behind her.

"Oh, hi. Where did you come from?"

"The princess wants to see you again."

"Any idea why?"

"We have a few minutes," Alaric said. She took Lela by the elbow and led her back to her room.

Once they were inside and had the door closed, Alaric leaned over and kissed her.

Surprised by this, but not opposed to it, Lela let herself be taken away by Alaric's desire. Alaric slowly turned them around as the kiss deepened, and Lela could feel her back being pressed against the wall. Alaric's right hand found Lela's breast, and the way the fabric rubbed against her hard nipples almost made her swoon. Alaric continued kissing her, with her lips leaving Lela's just long enough to graze her throat and her earlobe, bringing the most delightful sensations to Lela's entire body.

Lela wanted to be in bed with her where she could feel Alaric's skin on hers, but Alaric kept an arm around her and held her up as she opened Lela's uniform and took a nipple into her mouth.

"Oh . . . please . . . oh yes," Lela muttered while she helped get her own clothing off. Alaric kissed her way up Lela's chest and lingered at her throat before finding her lips once more. She sucked Lela's tongue into her mouth, and Lela felt weak with pleasure and hot with anticipation. In the back of her mind Lela knew she would come soon, and she wanted to make it last as long as possible. *Anticipation,* she thought. *Sweet anticipation is the ultimate seduction.*

Lela was naked in Alaric's arms, and Alaric gently opened her and caressed the wetness between Lela's legs, the wetness that begged for her touch, that begged for complete attention.

"How does this feel?" Alaric whispered while her tongue outlined Lela's ear.

"Fabulous," Lela said with difficulty. She couldn't talk. She couldn't breathe. All she could do was move against Alaric's fingers, which were stroking her into oblivion. "Don't stop," she mumbled. "Don't stop. Please."

As the warmth began to spread through her body, Lela searched wildly for Alaric's mouth. "Kiss me," she whispered. "Kiss me."

Alaric's mouth covered hers, and her tongue began working its magic again, probing Lela's mouth, bringing her closer and closer to the edge. Lela wrapped her arms tightly around Alaric's neck and came with an intense shudder, throwing her head back and calling out Alaric's name.

Alaric held her and kissed the top of Lela's head. "That

sounded quite nice," Alaric said with her cheek resting against Lela's hair.

"Nice?" Lela managed to say. "Yes, indeed, that was nice." She kept her arms around Alaric's neck and kissed her tenderly. Lela felt warm and sleepy. "Come to bed with me. I want to make you feel nice too."

"The princess is waiting for you."

"Let her wait," Lela said as she took Alaric by the hand and led her to the bed. "We have more important things to do."

Chapter Fifteen

Command Suite

After Alaric escorted Lela to the command suite where the princess was waiting for her, she explained that she had to be at another security briefing where they were preparing for the arrival of Alpha Sector's delegation.

"There you are," Tavia said as the door closed behind Lela. "How was your visit to Ambrose?"

"It's an impressive place," Lela admitted. She thought about some of the things that had happened to her there and felt certain that she blushed. She remembered Alaric's cool bare skin next to hers and knew those memories were readily reflected in her face.

They sat down at a table on the far side of the room. Tavia

had tea ready for them and continued asking Lela questions about her impressions of Ambrose.

"It's the kind of place that's hard to leave," Lela said.

"Sometimes the children make it nearly impossible to leave, so I stay there for a few days and have the most delightful time," Tavia said as she stirred her tea. "At K Sector I understand you've been doing research in the area of synthetic food. Is this true?"

"Yes," Lela said. "That's what I've been working on for the past two years."

"Tell me about it."

Lela shrugged. "Our weather patterns have been changing, making it hard to predict how long our growing seasons will be. Recreating the perfect setting for some of our staples hasn't been as successful as we had hoped. Artificial environments can't replace the real thing, so for quite some time now K Sector has made food research and alternatives to our regular food sources a priority."

"How close are you to finishing with your research?"

"It's an ongoing project. I may never be finished with it."

Tavia leaned back in her chair. "Do you ever get tired of working on the same thing all the time?"

Lela smiled. "I like treating each day as if it were *the* day that something new and exciting will happen, so my answer is no. I don't get tired of it. Each day is different. I love what I do."

"Spoken like a true scientist," Tavia said with a sigh. "The proposition I had for you suddenly seems trivial in comparison."

Curious, Lela asked that she explain.

"You've been to Ambrose and seen the Amtec children," Tavia said. "I even requested that you dine with some of them. In particular, I wanted you to spend time with the four-year-olds."

Lela nodded. "What a cute, lively bunch they are."

"So true," Tavia said with a laugh. "But did you notice anything else about them during that time?"

"They played a lot and had an endless string of questions," Lela noted.

"How much food did you see them eat?"

Lela stopped to think about it. "I remember food being there, but I can't say that I noticed them eating any of it."

Tavia poured them both more tea. "They play with their food. They don't eat it."

"Isn't that what most four-year-olds do?"

"Maybe," Tavia said with a nod. "But if the food tasted better to them, then maybe they would eat more of it."

Lela nodded as well. "Maybe."

"So I thought of you when this idea occurred to me. I was wondering if you'd be interested in starting another project here in the Amtec laboratories, another food study. Developing a type of food that children will like."

"You have healthy children at Ambrose. No one is going hungry there."

"But if I can make things better for them," Tavia said, "then that's what I want to do. You would have your own lab and as many assistants as you need. This would be considered a major project, and it would have my complete support."

"Are you talking about now? Me conducting research in between meetings during the summit?"

Tavia laughed. "No, I mean after the summit. You could stay here and begin your research then."

"I can do this type of research at K Sector," Lela said. "Why would I have to be here?"

"The Amtec children are here."

"It can be tested on children anywhere. I'm sure you don't have the only four-year-olds who play with their food."

Tavia laughed again. "You're probably right, but that's the

proposition. A new project and your own lab. At the same time, you could also keep track of the life capsule and the testing with lidium."

"That's much more appealing to me than appetizing meals for children."

"I can see now that I've approached this all wrong."

Lela laughed. "This food project you're suggesting could take awhile. I might not be able to find something they'll like. Kids are fickle. I'm not even sure that four-year-olds are *supposed* to eat like the rest of us do. Have you discussed this with any of your child psychologists?"

"I have, and they all say that when children get hungry, they'll eat." At Lela's raised eyebrow, Tavia added, "But I've also talked to the children, and *they* say that the food is icky no matter how hungry they are."

"*Icky?*"

They both laughed this time. Tavia sipped her tea and looked at Lela over her cup. "Yes, *icky*. That's their word, and it's the basis for my proposal. Please think about it. I can't, in good conscience, keep serving Amtec children icky food. I'm asking for your help in fixing this problem."

"In the meantime, I can't just toss my other projects aside," Lela said. "The things I'm working on now could lead to significant changes for everyone. Including children. It could mean the difference between so-called icky food and no food."

"I see your point," Tavia said. Lela saw the disappointment registered on her face. "You must think this is petty."

"I understand your need to make things better for your people."

"Then is there any chance that I could convince you to work on both projects? Yours and mine?"

Lela smiled. "Possibly. But again, I could work on both projects at K Sector. I wouldn't have to be here."

"I can make resources available to you in the Amtec labs that you don't have at K Sector," Tavia said. She studied Lela for a moment. "You have your mind made up already, don't you?"

"You haven't convinced me that the Amtec labs are the perfect place to do any of this." Lela smiled and sipped her tea. "If I remember correctly, it was in a K Sector lab that someone successfully opened up the capsule that you were trapped in. A feat thought impossible by your Amtec researchers." She shrugged. "Maybe the Amtecs would benefit from moving their projects to K Sector laboratories instead."

Tavia raised an eyebrow and shook her head. "You have an interesting way of turning things around on me. You don't like us much, do you?"

"That's not true."

"But there is something."

Lela laughed nervously. How could she tell this woman that she thought having an army of warriors was a waste of human resources, and that living in something referred to as a *palace* was absurd? How could she tell her how ridiculous it was to have a group of "trained fighting machines," as Jaret had called them, let themselves be led around by someone referred to as a *princess*? Lela found it hard to take the Amtecs seriously. Many aspects of their existence irritated her in some way.

"Let me ask you this," Tavia said. "When you discovered who I was after my release from the capsule, what kind of response did you get from the Amtecs?"

Lela didn't have to think long about the question. She remembered Jaret's reaction to seeing the capsule and then to seeing Tavia when they had sent for her. When Jaret had knelt down in front of the princess, Lela had felt how powerful the Amtecs really were as a nation. They were united by their traditions, and to see someone as strong as Jaret be reduced to a humble, loyal follower was an eye-opening experience for Lela.

"Your people love you," Lela said.

"It's not just love," Tavia said. "There's also respect. My

mother was a gentle, caring woman. She loved her people as much as she loved me. I know what my responsibilities are, and I've made my share of mistakes. I consider it an honor to serve them, and I hope to do my best to make their lives easier and safer. I will always have their love, but there's a lot of work involved in earning and keeping their respect."

"I'm sure you'll have no difficulty with either."

There was a knock on the door, and Jaret came in. "The delegation from Alpha Sector will be arriving in a few minutes."

"Thank you, Lieutenant," Tavia said, and to Lela, "Will you join me in welcoming them?"

Amtec Reception Bay

Lela hadn't had much time to think about anything, but as she and Kricorian stood together among the swarm of people in the reception bay, she took a moment to reflect on the situation. Lela watched Alaric, Tavia, and Jaret as they discussed something in front of a warrior formation. Any time there were more than a handful of warriors together in one place, Lela had to admit that it was an impressive sight. Jaret was the one in charge of the formation, but it was Alaric who initiated the commands.

Alaric, Lela thought. *What is it about her that makes me want to be so cautious?* Lela remembered how distant Alaric had become once they were on the bed in her room. She had been responsive to Lela's touch, and she had allowed Lela to make love to her. But afterward it was obvious to Lela that all of it had been nothing more than sex for either of them. Alaric had a coldness about her that Lela didn't care for, and Lela was sure that Alaric wasn't investing much into their relationship either. Lela reminded herself that they were nothing more than two people spending time together during the summit. There would probably be a few other attendees doing the same thing as soon as the summit got underway. *But it was the best sex you've ever had,* Lela admitted with a smirk.

"There they are," Lela heard Kricorian say beside her.

There was a buzz of activity as Alpha Sector's spidercraft landed in the reception bay. Jaret called the formation to attention, did an about-face, and gave the commander a crisp salute. Alaric returned the salute, did an about-face, and saluted the princess.

A warrior suddenly appeared beside Lela and informed her that the princess wanted them both up front to help with the welcome. As predicted, Keda and Viscar were the representatives for Alpha Sector.

"Where were you?" Tavia whispered when Lela stepped up beside her.

"We had a nice view from the back," Lela said.

Keda and Viscar had removed their helmets and were smiling. Tavia gave them a warm welcome and let Alaric take over from there. Lela watched as Kricorian joined in and became part of a brief political discussion as well as a mini-reunion with her two friends. Lela greeted the new arrivals and felt a sense of relief at having the summit closer to being a reality.

As Alaric, Kricorian, and the two new delegates moved through the crowd, Lela and Tavia followed them at a more leisurely pace.

"My work is done for now," Tavia said. "Alaric will see to them."

"So you show up and shake a few hands and then turn them over to someone else?" Lela teased.

"Keda and Viscar will be more comfortable having Alaric show them around." Tavia gave her a shy smile. "You and Kricorian might have preferred the same thing, but I wanted you to have a more personal tour."

"We're both enjoying our stay, even though I find it a waste of time to have warriors posted everywhere. Is that all they do? Stand around guarding empty hallways?"

"Security will be —"

"Excuse me, Princess," Jaret said as she fell in step beside them. "We've heard from Corlon. They want to send a delegation of four instead of two."

"Tell them no," Tavia said. "Everyone else is sending two. Having four is unacceptable. Why can't they follow simple instructions?"

"And if they insist on four?"

"Only two will be allowed to attend the meetings, and only two can vote."

"I'll let them know." Jaret turned and left.

As they began walking again, Tavia said, "This will be an interesting time for all of us."

Chapter Sixteen

Command Suite

Lela and Kricorian accepted Tavia's invitation for dinner later that evening. Keda and Viscar would be joining them also. The Tracon delegation had been delayed until the following day, and negotiations were still going on with Corlon about the number of delegates they were sending. Lela had seen Alaric only once in passing that afternoon, and they had barely spoken. Lela sensed a certain degree of embarrassment for Alaric. It was obvious to Lela that Alaric didn't want anyone to know what had happened between them. Lela was in agreement with that on several levels. She also agreed that nothing should upstage the reason they were all there in the first place. The summit had to be the main focus now instead of who everyone was sleeping with. Lela regretted not having been more selective in how she had spent her time while she was there. Sex with Alaric had been a mistake.

Once she and Kricorian were in the command suite, Lela noticed how comfortable it was and wondered why she hadn't noticed that before. A work area as well as a place for entertaining up to thirty or so people took up the majority of the space. There were other rooms off to the side where Lela assumed Tavia's private quarters were maintained. The command suite's current setup had the work area as its primary layout. Toward the center of the room was an elaborate table festively decorated and set for five. Viscar and Kricorian were already in the work area making use of two scanners capable of zooming in on the Intergalactic Corridor. They were also keeping in contact with Jaret to see how negotiations were going with Corlon.

Once everyone sat down to dinner, there were discussions about the summit's agenda, with subsequent items to be added and deleted from it. Eventually it was decided that the agenda couldn't be completed until all delegates were present. Lela liked the way Tavia kept trying to shift the conversation away from anything too serious. There would be enough of that going on over the next few days. As the evening progressed, the wine flowed freely and the food was excellent. Keda and Viscar were enjoying themselves as though they hadn't been away from home in quite some time.

"Tell me, Princess," Viscar said. She was sitting at the opposite end of the table from Tavia and had already consumed several glasses of wine. "Is it true what they say about these warriors of yours?"

"What exactly is it that's been said?" Tavia asked innocently. Everyone at the table laughed.

"Oh, I'm sure we all know which rumor I'm referring to. Is there some sort of special instruction your warriors have to go through to become such good lovers?" Viscar asked. "Is this something that can be taught?" She cleared her throat.

"Because if it is, I'd like to volunteer my services during their practice sessions."

That produced another smattering of laughter. Tavia passed a new bottle of wine around the table.

"Subjects taught at the warrior academy are a secret, I'm afraid," Tavia informed them. Then she looked directly at Viscar and said, "Are you aware that I'm also a graduate of the Amtec warrior academy?"

Viscar let out a little gasp, and then her eyes popped open. "Well, well," she cooed. "I wasn't aware of that!"

"Oh yes," Tavia said. The wine bottle had made its way around the table already, and Lela watched as Tavia again filled their glasses. "My mother insisted that I be trained as a warrior. I could not lead them if I were not thought of as one of them."

"So you know the secrets," Viscar said with a playful gleam in her eye.

Tavia smiled. "Those and more."

Kricorian picked up her glass and shook her head. "I'm learning a lot tonight," she said, and waved her hand in front of her face like an imaginary fan.

As the chuckles died down, Lela spoke up. "Then I have a question for you," she said. Lela, sitting next to the princess, had spent most of the evening watching Viscar flirt shamelessly with Tavia. This annoyed Lela. It wasn't as though Tavia was flirting back with her — or flirting with anyone else for that matter. Lela was quick to blame her silliness on the wine, and she decided to have just one glass last her until the end of the evening.

"What's your question?" Tavia asked. Her head tilted to the side, she gave Lela her full attention. Lela realized how attractive the princess was.

"We're waiting," Keda said in a wine-induced singsong voice.

"Yes," Tavia agreed with an engaging smile. "We're waiting."

Lela had already changed her mind about bringing this subject up, but now she wasn't sure how to get out of it. She was suddenly put on the spot.

"Well?" Keda prompted.

"I was just wondering about you being a warrior," Lela said slowly, "and how it was possible for a warrior to be abducted the way you were. Why didn't you just kill them? Isn't that what warriors do?"

"Warriors aren't indestructible," Kricorian said.

"According to whom?" Lela asked with a raised eyebrow. "Ask any Amtec warrior around here, and she'll tell you differently."

They roared with laughter again.

"I have a question, too," Viscar said. "I was wondering how many women a warrior can satisfy at one time?"

After the howling laughter died down, Tavia announced that the record for the most women satisfied at one time by an Amtec warrior was only three.

"But that's not always something that can be taught," she added. "For some of us it just comes naturally."

Much later, Lela overheard Viscar ask the princess if there was anyone special in her life. Lela had met Viscar on several occasions, but had never seen her quite so chatty before. Keda and Kricorian made sure that Viscar stayed on her feet as they all left the command suite and followed Tavia through the palace. Lela walked beside the princess as they led the way, and neither could stop smiling as they listened to the three older women behind them talk.

"You can't keep serving us that wine and expect to have delegates in any shape to work the next day," Lela said good-naturedly.

"They should be fine in the morning," Tavia assured her. Turning around and walking backward, she pointed out things along the way that had significant meaning for the Amtecs. Each item that Tavia showed them was something interesting that hadn't been mentioned before. Lela was beginning to see why the Amtecs were such a proud people.

They finally came to the part of the palace where the visitors' quarters were. As usual, a warrior was posted at both ends of the long hallway. Upon seeing the princess, the first warrior snapped to attention and saluted.

Tavia returned the salute and put the warrior at ease. "Has it been quiet tonight?" she asked her.

"Yes, Princess," came the reply. The warrior was in her early twenties and had an oval-shaped face and the same shaggy haircut that all warriors had. This one was a redhead and parted her hair in the middle, but the sides were pushed back behind her ears, giving her a softer, more feminine look.

Tavia chuckled and nodded toward the three delegates behind her. "Let's hope it stays that way." She turned toward Keda, Viscar, and Kricorian and said, "Those two rooms at the end of the hallway have been designated for Alpha Sector."

Keda and Kricorian steered Viscar toward the closer of the two rooms that Tavia had pointed to.

"And if you see a door in the area that has a warrior posted outside of it," Tavia went on to explain, "that usually means there's some sort of interesting activity going on inside."

"What kind of interesting activity?" Keda asked.

Tavia smiled. "It could be personal, classified, or sexual in nature. Usually the latter. Either way, it's advisable not to disturb whoever is in there."

Keda and Viscar roared with laughter.

"How can there be any good sexual activity going on if the warrior is *outside* the door?" Viscar asked.

But it wasn't until Lela saw Kricorian's face glowing a bright shade of red that she realized what the princess had said. Kricorian met Lela's wide eyes and acknowledged her shocked, surprised expression. Kricorian shrugged guiltily.

"You?" was the only thing Lela could think of to say. Her

mind became a blank for several seconds before she remembered that Jaret had come out of Kricorian's room earlier that day. Then suddenly Lela looked at Kricorian again and managed to mutter, "And Jaret?"

Kricorian became quite busy getting Viscar's door open and showing the two new delegates around. The five of them were then inside Viscar's room, and Keda and Tavia stretched out in the two chaise longues.

"I think I'm ready for bed," Viscar announced.

Kricorian nudged her over to the bed and helped her take off her boots. Viscar stretched an arm out toward the others and said sleepily, "My apologies. You should all leave now before I really embarrass myself."

"Like you haven't already?" Keda said.

Once the other four were out in the hallway again, Kricorian made a show of introducing Keda to a room of her own. Since all the rooms were identical, this bit of hospitality on Kricorian's part made her nervousness even more evident.

"Breakfast in the command suite in the morning," Tavia announced. "Afterward we'll work on the agenda again and hopefully Tracon and Corlon delegates will be here by then."

"It's been a long day," Keda said. "I'll see all of you at breakfast then." She stopped the princess at the door. "It's always a pleasure to be here. Your mother would be proud of you."

Tavia gave her a hug and thanked her.

"Well," Kricorian said as soon as the three of them were alone in the hallway. Avoiding Lela's attempt at eye contact, Kricorian said, "I'm going to the communications center to see if they've made any progress on the Corlon negotiations."

"That's where I was headed, too," Tavia said.

Lela had no intention of being left behind. She wanted more information about what Kricorian had been up to lately, so she followed them.

~ ~ ~

146

Amtec Communications Center

Lela saw Alaric right away when the three of them arrived. She acknowledged Alaric's nod, but they didn't speak. The center was huge. Several walls were lined with equipment that looked vaguely familiar. Lela knew that K Sector had a similar place at Security Command, but she had no idea how to work anything or what most of the gadgets were used for. Jaret was there also, and Lela watched Kricorian's face light up the moment they saw each other. Lela was still recovering from the initial shock of their being together. This side of Kricorian was something Lela hadn't seen in a long time.

"What's the status?" the princess asked Alaric.

"Corlon insists on bringing four delegates," Alaric said. "Their reasoning is that Corlon is the largest sector and that they represent more people."

"That was their answer to our two-delegates-two-votes proposal?"

"Yes. Jaret is working with one of the delegates now. There's some indication that they might consider four delegates with two votes."

Tavia shook her head. "That's ridiculous. Tell me who you've been talking to there."

"They aren't giving us much information," Alaric said.

"We don't even know who we're negotiating with?"

"No. They're always uncooperative."

Tavia joined Kricorian and Jaret at a scanner on the other side of the room. Lela moved closer too in order to hear what was going on. She watched as Tavia pushed a button on one of the control panels.

"This is the Amtec princess," she said. "Who am I speaking with?"

There was silence on the other end. Lela could see the frustration on Jaret's face, but it wasn't clear to her if it was because Tavia had arrived and was taking over or because they were getting no cooperation on the other end. Lela focused on Kricorian and Jaret standing together, and she felt good about the possibilities for them. Lela moved closer and stood next to Kricorian, putting her arm around Kricorian's waist and giving her a hug. Kricorian returned the squeeze. Just then everyone jumped at the sound of Tavia's loud, impatient voice repeating what she had said earlier.

"The only person we will talk to now is Exidor," Tavia said to the blank red screen. "We're wasting valuable time."

A few more seconds of silence followed, and then everyone jumped again when a deep male voice reached them from Corlon. He asked if she was really the Amtec princess.

Tavia smiled. "Exidor," she said sweetly. "What's all this nonsense about you trying to send four delegates to our summit?"

Everyone in the room was fascinated by the exchange that followed between the elusive Corlon leader and the Amtec princess. The discussion began with Exidor making a demand to send six delegates. Tavia laughed before reconfirming the two-delegates-two-votes rule.

"I'm telling you this," Tavia said at one point. "If you try to bring more than two delegates, I'll have a fleet of warriors in the air intercepting you so fast you won't even know we're there until it's too late and we're escorting you back home again."

"That's not very neighborly of you, Princess," Exidor droned.

"Well, you're not my neighbor of choice either," Tavia reminded him.

So the stalemate continued, as did the banter. Exidor said he believed that Corlon deserved to have more delegates because of its size and population, and Tavia continued to repeat that the consensus of the other sectors was two-delegates-two-votes.

"If I were to agree to that," Exidor finally said, "how would you provide for my safety while I'm there?"

"The same way I'm providing for everyone else's safety," Tavia said.

Lela watched Tavia motion for Jaret. As they whispered to each other, Tavia's expression changed. She smiled at Jaret and nodded approval at whatever had been discussed.

"We're getting nowhere with this, Exidor," Tavia said. "Maybe there's another way to accomplish our goal. You choose two delegates, and we'll let them attend the summit via the teleconference communications link. We'll stay here and your Corlon delegation can remain there. Then we'll all feel safer."

"That doesn't resolve my need to have more than two delegates."

"It doesn't matter how many delegates you have if you stay there," Tavia said. "You still get only two votes."

"Unacceptable."

"If that's your answer, then I'm sorry we couldn't work something out. The summit will go on without you."

"The teleconference communications link," he said after a moment.

"We can make it happen on this end. Is there anyone at Corlon who can capture a commo link?" Tavia asked.

Lela joined in the chuckling that scattered throughout the room. *Even the children at Ambrose can set up a commo link,* Lela thought.

"I'm sure there is," Exidor said dryly. "You'll have my answer tomorrow."

The connection was broken. Tavia asked Jaret how long it would take to have teleconference capabilities.

"About ten minutes."

"Then we'll worry about it tomorrow." The princess turned to Alaric and said, "Watch him closely. I want no surprises."

Chapter Seventeen

Lela and Tavia left the communications center together and walked through the main hall, occasionally meeting others in passing. The palace was quiet, and few people were moving about. Military customs didn't apply to everyone who lived there, and Lela noticed how casual the ordinary Amtecs were compared to warriors.

Lela thought about Alaric and how strange it was to see her now. She was disappointed in Alaric's ability to shut her out so easily, but Lela was glad things hadn't gotten complicated for them. Getting too attached to someone from another sector was never a good idea. She had dabbled in a sexual flirtation and had been attracted to the warrior charm that

Alaric possessed. Lela was now ready to put that behind her and concentrate on why she was there in the first place.

"Are you tired?" Tavia asked. "I know it's late."

"I've had a busy day," Lela said, "but I'm not tired." She wasn't sure she would be able to sleep after all that had happened. Her mind mulled over the details of being with Alaric at Ambrose and then seeing her again later in the communications center only to be ignored. As many times as she had told herself that it had been fun and that she needed to concentrate on other things, it still surprised Lela when her psyche refused to listen to reason. One minute she was happy that things had happened but even more happy that it was all over, and then the next minute she was angry for having let Alaric decide when things were finished between them. Each time they had made love Lela had expected to feel closer to Alaric, had expected to know her better and understand some of the things about her that made no sense, but Alaric wasn't able to let go of that formidable exterior of hers.

The things that intrigued Lela the most about Alaric were the characteristics that made her such a good warrior: her unyielding confidence and courage. But those same things were also what Lela found to be infuriating. The incident in the cave when Alaric insisted that Lela would be safe there alone, for instance. Alaric had been so confident in her interpretation of the situation that she made Lela feel safe even though she had been alone in a dangerous place. Alaric's courage during the rescue had been phenomenal despite the fact that her interactions with Lela during the entire crisis were annoying.

Lela wondered if Kricorian had noticed the same things about Jaret. Maybe the inability to connect with someone was a shortcoming that all warriors had in common. Even though Amtec warriors were good at the physical and technical aspects of pleasing a woman, perhaps warriors were only capable of communicating with each other.

"If you're not too tired," Tavia said, "maybe I could give

151

you a more thorough tour of the Amtec laboratory and answer any questions you might have."

"You haven't given up on that yet?"

"Me? I never give up," Tavia said.

They turned down another hallway before coming to a door at the end of a long corridor. Tavia entered a code into the panel. The door swooshed open, letting them in.

"What do you think Exidor will do?" Lela asked. "I was impressed with the way you handled him earlier," she admitted. It made Lela realize how little she actually knew about this woman.

"Exidor will do what he always does," Tavia said. "He'll make demands we can't meet and then will accuse us of being unreasonable and not cooperating."

They reached the Amtec laboratory. Everything was new, and Lela could see several active projects. She liked the layout as well as the resources.

"Exidor likes to play these games all the time," Tavia continued. "As I'm sure you know."

"What if he shows up with five delegates?" Lela asked. "What would stop us from delaying the summit long enough for the other sectors to send for three more delegates of their own?"

Tavia tilted her head back and laughed. "He would be furious, but I like the way you think."

"Exidor would be a fool to come here with anything other than his own army," Lela said. "His Star Fighters killed my mother and sister. I'd love to see him dead."

"They killed my mother, too," Tavia said quietly. "Even though there were retaliations at the time, no one feels as though Exidor has been adequately punished for what he's done. All of that is a part of why we're here now. As delegates we have to get beyond that."

They came to another door that Tavia opened.

"Then it might be best that the Corlon delegation not be

here at all," Lela said. "An item on the agenda might have to involve what we do about him."

Even though it was late, some researchers were still in various parts of the lab. Tavia opened another door to a restricted area, and she and Lela went inside. There Lela saw the soft green glow of the life capsule that the princess had been in when they first met.

Nearly speechless, Lela moved closer and gently touched it with the palms of her hands. "It's still magnificent," she whispered. Looking at Tavia standing at the end of the cylinder, Lela said, "For this I would consider staying here to work. This thing fascinates me. It makes me want to know absolutely everything there is to know about it."

Tavia smiled. "Good. I was hoping you would say that."

Lela couldn't stop touching it and could almost feel the capsule breathing through her fingertips. "You certainly know how to get my attention. As far as research goes, nothing has ever captured my interest the way this has."

Tracing one of the intricate carvings with a fingertip, Lela asked, "Would I have to come up with a tasty food for four-year-olds before I could work on this?"

Tavia laughed. "I'll make sure all our records are made available to you while you're here."

"That's very generous," Lela said. She wasn't sure what was involved with the offer, but Tavia seemed to be going to a lot of trouble to keep her around.

"Right now all I want you to do is think about the things we've discussed," Tavia said. "We need to get through the summit first."

Lela knew it was Kricorian in her room even before her eyes were opened all the way. Standing beside Lela's bed, Kricorian didn't have to say anything. Lela got up and followed her over to the chaise longues and sat down in one while Kricorian eased into the other.

"What's going on between you and that cute little warrior you've been seeing?" Lela asked with a yawn. She decided that it was probably much later than she realized.

"Oh, Lela, she says she loves me. What am I going to do?"

Lela didn't know what to say. Their midnight chats had always involved Lela's affairs of the heart. The two of them had never had one where Kricorian's personal life was the topic of discussion.

"Tell me how you feel about her."

"I'm old enough to be her mother."

"But tell me how you feel. Do you love her?"

Kricorian didn't answer, and Lela wasn't sure what else to say. She reached over and took Kricorian's hand.

"You deserve to be happy," Lela whispered.

"I was happy with your mother."

"And maybe you'll be lucky enough to have that again with someone else." She gave Kricorian's hand a reassuring squeeze. "Jaret doesn't seem to be bothered by the age difference."

"She isn't."

"Then do whatever it takes to get yourself past that," Lela said. She felt her heart swell when she realized that Kricorian was crying.

"Everything seems to have happened so fast," Kricorian said.

Earlier Lela had felt the same way. Good sex wasn't everything. Lela didn't like the way Alaric made her feel *after* they made love.

"Is Jaret working now?" Lela asked.

"She should be looking for me soon," Kricorian said, "but I needed to see you first." She took Lela's hand and laced their fingers together. "I have to know that you're all right with this."

Lela smiled and got up. She took both of Kricorian's hands

and pulled her to her feet. "I just want you to be happy. And if Jaret makes you happy, then it's fine with me." Lela gave her a hug, and she felt Kricorian relax in her arms.

After a moment they let go of each other and Kricorian asked where Alaric was. "I thought she'd be here, or maybe neither of you would be here."

"I'm not really sure what's going on with that," Lela said awkwardly. "Soon we should both be too busy to worry about it."

They walked to the door, where Kricorian gave her another quick hug. "Thank you, little one. I can't do this without your blessing."

"You have it. Stop thinking so much."

Lela woke up to voices in the hallway and realized everyone was on their way to breakfast with the princess. She hadn't gotten much sleep and wondered why Kricorian hadn't come to wake her. *Unless she isn't sleeping alone,* she thought with a smile. Lela felt happy for her and briefly wondered how their lives would change because of it.

She got ready for the day and fluffed up the back of her damp hair as she left her room. Going out of the door, Lela ran into Alaric.

"Good morning," Alaric said. "I was sent to look for you."

"I'm running a little late."

"Can I come in for a minute?"

"No need for that," Lela said. "We can talk on the way if you like."

They walked side by side in silence, with warriors snapping to attention as soon as they saw their commander. Lela was surprised at how angry she was at Alaric and how disappointed she was with herself for having had so little self-control while dealing with her.

"The Tracon delegation will arrive in about an hour," Alaric said.

"What's the latest on the Corlon fiasco?"

"Jaret has the commo link in place. Exidor will attend the summit that way, which makes my job a lot easier."

"That's good news."

"Lela," Alaric said. She stopped in the middle of the hall-way, which made Lela have to slow down and turn around. Alaric held out her hand and asked if they could talk privately for a moment.

"I'm already late," Lela reminded her.

"A few more minutes won't matter that much."

Alaric opened a door and held it for Lela.

"You're upset with me," Alaric said as she closed the door behind them. "Have I done something to offend you?"

"We both have jobs to do here, Alaric. Let's concentrate on that now."

"So I have done something," Alaric said simply. "Tell me what it is."

"You've done nothing but be yourself."

"That's not a compliment, is it?" she asked with a slight smile.

"We had fun, Alaric, and we got to know each other a little better."

"But?"

Lela shrugged. "But what?" It surprised her that Alaric looked so confused all of a sudden. "The sex was everything I've heard it would be," Lela said, "but it's not enough. I need what goes along with it."

Alaric moved closer to her. There was no furniture in the long, empty room, which made their voices echo a little.

"What kinds of things go along with it?" Alaric asked in a low, curious voice.

Lela shrugged again. "I can't be rolling around on my bed with you one minute and then be ignored by you the next. I usually don't give myself to someone so casually." To hear herself, Lela knew she was sounding fickle and trite, but she was also trying to be honest. "I prefer having a lover instead of just a sex partner. I learned something about me while I was here, and I have you to thank for that. And I mean that sincerely."

"There can be a certain comfort in being with a stranger," Alaric said. She reached over to touch Lela's hair and grazed the side of her face with the back of her fingers. Lela's body betrayed her with a tremble.

"I don't need comforting right now," Lela managed to say.

Alaric's fingers continued mingling in her hair, delicately touching Lela's ear and the back of her neck.

"Is there anything I can do to change your mind?"

Lela slowly shook her head. She knew that her body wasn't fooling either of them, but a purely physical relationship with Alaric wasn't what she wanted. Lela knew in her heart what was best for her.

"You still haven't told me what happened," Alaric said.

"I'm late for breakfast with the princess."

Alaric nodded and stepped back away from her. "Very well," she said and opened the door. "You're underestimating my ability to care about you."

"It's obvious where your loyalties are and where your commitment belongs, Commander."

"I can see that I've made a mistake," Alaric said. They were back in the main hallway again. "I'll try to redeem myself," she said with an engaging smile. "Don't underestimate me. I might still surprise you."

Chapter Eighteen

Amtec Reception Bay

Lela and Kricorian had a few minutes together as they stood at the edge of the Amtec reception bay waiting for the arrival of the Tracon delegation. Breakfast with the princess had been more of the same, with the talk of the morning being Exidor's decision to participate in the summit via a commo link. Viscar and Keda were also relieved to hear about that new development.

"Jaret and I have discussed this at great length," Kricorian said quietly. She and Lela had their heads close together so they could hear each other over the chatter in the reception bay. "She wants to request an assignment at K Sector helping me with the lidium project. I need to know if you would support such a recommendation if I were to bring it up as an agenda item."

"Of course I would!"

Kricorian nodded. "Thank you."

Lela saw Kricorian look over at Jaret, who was standing in front of the warrior formation. Jaret was already looking at them smiling. *That's what's missing with Alaric. Having her be aware of someone across a crowded room or having her search for me that way when we're not physically together.* Lela knew that such things didn't just happen. Those feelings were either there or they weren't. She was happy to see that Jaret apparently felt the same way about Kricorian that Kricorian was feeling about her. They actually looked as though they were falling in love.

Lela was also beginning to realize that she had never had that type of feeling before. Not with Colby. Not with anyone. Lela pushed the thought away and glanced over at Kricorian again. Lela wondered what she would do if Kricorian got hurt over this new relationship. *She's fallen hard for Jaret. I hope things work out for them.*

"There they are," Kricorian said. "Let's move up closer with the others before the princess sends someone to look for us again."

They made their way through the throng of people and were able to stand beside Keda and Viscar. A few seconds later the Tracon spidercraft landed to a hearty cheer from the crowd. Jaret called the formation to attention, and the saluting began again. Lela was surprised at how bored she was with all the military customs and courtesies going on. After only a few days it had gotten old.

By the time the princess was finished with the military presentation of the troops, the spidercraft had docked and its occupants were getting out. Tavia was up front greeting the three dignitaries from Tracon, with Meega being the first one on the flight deck, followed by Sporae and the Rufkin leader. Meega had her bright pink hair piled high on her head in a more conservative style than usual, and she wore a matching pink flight suit that made her appear a lot younger than Lela imagined her to be. Sporae was visibly tired and frail, but he still had an uncanny wisdom in his eyes. He smiled and nodded when he saw Lela. The Rufkin leader stayed close to him and helped Sporae remain steady on his feet.

"Tavia, babe!" Meega squealed. She took the princess into her arms and nearly picked her up off the ground in a hug. Meega kissed Tavia on the mouth with a loud smacking noise and then let go of her. "I haven't seen you since those awful pirates snatched your butt! You look fabulous!"

Meega, Lela thought. *How could I have forgotten that she would be here!* Lela leaned over to Kricorian and whispered, "If she touches me, I'll knock the —"

"She won't," Kricorian said with a chuckle. "I'll make sure of it."

Meega was making her way down the line, shaking hands and talking to Keda and Viscar. She squealed again when she saw Kricorian and swooped her up in another one of her bone-crunching hugs.

"Good to see you again, Meega," Kricorian said. "Put me down, and welcome to the summit." In Meega's ear she whispered, "If you touch Lela, her girlfriend will probably kill you right where you stand."

Meega threw her head back and laughed. "So my little Lela has a girlfriend now, eh?"

Lela rolled her eyes, but was glad Kricorian had found a way to keep Meega from getting close to her. What Meega did with everyone else didn't bother Lela in the least, but she wanted nothing whatsoever to do with the sleazy saloon keeper.

Meega winked at her and made a little clucking noise with her tongue. "Is it a warrior, Lela-babe? You know those rumors about warriors in bed," she said with an exaggerated wink. "Where do you think they learned all those tricks from, my friend?"

Lela ignored her and stepped out of line to speak with Sporae. He was the one and only thing Lela missed about Tracon. When Lela and Romney were children, their mother and Kricorian would take them to shop at Tracon, and they would visit with Sporae for several hours while they were there. Lela could still remember the spicy smell of the tea he had made for them and the layers and layers of scarves hanging from the tops of his doors, giving his boutique such a mystical look. He always had interesting things for Lela and Romney to do while they were there and unusual toys for them to play with. Visiting Sporae had always been the highlight of any shopping trip at Tracon, and Lela still despised Meega for ruining that for her.

Lela knelt down and gave Sporae a hug; she could feel his fragile bones through his robe.

"How are you?" Lela asked him.

"I always forget how small a spidercraft can be until I'm in one with certain people."

Lela laughed. "You certainly have my sympathy," she assured him. "Please tell me that Tracon didn't send three delegates."

Sporae signed wearily. "Yes, we are a delegation of three. The Rufkins wouldn't let us leave until they were represented. That's why we're so late. We finally stopped arguing and just brought one of them with us. Otherwise we'd still be there arguing."

"This isn't good," Lela said just before she heard the princess talking to Meega about the same thing.

"You wouldn't believe the problems we've had with Corlon over this issue," Tavia was saying in exasperation. "I can't believe there are three of you here!"

Meega put her arm around Tavia's shoulder and pulled her close. "Now don't get your tiara in a knot. We'll figure something out."

While the princess handled the delicate matter of how to keep the summit on track and all the delegates on board and happy, Lela and Kricorian helped arrange to get Sporae settled in his quarters.

Later that afternoon, Jaret closed the door to Kricorian's room and pulled Kricorian into her arms, kissing her deeply. Kricorian immediately responded to her touch and felt wonderfully alive.

"I've missed you," Jaret whispered as she opened the front of Kricorian's uniform and filled her hand with a soft breast. Kricorian wanted her.

"How much time do you have?"

"An hour," Jaret whispered as she kissed her again.

"Then you first," Kricorian said in between nibbles on Jaret's neck. She maneuvered her to the bed where they helped each other out of their clothes. To lie down on a bed and feel Jaret's warm skin next to hers was like a little miracle whenever it happened.

The last few times they had made love Kricorian had been exhausted afterward. Jaret enjoyed giving her several orgasms in a row with little opportunity to recover between each one. The excuse about her body being old hadn't worked since their first night together. Kricorian was also surprised at how totally responsive she had become over the last few days, as if Jaret had discovered something in her that Kricorian had never before known existed. And just when Kricorian was certain that she couldn't come again for at least several more hours, Jaret would touch one of Kricorian's nipples with the tip of her tongue and then slip her hand down between Kricorian's legs again. The most Kricorian could do when that happened was smile in a dreamlike stupor and mumble something silly, like "I can't possibly do it again" or "There's no way another one can be in there."

Jaret would find Kricorian's ear and whisper to her as her fingers did their magic below. "Is it all right if I just play with you this way?"

Jaret would then gently kiss Kricorian on the cheek and tell her to relax; all the while Kricorian's body was already tingling from Jaret's touch. In Kricorian's mind there was no pressure to come ... no pressure about having to give her lover any evidence that she was enjoying what was happening to her. The moment Kricorian began to move, Jaret would kiss her ear and whisper, "It's time again, lover. Time for something different. I think my mouth belongs down there now."

Those words would send heat throbbing through Kricorian's body.

"It does belong there," Jaret would whisper, and Kricorian's moaning would invariably get louder.

"Would you like that?" Jaret would then ask her. "Would you like my mouth there?"

Kricorian would never answer, but her body talked for her. Once again they would be off in search of an orgasm that Kricorian was certain couldn't possibly exist. But if her lover wanted to try again, who was she to deny her that?

And then, as if by way of another miracle, Kricorian could feel the magic of Jaret's tongue as it worked on her, never in the same place and never teasing her, just a series of oral encouragements and direct stimulation in exactly the place where Kricorian needed her to be.

"You first this time," Kricorian said again as they continued kissing. "Turn over."

Jaret looked at her and smiled before turning over on her stomach.

"You always make me too sleepy to take care of you properly," Kricorian said as she drew her neatly trimmed fingernails down along Jaret's back.

"Mmm. That feels good."

Kricorian kissed Jaret's bare shoulder. She liked seeing the relaxed, dreamy expression on Jaret's young face and had no idea why this beautiful woman half her own age would fall in love with her. It had come to the point where Kricorian no longer wanted to think about why something like this had happened. She was too grateful to question it any longer.

With the palm of her hand, Kricorian rubbed along Jaret's lower back and then moved down even farther. She used her fingernails again up around Jaret's shoulders and worked her way down once more to the lower back.

"This feels so good," Jaret purred.

Kricorian propped herself up so that her upper body was more comfortable and her breasts could touch Jaret's back. She kissed Jaret's shoulder and neck while her hand rubbed along the top of her thigh.

"Open your legs," Kricorian whispered, and she was rewarded with a moan from her lover as Jaret spread her legs.

Kricorian slipped a finger inside of her from behind and knew exactly how good it felt. Kricorian loved being taken this way, and she could hear Jaret's breathing change as she began to squirm with pleasure.

"Does this feel good?" Kricorian whispered in her ear, knowing already that it did.

Jaret's arms were crossed, and she cradled her head as she continued to moan her pleasure. The position Jaret was in left her breast free to be touched, and as Kricorian worked two fingers in and out of her, Kricorian was also able to take advantage of Jaret's breast with the other. It made Kricorian feel wonderful to have Jaret so out of control.

Before they got too far along, Kricorian asked her to turn over again. Keeping her fingers in place she said, "I need to see you come."

Jaret turned over, careful not to lose the physical connection they had. "But I already came once."

"That's right," Kricorian said as she briefly covered one of

164

Jaret's nipples with her mouth. "But I'm just getting started with you. Relax and let's see what happens."

Command Suite

Lela was amused at the way the princess was handling her anger about three delegates from Tracon showing up. Meega had been oblivious to the problem until the princess informed her and the Rufkin leader that Tracon could only have two votes at the summit.

"We all know that Sporae didn't travel all this way to not have his vote counted," Tavia reminded them.

"Well, neither did I!" the Rufkin leader said.

"Then the Tracon delegation needs to work something out among the three of you," Tavia said. "I won't have us looking like fools in front of Exidor when we all finally get together. It needs to be settled and taken care of now."

Lela had seen her be more diplomatic over the last few days, but the princess apparently knew what it took to handle the two of them. Tavia announced to all the delegates present that there would be a working dinner that evening where they would firm up the agenda. The summit would officially begin in the morning.

"So anything you want discussed at the summit," Tavia said, "be prepared to present it and defend it this evening."

"Where's Kricorian?" Viscar asked.

Lela tried hard not to smile when Keda suggested that Kricorian must be in a meeting since she saw a warrior posted outside of her door earlier.

"She's helping with security while she's here," Tavia said.

Helping with security, Lela thought. *I know exactly what she's securing right now.*

"And what's all this nonsense about me having my own room?" Meega asked the princess.

"Everyone has their own room," Tavia said.

"I thought I'd stay here with you," Meega said as she ran a fingertip along the sleeve of Tavia's uniform. "Like last time."

"Like last time?" Tavia said with a laugh. "You've never stayed here with me."

"Well, almost like last time."

Lela had no desire to find out what had ever happened between these two. Anyone who would voluntarily associate with Meega on a personal level became suspect in Lela's mind. Meega could be quite pleasing to the eye at times, but Lela found her to be manipulative and sleazy. Lela did, however, have several hours free before needing to be back for the agenda meeting later, and since it didn't look like Meega was letting go of the princess anytime soon, Lela went over and interrupted them to ask Tavia for a favor.

"Where's your girlfriend?" Meega asked Lela. She stayed close to the princess without really touching her, attempting to give the impression that they were together.

Tavia gave Lela a curious look. "You're seeing someone here?"

"Only if it keeps Meega away from me," Lela said with a smile. She returned Tavia's steady look and then nodded toward Meega. "You can do better, Princess."

"Don't talk about me like I'm not here!" Meega said incredulously.

"I'll be fine," Tavia assured her. "Thank you."

Lela then asked if she could have access to the lab for a few hours. Tavia smiled and seemed pleased by her request.

"I'll have someone escort you there right away."

Chapter Nineteen

Amtec Laboratory

Lela couldn't believe that Alaric was the only person available to get her into the lab.

"Don't you have other things you need to be doing?" Lela asked as Alaric opened the first door to let her in.

"This shouldn't take long," Alaric assured her. "And yes. I have other things to do." Once they were in the main part of the research center, Alaric asked her what in particular she wanted to do while she was there.

"Archived records for the life capsule," Lela said. "The princess promised that I could see them whenever I wanted to."

Alaric smiled. "She's given you unlimited access to everything in the lab while you're here. We haven't had time to reprogram special codes for you yet. I'm sorry. I'll have Jaret do it right away. The archives are in here," she said.

"I appreciate this. Thanks."

"If you need anything," Alaric said as she looked directly at her. "Anything," she repeated. "I'll make sure it's available for you."

Anything, Lela thought with a smirk.

There was a flash of anger in Alaric's eyes, but Lela wasn't afraid to provoke it. Part of the reason she had found Alaric so attractive in the beginning was the undercurrent of passion she could see bubbling near the surface; another part was Alaric's need to always be so in control of herself. Lela had been able to penetrate that cold exterior on only two occasions when they had made love, and the person she had found was the person Lela wanted to see more of and get to know better.

But that's not possible. Alaric kept that person closely guarded and out of sight, as if the two times Lela had touched the real Alaric had been too much for her to handle. Their time together was limited and it was easier to leave things unresolved than to try to untangle the mess they had made of it already.

"I'll leave you alone," Alaric said. She turned and was gone.

Command Suite

Tavia and Jaret were the only ones there when Alaric arrived. Jaret was briefing the princess on the additional security measures that had been put in place around the Amtec perimeter.

"There's new activity in the Intergalactic Corridor," Jaret said. "It's not clear whether these are Star Fighters or pirates."

"So we're going under the assumption that they could be two different factions?" Tavia asked.

"For now," Jaret said. "The other possibility is that Corlon is feeding information directly to whoever these pirates are. This way Exidor lets them do his fighting and raiding, and all the while he claims to be innocent."

"Watch him," Tavia said. "And keep me informed about what's going on."

Jaret gave the princess a sharp salute and left the room. Tavia looked up at Alaric and invited her to sit down.

"I take it that Lela is settled in the lab," Tavia said. "And your charms are still working on her?"

Alaric glared at her for a moment. "Apparently I'm losing my touch."

"I doubt that." When Tavia didn't see Alaric's expression change, she looked at her more closely. "Explain what you meant by that."

Alaric looked away and didn't say anything.

"When was the last time the two of you made love?" Tavia asked.

Alaric seemed to be making an effort to control herself.

"Alaric," Tavia said gently. "Please answer me. This is important." When Alaric still said nothing, the princess continued. "We know that she's attracted to you, so what seems to be the problem here?"

"I'm not sure exactly."

"Is there still a physical relationship?"

"No," Alaric said. "She's no longer interested in that."

Tavia put her hands on the table and folded them in front of her. "Is this fixable?" she asked calmly. "Or is this a chemistry problem between the two of you?"

"I don't know."

"Is there anything I can do to help?" Tavia asked. "I can't emphasize strongly enough how important it is that we keep Lela happy while she's here." The princess rubbed her arms as if to ward off a sudden chill. "I feel a sense of urgency about several things," she said, "and one of those things is convincing Lela to come here and continue her research. Her talents are being wasted at K Sector. Anyone there could do what she's doing. Lela was the one who saved me from being trapped in the capsule. There's no telling how long I would have stayed in there had K Sector not been involved with finding me. It's safe to say that not just anyone could have freed me the way she did. Zigrid was the first to bring this to our attention while we were all still there. Lela's talents are exceptional, Alaric, and I want her working here with us. In the Amtec labs."

Their eyes met again, and the tension seemed to ease.

"I told her about one project that was important to me," Tavia continued, "but it wasn't of much interest to her. It's obvious that she only wants to work with the capsule right now, so that's where our focus needs to be. I have other things that will pique her interest as far as research goes, but it made sense to me at the time that having someone here at the palace to physically attract her would make any offer to stay here with us seem more appealing. That's where you come in. She likes you," Tavia said quietly. "She's attracted to you, and I'm almost certain that she would stay here for you."

"So you're using me to make her stay."

Tavia forced herself to keep looking at Alaric as she got this confession out of the way. "It doesn't sound as nice when you say it like that."

"You're not fooling me," Alaric said. "It's becoming clear to me that you're also attracted to her. When Lela and I were by the lake at Ambrose, you tried to watch, but you couldn't. I knew —"

"What I feel doesn't matter," Tavia said, interrupting her.

"It matters to me."

"You're the one she wants," Tavia whispered. "You're the one she'll stay here for."

"Why didn't you tell me how you felt about her?"

Tavia shrugged. "I didn't know myself until I actually saw you kiss her by the lake. You're right. I couldn't watch anything else after that."

"You know that this changes everything, don't you?"

"I don't know that at all," Tavia said. Her voice was low, and she was on the verge of crying. "I can make this work for both of you. I promise."

"I can't continue seeing her knowing how you feel."

"That's no longer an option available to you, Commander," Tavia said quietly. "Our goal is to convince her to work here. If you happen to be one of the reasons she will want to stay, then that's the way it has to be." She stopped for a moment to get her runaway emotions under control. She dabbed her eyes on the sleeve of her uniform. "There's something else I need to talk to you about while you're here. The Amtecs will also have two delegates at the summit. I'm one, and I want you to be the other. Put Jaret totally in charge of security. All I want you thinking about is what's best for our people. This will also give you more time to spend with Lela."

"It's an honor to be asked to serve with you at the summit."

Tavia smiled. "There's no one else I'd rather have beside me right now."

Keda and Viscar sat Sporae down at the head of the table after having carried him in on a mini-throne. At first Sporae had protested getting special treatment, but once he heard how far the walk was to the command suite from his room, he climbed up on the portable throne and let them take him away.

Meega, the Rufkin leader, Kricorian, Alaric, and Tavia were already in the command suite when the other two came in carrying him. Lela, the last to arrive, came directly from the lab.

"Where did you find that thing?" Tavia asked with a laugh when she saw what they had carried him in on. "That was made for my mother as a joke," Tavia said, nodding toward the little throne. "She used to prop her feet on it when she took a nap. I haven't seen it in years."

Without any royal flourish, the food was brought in and wineglasses were filled. The delegates sat together around the table, with Tavia at one end, Alaric on her right, and Lela on her left. Meega sat beside Alaric, and the Rufkin leader and Sporae were at the other end of the table. To Sporae's right were Keda and Viscar; Kricorian was next to Lela. Tavia made it clear that by morning the Tracon delegation had to agree on how their two votes would be cast during the proceedings. All three could attend the summit, but only two votes would be allowed once policies were to be decided upon.

"Let's hope that Exidor doesn't count the delegates when the link is activated later," Tavia said.

The conversation at dinner consisted of talk about the palace and the food that was being served. Viscar was still swooning over the wine, but had vowed not to drink more than one glass with her dinner.

"You don't want her carrying you on that throne thing after she's had too much wine," Keda told Sporae to a burst of laughter. "We ended up pouring her into bed last night."

Meega was whispering in Alaric's ear. Alaric was a polite listener. Even from across the table it was obvious to Lela that Meega's hand was on Alaric's thigh, but no one gave it much thought.

"Four scruffy Star Fighters brought the capsule to my shop one night," Sporae said. "They wanted credits for gambling at the casino." He smiled, which made his eyes naturally squint. "It was a magnificent piece, and they were willing to let it go for two hundred credits."

Tavia laughed. "So at least *you* were willing to pay what I was worth?"

"I do apologize, Princess, for not realizing what I had."

"No apology necessary, my friend."

"I need to talk to you about something," Lela said as she leaned closer to Kricorian. "The princess has made me an interesting offer about coming here and continuing my research."

"Coming here for how long?" Kricorian asked.

"That part wasn't discussed, but she's given me complete access to the notes on how the capsule was developed. That's where I've been all afternoon."

"Would you be here for days? Weeks? How long?"

"Longer than that probably," Lela said. She had been dreading this conversation, and already she had an idea how Kricorian would take the news.

"What about your research at K Sector?"

"Tavia says I can do it here."

"Then it's settled?"

"I haven't given her a definite answer," Lela said. "It's not like you'll never see me again. We'll only be a few hours apart."

"But you'll be leaving home!" Kricorian said emphatically. "Excuse me," she said and pushed her chair away from the table.

Leaning toward Lela, Tavia asked if everything was all right.

"Not exactly," Lela said. "Excuse us for a few minutes." She placed her napkin beside her virtually untouched plate and followed Kricorian out the door. "Kricorian," she called once she was in the hallway. Kricorian stopped. Luckily Lela found a door like the one Alaric had used earlier that day. Lela opened it and motioned for Kricorian to go inside with her.

"I'm sorry I got so upset," Kricorian said once they were inside the empty room.

"It's just an offer," Lela said gently. "I haven't agreed to anything yet."

"I know how disappointed you were when they took the capsule back. This is something that's important to you."

"Again, it's just an offer," Lela said. "Other things are even more important to me than any of this. And you happen to be one of them."

Kricorian pulled Lela into her arms and gave her a fierce hug. "You just took me by surprise, that's all."

"A lot has happened over the last few days," Lela said. "Things that we're both still getting used to. Don't forget that it's been a shock to hear that you had a lover already."

Kricorian let go of her. "I think it was more of a shock to me than you," she said. "Come on. We need to get back to the meeting."

As they went out into the main hallway again, Kricorian looked back over her shoulder and shook her head. "How do you know about all these secret rooms and passages and things?"

"I've been all over this place."

Chapter Twenty

Command Suite

It was the first morning of the summit and Lela was more nervous than she thought she would be. Being a delegate was a big responsibility that she took seriously, but she wasn't quite sure what to expect. Lela had gotten plenty of rest the night before and had concluded that she was one of the few delegates who had slept alone. Warriors were standing outside everyone's door except for Sporae's and the Rufkin leader's. It was obvious that the others had spent their evening with company, and Lela was interested in seeing how they would hold up to hours of bickering and committee work during the summit. Undoubtedly there would be a few cranky delegates to deal with.

After a brief breakfast in the command suite with the princess, everyone seemed eager to get started. Lela watched Jaret finish checking the commo link so Corlon could join them at the meeting. The red screen indicated that the feed was working, but no one on the other end was yet available.

"Does he think we'll wait for him?" Viscar asked.

"He knows what time we start," Tavia said. "If he's not here, then he's not here. We aren't waiting for anyone."

At the designated time, Keda got the meeting underway. There was an official roll call and an explanation why Bravo Sector was not sending any delegates, a notation about the extra delegate from Tracon and about Corlon's absence via the commo link. An audio recording was being made with Keda moderating the proceedings. Once the preliminaries were behind them, which included a brief explanation about how the two delegates from each sector would be representing the views and needs of their people, they moved through the first few agenda items quickly.

"The next issue up for discussion is price-fixing at Tracon," Keda announced.

Everyone at the table began to squirm a little. This one promised to inspire a lively discussion.

"I move that we take a break first," Viscar said.

"We'll be here for days if we start taking too many breaks," Meega said. "I say we keep going."

Lela noticed that Viscar was having trouble staying awake. There was a lot of twitching going on at the other end of the table. The Rufkin leader had dozed through most of the proceedings already, but he sat up straight and appeared to be listening to what was going on. The fact that a fair amount of calico fur covered his eyes made his actions look less obvious, but the consensus was that the next few issues were going to be quite tedious.

"If frequent breaks will keep our minds fresh," Sporae said diplomatically, "then I suggest we take them when needed."

"Maybe it would help if we didn't take the agenda items

in order," Meega said. "Some of this is nothing more than dull policymaking."

"Are we taking a break or not?" Viscar asked.

With his eyes still closed, the Rufkin leader said, "I vote for a break."

"You don't even *have* a vote," Meega reminded him.

With a sigh Lela asked, "Did we vote on who gets to vote yet?" she asked.

"We will be here forever at this rate," Keda mumbled.

As soon as it was decided that a break was in order, Lela got some tea from a table of refreshments on the other side of the room. She noticed Jaret slipping in just as everyone began to mingle. Jaret whispered something to Alaric, and they left together. Kricorian followed them out, but she returned after only a few minutes. The other delegates, who were involved in discussions of their own, didn't indicate that they had noticed anything.

Meega seemed to be at a loss as to who to lavish her attention on with Alaric gone. Lela could hear her teasing Kricorian about her "new little warrior" friend. Meega then threw all her attention on the princess, who was attempting to have a serious conversation with Viscar about a new spidercraft that Alpha Sector was developing. Meega stood close to the princess, and Lela noticed that Meega made sure her breast brushed against Tavia's upper arm. Meega could be quite entertaining when in hot pursuit of a potential conquest. Lela had seen her in action and knew how to avoid being the object of that type of attention.

Lela stirred her tea and reached for a scone on one of several platters on the table.

"Were the archives helpful to you?" Tavia asked her as she poured herself some tea.

Lela glanced over her shoulder to see Meega now pressing

her breast against Viscar's arm while joining in on a conversation with another small group.

"I'm enjoying your reference library immensely," Lela said. "I appreciate the opportunity you're giving me."

"Have you thought any more about my offer of having your own lab?"

Lela smiled and remembered the panic on Kricorian's face when they had briefly discussed it the night before. "I've thought about it."

With a sigh Tavia said, "Your degree of enthusiasm doesn't sound like good news for me."

"There's more to consider than just what I want."

Tavia looked at her with serious, searching eyes, then asked, "So it's possible that this is something you might want?"

"I'm intrigued by the type of research done here, and I'm humbled by your generosity to share it," Lela said quietly. "But my responsibilities at K Sector may have to come first. I haven't decided what I want to do about any of it yet."

Tavia nodded. "Then it would be totally inappropriate for me to introduce you to any more intriguing things right now. Is that it? That would be a totally unfair thing for me to do?"

"What could possibly be more intriguing than the life capsule?"

"The Cirala Project," Tavia said. "Or Project C, as it was called at the time." She reached for a cookie. "My mother was a researcher. Did you know that?"

Surprised, Lela said no. "I thought she was a Princess like you."

Tavia laughed. "She was, but she also had the healing gift and was an amazingly brilliant woman. She developed the protocol for the life capsule and then turned it over to others for further research. What we have now is a result of that research, but no one has worked on it for years. But the capsule wasn't what my mother devoted her life to. She worked on Project C until she was killed. No one has touched it since."

Lela was curious now. Someone with genius enough to have developed the life capsule actually had another project that was even more important to her. This new information immediately captured Lela's interest.

"Break's over," Keda announced. "Let's get back to work."

After the price-fixing debate, Meega and Sporae were no longer speaking to each other. Sporae had eventually sided with the other delegates on the unfairness of price gouging, while Meega saw it as a supply-and-demand issue.

"I'm taking all the risk by dealing with these unsavory pirates for hard-to-get goods that all of you want," Meega said. "I should be able to charge what I think it's worth to me for that. If you don't want to pay my prices, then buy it from someone else."

"That's the point," Keda said. "There *is* no one else!"

The Rufkin leader actually growled at Keda during one heated discussion and was almost banished from the room and the summit until Kricorian got everyone calmed down. The riff between Meega and Sporae would have to be settled between them on their own time. Meega made no secret of the fact that she saw him as weak and political.

"You're here to help protect Tracon's interests," Meega told him pointedly. "You can't side with your friends, and you can't let these women intimidate you. Have you forgotten that you're a Tracon delegate? If not, then act like one. We're both here to get the best deal we can for Tracon vendors. How about a little support? We're supposed to be a team."

In a calm voice, Sporae said, "Meega, dear. No one will come away from the summit as having totally won anything. We all will have to make compromises and concessions for the good of the whole. Now let's move on to the next agenda item."

They kept working and had lunch served to them while discussions continued. Lela had to admit that Meega was a convincing advocate for vendors' rights at Tracon. As a businesswoman, she was to be respected, but as a person with an out-of-control libido, Lela still found her to be sleazy and disgusting.

Things were going slowly, but they were making good progress in the quality of the decisions being made. Other than the price-fixing agenda item, there had been no other major disagreements. Sporae had been correct in his assessment of how the compromise issue would work. No one was getting exactly what was wanted, but no one was given a deal that he or she couldn't learn to live with either.

"I move that we adjourn for the day," Sporae said tiredly.

"I second the motion," Alaric said.

The princess announced that dinner would be served in the atrium later. "We all need a break from having to spend too much time in here," she explained. "There will also be music and dancing if anyone is interested."

"Dancing," Meega cooed. "Can I have the first dance with you, Princess?"

Tavia laughed and didn't answer.

"Make sure there's plenty of that wine available too," Viscar said. "I've grown quite fond of it already."

"Like *that's* a big secret," Keda said.

"We're back here at the same time in the morning?" Viscar asked.

"Yes," Kricorian said. "I think we covered a lot today. And most of us are still speaking," she said with a laugh.

"Most of us," Meega said as she gave Sporae a piercing look.

Lela wanted to have a word with Kricorian before heading over to the lab for the evening. She tugged on her elbow and got Kricorian off to the side.

"What's going on with Jaret?" Lela asked. "Why was she in here this morning and then didn't even acknowledge you?"

Kricorian looked around before answering. "We can't talk here."

"Fine," Lela said. She took Kricorian by the hand and slipped out the door and into the hallway. "This better?"

Kricorian spoke quietly with her head close to Lela's. "There was activity outside the Amtec perimeter this morning. Jaret doubled the patrol, which was already quite sufficient, and whoever it was went away." Kricorian stopped and took a deep breath. "There have been other indications that more are on the way. We aren't sure what they want or what they'll do once they get here, but the Amtec leadership has decided to be on the offensive once it's clear that they're coming back this way."

"What kind of danger are we in?" Lela asked.

"We? None," Kricorian said. "If they return, the Amtecs could possibly lose a few warriors in a skirmish, but Jaret doesn't think so. The Amtecs have confidence in their ability to hold the perimeter. That's not a concern for them, but they take immediate offense to anyone entering their air space uninvited. That's considered an act of war, and that's where everything is right now."

"Will Jaret be one of the fighters defending the Amtec air space?" Lela asked.

Kricorian shook her head. "No, but she'll be upset if she loses even one warrior."

"I understand," Lela said and gave her a hug.

"Let's go back inside," Kricorian said. "I need to help patch this thing between Sporae and Meega."

"I'm going to the lab," Lela said. "I probably won't see you again until the morning."

Lela felt safe at the palace even though she wondered if Kricorian was telling her the complete truth about the amount of danger they were in. She decided that there wasn't much she could do one way or the other, so she buried herself in the notes from the life capsule research.

From what Lela was able to extract from the information available, adrenaline was the key to activating the capsule. It had been specifically designed for Tavia's DNA, with a rush of adrenaline being the triggering factor in the capsule's release. One of the things that Lela found to be so fascinating was the way it had been used. It had been saved for Amtec royalty instead of refined and perfected to be used by all Amtecs. *Doesn't everyone deserve to be protected in this way?* she wondered.

Lela pored over the research. One of the first things Lela wanted to do was find a way to make the capsule smaller and still be able to protect its contents, an idea on a similar scale to the one now being devised to protect lidium. She also reasoned that if a capsule were made to look less majestic and ornamental, it wouldn't draw so much attention to itself. There had to be a way to use the technology to help everyone, and it was something Lela wanted desperately to be a part of now that she had seen the capsule again. She decided to have another talk with Kricorian about staying on here for a while.

Lela was rubbing the back of her neck when she heard something. She looked up to see the princess by the door.

"I thought I'd find you here," Tavia said. "I was wondering if you'd have dinner with me."

Lela was surprised by the suggestion, but then realized that she was hungry. Her body was tired from sitting so much that day.

"Is it that late already?" Lela asked as she rubbed her neck again.

"It's late. We can either go back to the command suite and have dinner there or," Tavia said as she went out the door and then came back in again with a tray, "or we can dine here. Which would you prefer?"

Lela smiled and was pleased by her thoughtfulness. "We should probably just stay here."

"Good idea," Tavia said and set the tray down. "How is it going? Have you learned anything?"

"Volumes. Among other things, I've learned what a genius your mother was."

Tavia nodded. "Yes, I know. It was hard for her to have to devote so much time to leading our people. That gave her less time to do the things she really wanted to do."

"Why hasn't there been any further research done on the life capsule?" Lela asked. "That's amazing to me. This is a major breakthrough, and nothing's been done with it for nearly twenty years."

Tavia put some vegetables and meat-filled pastries on their plates and poured them some wine.

"The truth is," Tavia said, setting the empty tray on the counter behind her, "no one remembered that the capsule technology existed until K Sector notified the Amtecs that you had found me."

Lela was puzzled.

"My people believed that I'd been abducted but that whoever had me wasn't making contact with the Amtecs. Apparently I was taken away someplace where they attempted to open the capsule, but it's impossible to get it open by prying or jabbing or using explosives," she said before taking a bite of a steamy carrot.

"You're saying that until K Sector got in touch with the Amtecs and told them that we had you and explained how we found you —"

"Then the older researchers who remembered what my mother had been working on realized what had happened."

Lela was even more excited about the capsule now than she had been before. They ate in silence for a moment before Lela asked, "Do you remember what it was like being inside?"

Tavia smiled. "No. Sorry."

"What's the last thing you remember?"

"Being grabbed from behind and being very scared. That's it. Nothing more." Tavia took another bite of the pastry. "This is where I should thank you again for rescuing me."

"You don't have to thank me," Lela said. "I was only interested in the capsule, remember? I had to get you out of there so I could finally play with the inside of it."

They laughed together for a moment, and then the princess became serious again. "I do want to thank you again, and I also want you to know that I'm going to try very hard to convince you to stay and continue my mother's work."

It finally became clear to Lela that this was what Tavia was doing.

"I'm sure that you have good Amtec researchers here who could do that for you," Lela said, flattered.

"I don't want them working on any of this. They have other things to do that are just as important and interesting in their own way." Tavia sipped from her wineglass. "I want you. An outsider. Someone just as brilliant and daring as my mother was. It has to be you, or it'll be no one."

"And why is that? Why does it have to be an outsider?"

"I hope to be able to tell you soon."

Lela didn't know what to say to that. "What makes you think there's any brilliance in me? I'm a trained healer who graduated on to research. Not a lot of brilliance involved in that."

Tavia smiled. "You opened the capsule without killing me. That's brilliance enough for me."

It was Lela's turn to take a gulp of wine. Again, she didn't know what to say.

"But there's something I mentioned earlier that you didn't take the hint about." Tavia laughed lightly. "Has anyone ever told you that you don't take hints well?"

Lela shook her head no.

"There are times when you have such a wonderful sense of humor," Tavia said. "Other times it's not so wonderful. You're a little cynical, and you tend to tune things right out."

Curious, Lela asked what hint she hadn't taken.

"The hint about the Cirala Project. Project C has the potential to be even more fascinating than anything else you've seen so far. I was hoping you'd agree to spend some time going over that information before you make a decision whether to come here and work."

Lela thought of it as a small request. "I'll check out your Project C tomorrow after the summit adjourns for the day."

"Thank you." Tavia sipped more of her wine. "How much work were you planning to do here tonight?"

"I'm at a good stopping place now," Lela said and rubbed the back of her neck again. "This has been nice. Thank you."

Tavia filled their glasses again and smiled at her.

Chapter Twenty-One

Amtec Atrium

The music was loud and lively, and the delegates from the summit were dancing with Amtecs as well as with each other. Kricorian, Meega, and the Rufkin leader stood near the grape arbor discussing the events of the day. Meega excused herself when Alaric came in. She went over to her and dragged Alaric onto the busy dance floor. Kricorian then asked the Rufkin leader to dance, which brought hoots of laughter and applause the moment they began moving to the music.

Kricorian's plan all along had been to make an appearance at the festivities and then to slip off to the communications center to get an update on the latest activity outside the Amtec perimeter. So far nothing else had changed, but she knew that things tended to happen quickly when it came to Star Fighters or pirates.

Lela and the princess walked down the main hall. Lela had decided to spend all her free time over the next few days going over whatever notes she could find on Project C.

"I wonder how much wine has been consumed there already," Tavia said, nodding toward the atrium ahead. "Viscar has become quite fond of that particular vintage."

"I'm sure they all have by now." As they continued walking, Lela asked about the suspected pirate activity in the corridor. "Kricorian told me about it earlier today."

"We're patrolling heavily around the Amtec perimeter," Tavia said, "but another concern is Corlon. There's been no communication from them. It's not just the summit that Exidor is ignoring. It's everything. We'll be sending a group of warriors close by there within the next few hours to see if there's anything new to worry about."

"That's a dangerous thing to do," Lela said.

"We need to know what's going on, and there's no other way to get the information." Tavia glanced over at her. "A large number of warriors have already volunteered to go. Those who aren't chosen for the mission will be disappointed."

"There's a thin line between bravery and stupidity," Lela said philosophically.

Tavia shrugged and laughed. "Not to a warrior."

They rounded the corner that led to the atrium and went inside. Lela joined Kricorian and the Rufkin leader on the dance floor, and much to Lela's surprise the princess immediately did the same. There was more applause and laughter once people began to recognize the new dancers. Tavia moved well and gave a few onlookers at the edge of the dance floor a brief spin around the room.

When the song was over, several delegates went looking

for the wine again. Meega stepped over to the refreshment table and asked if anyone had seen Alaric.

"We were just dancing," she said. "Now I can't find her anywhere!"

"Maybe you grabbed her butt one too many times," Viscar suggested as she poured them all more wine.

"That couldn't be the problem. She likes it," Meega said with a wink. Then she spotted Lela. Meega worked her way past a few other delegates and sidled up next to her. "Where's your new warrior girlfriend? I haven't seen you with anyone since I got here." As she pressed her ample breast into Lela's upper arm, Meega touched the back of Lela's hand with a bright pink fingernail. "Since you're here alone, why don't we dance a little?"

Lela closed her eyes and said calmly, "Get away from me."

"Now, Lela. Whatever it was that happened between us before, well, you can't blame me for wanting to spend time with you." Meega moved away from her, but she was still too close for Lela's liking. "Why don't you let me make it up to you?" Meega asked. "I can show you a good time no matter where we are."

With a fake smile, Lela said, "I'd rather drown in pig excrement than spend five seconds alone with you."

Meega laughed so loudly that heads turned to see what was going on. "If I thought you really meant that —"

"Without a doubt, Meega, I really mean that."

"Where's this mysterious girlfriend of yours?" Meega persisted. "I haven't seen anyone —"

"She's with me," came a voice behind them.

Lela and Meega both turned to find the princess standing there. Lela made an attempt to keep her surprise from showing.

"With *you*?" Meega said. "Since when?"

Ignoring the question, Tavia asked Lela to dance. "Pretend that I've just said something incredibly funny," Tavia whispered in Lela's ear.

Being in Tavia's arms as they whirled around the room had Lela speechless, but she did manage to laugh for Meega's benefit. She sensed that everyone in the room was watching them, and it was nice being the center of attention. Lela had another surprise when her knees became unexpectedly weak each time Tavia's lips brushed against her ear whenever the princess said something to her.

"Are you all right?" Tavia asked, whispering in her ear again.

Lela could feel a slow, warm sensation begin to spread through her body, but she managed to nod her reply.

"What's the story with you and Meega?" Tavia asked. "You make no secret of your dislike for her. And knowing Meega the way I do, she considers that a challenge and will usually try harder."

"It's a long story," Lela said, "but basically I was in the cantina one night when she drugged me. She was in the process of hauling me off to her bedroom for some fun when Kricorian came looking for me. I have no use for the woman."

Tavia smiled. "I can see that, and you have a good reason."

The rubbery feeling in Lela's legs was going away, but the fluttering in her stomach at the closeness she was sharing with Tavia was a revelation of how much she liked being held by her.

"You and Meega have been lovers," Lela said. It was a statement, not a question.

"I enjoy the casinos at Tracon," Tavia admitted. "I usually go there with a warrior escort."

"Was that a yes or a no?"

Tavia smiled. "Have Meega and I ever been lovers? The answer is no. Not officially."

"And what does 'not officially' mean?"

"Physical things have never progressed as far along as Meega would have liked for them to."

"So you're a tease," Lela said. *Here I go again. Now I'm flirting with her.*

Tavia laughed. "No. Not at all. It's just that in order for things to have gotten to a certain point, there would have been several warriors there with us, and that's never as romantic as one might think."

"Meega would have liked having you and a few warriors at the same time," Lela said.

Tavia didn't deny it. "But I wouldn't have liked it. So things never went very far with us." She glanced at Lela. "Is that all right with you?"

"With me? My opinion shouldn't mean anything to you."

"It probably shouldn't," Tavia said, "but it does."

"Well, then," Lela said as her stomach did a few somersaults. "You haven't slept with her either. I'm glad we both at least have that in common."

The music stopped, and it was several seconds before Tavia let go of her. They stood close in the middle of the dance floor, their eyes searching and connecting in such a way that Lela's legs became rubbery again. Another song began, and they still couldn't stop looking at each other. Then someone was beside them, and Lela heard Alaric's voice.

"Excuse me, Princess," Alaric said. "Can I speak with you for a moment?"

Tavia was led away, and Lela felt an overwhelming need to follow them just to be close to her again. She pushed those thoughts away and refused to deal with any of it right then. Lela left the atrium and went to her room. She was tired enough for sleep to come easily.

Kricorian saw Alaric and Tavia leave together and wondered if they had gotten more information on what was happening in the Intergalactic Corridor. Once the music started up again and the dancing began, it was easy to slip away from the party and follow them to the communications center. Kricorian reasoned that it would also give her a chance to spend more time with Jaret even if they just ended up working together. Jaret had been working late and getting up early for so long that all she had wanted to do the last time they were alone was fall asleep in Kricorian's arms. Kricorian wasn't complaining about that, but she didn't like the pressure that Jaret was under.

Kricorian entered the communications center, which was busier than she had ever seen it. Tavia, Jaret, and Alaric were in the middle of the room talking. Tavia saw Kricorian first and waved her over to join them.

"Jaret tells me that Corlon was attacked this morning," Tavia said. "We've just confirmed it. That's why Exidor didn't meet us for the summit."

This is bad news for everyone, Kricorian thought. With Corlon being attacked, it meant that there really was an outside enemy. There would be a different type of strategy involved in fighting the unknown. They were all accustomed to battling Exidor and his Corlon Star Fighters, but now it looked as though Corlon would have to join them in defending this part of the galaxy. Corlon as an ally seemed inconceivable.

"Any idea who attacked them?" Kricorian asked.

"Renegade pirates," Jaret said. "They could be disgruntled Star Fighters or they could be coming from several other places."

"How badly was Corlon hit?"

Jaret sighed. Kricorian could see the weariness in her eyes, and she wanted to hold her right then.

"Severe damage to their perimeter," Jaret said. "And some of that could've been caused by low lidium levels. Corlon paid no attention to the warnings we gave them once we found out how serious the lidium problem was." Jaret cleared her throat. "They've got hundreds dead and no power sources functioning. We've received a weak signal from them requesting that we take some of their wounded."

The princess breathed deeply as she stood there thinking. "If we decide to help, we can only take women and children."

"Male children, too?" Alaric asked.

"Male children are still children. All adult males wanting to leave Corlon will have to go to either Bravo Sector or Tracon. Adult males are there already."

"Once things are more normal again at Corlon," Alaric said, "Exidor will try to take any male children back. He'll come looking for them without warning and won't stop until he finds them."

"We won't be holding anyone hostage," Tavia said. "No one stays here against their will."

"In my opinion," Alaric said, "it's a mistake to bring male children here."

Tavia turned to Kricorian. "Your opinion on this?"

Kricorian shrugged. "I agree that children are children, but I'm not the one who'll have to face Exidor's wrath once he realizes where they are. We all know how Exidor feels about us. Corlon children would be tainted in his eyes if we did anything to help them. I personally don't like the idea of Exidor asking for our help at all. Exidor wouldn't do that. He'd let his people die first. Something isn't right here."

Tavia nodded at that particular reasoning and looked over at Jaret. "Who at Corlon has requested our help?"

"As I said before, it's a weak signal one of our patrols picked up."

"That could mean anything," Kricorian said. "Even a trap to lure us there."

Jaret agreed on that possibility. "But we've already confirmed that Corlon has been attacked. It's at least feasible that we do more checking on Corlon's problems."

"You're leaning toward attempting a rescue mission?" Alaric asked. "If so, then I agree with the princess about only taking women and children. That should be our choice to make, and it's something that can be arranged beforehand."

Tavia agreed, and to Jaret she said, "First confirm the amount of destruction and ask for warrior volunteers to go get the refugees immediately. There should also be at least one healer going with them."

"I'll check to see how many wounded we can accommodate at one time," Jaret said. She touched Kricorian's hand quickly and went back to work.

Kricorian waited as long as she could before going in to wake Lela. The refugees were on their way, and every healer was needed. She knelt beside Lela's bed and gave her a shake.

"Wake up, little one," Kricorian said quietly.

Lela turned over with a start and then sat up. "Are you okay? What time is it?"

"Late," Kricorian said. "We need you. Get dressed."

"Is it Exidor? Did they get through the perimeter?" Lela was wide awake. She was out of bed, pulling on her clothes.

"No," Kricorian said. "The perimeter's fine. It's —"

"Are you sick?" she asked as she gave Kricorian a visual check. "Or is it Sporae?"

Kricorian explained about the fifteen Corlon children who would be arriving soon and about Corlon being attacked and asking for help.

With a sigh of relief Lela asked, "Are we sure Exidor didn't attack himself just to get some sympathy?"

Kricorian smiled. "Nothing would surprise me."

"I haven't seriously healed anyone in a while, Kricorian. Research is what I do best these days."

"You'll be fine. This is something you never forget."

"Do we know what injuries these children have?"

"Broken bones mostly, from the report we received."

"Poor things," Lela said. "Let's go."

Chapter Twenty-two

Amtec Reception Bay

The Amtec reception bay had plenty of room for the transport to land, despite the extra spidercrafts belonging to the delegates. A few warriors were there to help, but mostly the volunteers consisted of Amtec women who were carrying the children from the transport to the infirmary. The most seriously injured were the first to come off. Lela was one of nearly a dozen healers available, and they were soon overwhelmed with sick patients.

"Tell me what we can do to help," Kricorian said as she carried in a seven-year-old girl and carefully put her on a bed in the infirmary. The princess placed another girl about the same age in the bed next to her.

"We need to cut them out of their clothes," Lela said.

Lela worked quickly and got an initial assessment of three children's injuries within a few minutes. By holding a child's head in both of her hands, Lela could locate where the pain was and draw it out with the tips of her fingers. All the children had been sedated for the trip, which made it harder for her to pinpoint exactly where the problem areas were. What Lela felt and the impressions she received were relayed to someone else for documentation and eventually other treatment.

Lela found concussions, broken bones, and internal injuries. She was in a trancelike state as she calmly spoke about what she perceived to be happening with each small patient. Kricorian, Tavia, and several other volunteers annotated and acted upon Lela's impressions. It was exhausting work for Lela, and by the time she had finished with the first five children, she felt a weakening in her shoulders and legs. Each time she mentally reached deep to locate the source of a child's pain, it drained more of her energy. Lela tried standing differently and shifting her weight, but her legs were tiring. Her shoulders weren't faring any better, but she held on and knew it would be over soon.

Leaning over and whispering to Kricorian, Tavia asked if she understood what was happening. "How can she know so much from just touching them?"

Kricorian shook her head as she watched Lela work. "She's always been able to do it. Did you see the group over there in the corner?" Kricorian asked as she nodded toward the back. "They're mending broken bones right now."

It wasn't until then that Tavia noticed how things were set up in the infirmary and which healers were doing what. Lela was being used to relieve pain and determine what injuries the children had. Once she was finished with a patient she moved on to another one, repeating the same procedure over and over again. From there the other healers went to work, using the information they had gotten from Lela. The healers worked as a team even though there was almost no verbal communication between them. Each healer worked hard at what she did best, and it came together for the good of the patient.

"This is truly amazing," the princess said. "No matter how many times I've seen it happen, it *still* amazes me."

"I know," Kricorian whispered.

By the time Lela had finished treating each child, she was totally exhausted. It would take awhile to regain her strength and shake off the threatening nausea.

"What can I do for you, little one?" Kricorian asked as she rubbed the back of Lela's neck and shoulders.

"I'll be better in a minute." Lela felt completely drained, but Kricorian's hands eased the tension from her body. After a moment, Lela cleared her throat and asked Kricorian and Tavia to locate children with bruises or scrapes. "That's the other thing I'm good at," she said tiredly.

From there Lela went from bed to bed, making bruises disappear and abrasions go away without scarring. While she was doing that, other healers mended broken bones, reduced swelling, and treated several children for shock. Once all patients were stabilized, each healer began to show true signs of exhaustion.

"I got tired watching them work," Kricorian confessed to the princess a while later. Even from across the room, Kricorian could see the weariness on Lela's face. Lela and the other healers were visibly drained.

"I'm going back to bed," Lela said as soon as she got close enough to talk without exerting much energy. "There's nothing more I can do here." To Tavia she said, "I've strongly suggested to the others that psychologists from Ambrose be brought here to see the children tomorrow. You have good, caring healers here, Princess, but we're all too tired to make a decision on what should be done next."

Kricorian looked over at Tavia, who appeared to be waiting for Lela to say something else.

"Tavia," Kricorian said. "Child psychologists sound like a good idea to me, too."

"Of course," Tavia said. She was still looking at Lela, which Kricorian had noticed throughout the entire healing ordeal. "Thank you for helping," Tavia said.

"I'm out of shape for this," Lela said. "I need some sleep."

Lela let Kricorian help her get her boots off as soon as they were in Lela's room again.

"Not only were we sent fifteen little girls," Lela said, "but all fifteen of them are genetically dispositioned to be female identified like us." She waited a moment for that to sink in. "Like us, Kricorian. These fifteen girls are like us. And they're from Corlon." Lela waited for Kricorian to see the connection, but Kricorian seemed more intent on getting Lela comfortable and tucked in than anything else. "Are you listening to me?"

Kricorian set Lela's boots down. "How do you know what their sexual orientation is? You could tell that just by touching their heads?"

"I could tell that and more."

Kricorian had the beginnings of a smile. "But they're from Corlon, and Corlon has no homosexuals."

"Well, they do now," Lela said. "Or at least they *did*. I guess technically the Amtecs have them now." She eased back on the bed and willed her body to relax. "Those children were sent here for a reason, Kricorian. All girls and all female identified. Exidor has either put them in exile — and if that's the case, then their injuries are highly suspect — or there's an underground of women like us on Corlon. If at all possible, I want you to find out as much as you can about where these children have been, how we got them, and who on Corlon sent them to us. If more women like us or if more children like these exist, we need to find them and bring them here. This is too big of a coincidence," she said. "Too big . . ."

Lela woke up to voices in the hallway the next morning. Just as she opened her eyes, Kricorian came into her room to see how she was doing.

"Much better," Lela said. "Am I late for the summit?"

Easing down on the side of the bed, Kricorian gave Lela's leg a pat. "The summit will resume tomorrow, so there's no hurry. You caused quite a stir last night," Kricorian said. "The princess hasn't been to sleep yet. You were right about the children."

"Right in what way?"

"Girls, genetically dispositioned toward other girls, being here was more than a coincidence, just as you said. Jaret has isolated the signal coming from Corlon, and it's been confirmed that a small group of women there are responsible for getting the most seriously injured children to us."

"How are the children this morning?" Lela asked.

"Awake and hungry. They'll be going to Ambrose later today. Also, your suggestion about the psychologists," Kricorian said as she shook her head. "I have to tell you, little one. The princess is quite taken with you."

"How so?" Uncertain as to whether she was ready to start her day yet, Lela got comfortable again on the stack of pillows.

"You can do no wrong. She must've asked me thirty questions about you last night."

"She wants me to come here and work for her."

"It's much more than that."

"I doubt it." Lela didn't want to consider the possibility that Tavia was interested in her. She sat back up again and then decided to get out of bed and get dressed. "I have a question for you now," Lela said. "If Jaret gets reassigned to K Sector, will the two of you live together?"

Kricorian shrugged. "I haven't really thought about it."

"It makes sense to me that you would," Lela said. "You want to, right?"

Kricorian nodded shyly. "Yes."

"Our cubicle is barely big enough for two, much less three." *And those are some very thin walls.*

"You're really considering staying here?"

"Tavia is giving me a generous offer."

"I know. I guess I didn't realize it meant so much to you."

"Research is research. I can do it anywhere that has good facilities. But this might also be the right time for us to get something that you want too," Lela said. "If it gets to the point where the Amtecs don't want Jaret to come to K Sector, then we'll just tell the princess that I won't come to the palace to work unless Jaret can go to K Sector and work."

"I don't want to trade one of you for the other."

"Remember what Sporae said about compromise," Lela reminded her. "Not only that," she said with a wink, "I think you'll have a lot more fun with Jaret than you ever did with me as a cube mate."

Tavia called an emergency meeting of all the delegates, with Meega being the only one grumbling about it.

"First we get the day off and now a meeting," Meega said. "Can we make this quick? I've got two women waiting for me in my bed."

"And they're probably having a much better time together now that you're here with us," Lela said.

Everyone around the table laughed, including Meega.

"I have an announcement to make," Tavia said. She went on to tell those who didn't already know that Corlon had been raided and had suffered extensive damage. "They also have hundreds of casualties, and it's been reported that Exidor was one of them."

There was a hush around the table before Viscar finally spoke up. "I'm glad he's dead if it's true," she said, "but I've heard this before, and he always turns up again meaner and uglier than ever."

"Commander?" Tavia said as she turned to Alaric. "Tell them what you saw while you were there last night."

Lela listened as Alaric told them about flying the transport through Corlon air space without incident and seeing the destruction there firsthand.

"There were charred buildings everywhere, and few signs of life. We've all witnessed such devastation before with our own homes . . . devastation as a direct result of Corlon Star Fighters."

"There were survivors, Commander?" Sporae asked. Alaric nodded. "Has a new leader emerged?"

"Not yet," Alaric said. She then went on to tell about the rescue of the children and how a group of Corlon women had cared for them and prepared the children for the trip to the Amtec palace. Lela was fascinated by Alaric's account of what had happened. This was the first time she had heard that Alaric had been the one to fly the transport during the rescue.

"We're now debating whether to go back and see if we can

help others," Tavia said. "Communication is a problem, though, since Corlon is operating on little power. We don't want to be mistaken for looters."

"Maybe a small reconnaissance unit should go in and evaluate the situation," Keda suggested.

"I personally think we should leave them alone," Meega said. "If Exidor is really dead, then the Corlons need to find their own way out of this."

Mumbling and grumbling went around the table. Lela and Alaric shared brief eye contact and a mutual respect for each other. Alaric's courage and resourcefulness once again impressed Lela. *Saving people is one of the things she does best,* Lela thought as she remembered being trapped in a tunnel with Star Fighters all around her.

"I just wanted everyone brought up to date on what was happening," Tavia said. "We'll resume the summit tomorrow."

As they got up to leave, Meega reminded them of how each sector had become such an independently strong part of the Intergalactic Corridor.

"We've had friends and loved ones killed," Meega said. "Some of us have had our homes burned to the ground. Those experiences have made us who and what we are today. Corlon has to go through the same things. Bravo Sector is doing it now. Corlon needs to be angry enough to rebuild, and strong enough not to make the same mistakes again. This is Corlon's struggle. Not ours."

Keda shook her head in dismay. "Where's your compassion, Meega?"

"I have plenty of compassion," Meega said, "but when it gets right down to it, what good is a blanket and a cup of soup from a stranger going to do for you while you watch your home burn down and you bury your dead?"

"I think what Meega is trying to say," Lela announced to

the group, "is that if she can't be there to *sell* them the blanket and the cup of soup, then what's the point of doing anything?"

Making that familiar clucking noise with her tongue, Meega said, "Lela, Lela, Lela. Where did you get such a low opinion of me?"

Kricorian gave Lela a wink and said, "Meega, my friend. Lela probably knows you better than any of us."

Chapter Twenty-three

Command Suite

Tavia asked Kricorian and Alaric to stay after the others had gone. Jaret came in a few minutes later and sat down at the table with them.

"We've had more communication from Corlon," Jaret said. Kricorian could hear the excitement in her voice. "It's a weak signal, but the information we received was incredible. Apparently there is a small group of women who have been living in the foothills. They were the ones who sent us the injured children."

Kricorian's eyes popped open at this news. *So Lela was right,* she thought.

"Did you meet these women when you picked up the children, Alaric?" Tavia asked.

Alaric shook her head. "No. When we got there we received a message telling us where to land. Two women met us, and we all loaded the children on the transport. Then the women left. Nothing much was said."

"Things there are deteriorating," Jaret said. "An inner struggle for power is going on, according to our sources. I suggest that we go back for these women and the rest of the children they have with them."

"Have they asked for our help?" Kricorian wondered out loud.

"This morning they did," Jaret said. "There's nothing more they can do there now. They're safe for the time being, but it's uncertain how long that will last."

"Alaric?" Tavia said. "Can we get in and out again successfully?"

"That depends on whether the chaos continues. It was so easy the last time because of the turmoil."

"None of that has changed," Jaret said. "If anything, it's worse now. Instead of fighting pirates, the Corlons are fighting each other for control and power. Confusion, murder, raiding, and looting. The new regime may not be much better than what they had when Exidor was their leader. This is probably the best time to make another rescue attempt."

"If everyone agrees with that," Alaric said, "then I think we should do it as soon as possible."

When no one said anything, Alaric requested permission from the princess to take three warriors and a healer with her. The longer Kricorian thought about what the Amtecs were willing to risk for these total strangers, the more she wanted to be a part of it too. She couldn't ignore the danger involved, but Kricorian also knew that women could do extraordinary things in the face of adversity. The bravery and determination of the renegade Corlon women was to be admired and nurtured. It was because of women like them that K Sector, Alpha Sector, and the Amtec Nation had been founded to begin with. Kricorian was eager to do her part in creating something new. They all had something to gain by helping these women.

"I want to go with you," Kricorian said.

Jaret's reaction caught Kricorian off guard. "You're a delegate for the summit," Jaret said quickly. "We can't put you in that kind of danger."

"Alaric's a delegate too," Kricorian reminded her. "I also think it would be better if someone from another sector was a part of the mission. It would seem more like the humanitarian thing that it actually is rather than something that would appear to strictly benefit the Amtecs. Even more to the point, maybe we should limit the number of warriors that go and increase the number of delegates instead. We can ask Viscar and Keda if they want to help. Meega might also be interested."

"Meega?" Tavia said with a laugh. "If you aren't taking any warriors, then Meega won't be interested."

After sharing a brief chuckle at Meega's expense, Alaric agreed with Kricorian's reasoning to a point.

"Nothing personal, my friend," Alaric said to Kricorian, "but if we run into trouble with Star Fighters, I'd rather have three warriors with me than you, Viscar, and Meega."

Trying hard not to take offense to that, Kricorian had to agree with her. "So we'll leave Meega here."

For Kricorian, it wasn't easy picturing Meega doing something for humanitarian purposes anyway. That took more imagination than she had. Tavia suggested a compromise.

"We'll ask Viscar or Keda if they're interested in going. If so, then there should be room for two warriors and a healer. I think it's important that you have a healer with you."

"I agree," Kricorian said. "Thank you, Princess."

Jaret was visibly upset. "The more people you take," she

said, "the less room there'll be for refugees once you get there. And isn't that the purpose of the mission? To rescue as many as we can?"

"Then it looks to me like you need to find out how many there are to be rescued, Lieutenant," Alaric said.

Jaret was fuming. She looked across the table at Kricorian and then quickly looked away again. "I'll try to get an answer for you before you leave." Jaret stood up and abruptly left the room.

Amtec Laboratory

Lela found the information on the Cirala Project and was pleasantly surprised to see that special arrangements had been made so she could review the material. Tavia was the only one with access to some of her mother's work, but she said she would make sure Project C was immediately available for Lela's use.

From the overview Lela found, she discovered that Project C dealt with the blending of the finest cyborg technology, which involved the study of artificial limbs, eyes, or computer-enhanced brain capabilities given to humans, with the development of a humanoid prototype. Humanoids were bipedal humanlike aliens that had been part of the galaxy for nearly a hundred years. Corlon and Bravo Sector had thousands of humanoids in their population mix, and the humanoids were regarded as highly intelligent and productive members of society.

As Lela continued reading, she learned that the results of the study had produced a very efficient machine that looked amazingly human. The experiments that had been conducted over a two-year period had centered on perfecting the human aspects of the prototype. Humanoid DNA had been sequenced and genetically altered to suit the purpose. In conclusion, Lela read that the results of the first tests were so successful that the cyborg with the near-perfect human characteristics was introduced into the Amtec population to see if anyone would notice anything unusual.

Lela wondered briefly if Tavia's mother had been more mad than brilliant, but as she continued reading and delved more deeply into the scientific jargon of cyborg technology and humanoid research, she realized that the woman's brilliance surpassed whatever madness had been there. At this point Lela became very interested in how the human-machine's integration into ordinary Amtec society had gone. *Did it have communication skills immediately?* she wondered. *Could social skills be programmed? Was the project a success? Was the prototype well received by the Amtec people?*

She continued reading, and as the princess had promised, Lela became even more engrossed in finding out what had happened to the Cirala Project. Cyborg technology had been extremely popular at one time, but Lela had never been interested in it. Humanoid technology was a bit more controversial since it involved beings that were part human and part alien, but this in itself was what tended to make humanoid technology popular for some scientists. Lela could truthfully say that she had never heard of trying to combine the better of the two in order to produce a super cyborg. The concept was interesting.

Amtec Reception Bay

Kricorian was glad that Viscar had agreed to go with them. She felt better thinking that someone else also considered the rescue mission as a new beginning for some brave women. Kricorian saw Jaret come around the corner and then jog over toward her.

"Can I speak to you alone for a minute?" Jaret asked.

Kricorian already knew what she was going to say. She could see it in her eyes.

"Don't try to talk me out of this," Kricorian said.

"It's a dangerous mission!" Jaret hissed. "There's no need for you to do this."

"I *want* to do it," Kricorian said.

"Does Lela know where you're going?"

Kricorian didn't answer. She knew that Lela would be in the lab all day and would never even know she had been gone.

"I didn't think so," Jaret said angrily.

"If you'd been given the opportunity to go, we wouldn't be having this conversation."

"I'm trained for such things." Jaret was making an effort to keep her voice down. "I can't remember ever being so afraid before." Their eyes met, and Kricorian could see the fear and uncertainty in her lover's young, worried face. "Dying would be so easy compared to being alone again. If something happens to you —"

"Nothing's going to happen to me," Kricorian said as a lump formed in her throat. She gave her a weak smile. "I'll be with Alaric. She wouldn't dare let anything happen to me."

Jaret turned and walked away. Kricorian swallowed hard and got on the transport.

Amtec Laboratory

Lela sat in shock as she read one particular line over and over again. For a moment she couldn't think. She felt confused and leery about all the other information that had been in the document. She felt like a fool, as if someone had given her this little assignment to make fun of her and the things that interested her the most.

She turned the screen off and sat in semidarkness with her anger and disappointment rising to the surface. When Lela finally left the lab, she went to find Tavia. The princess owed her an explanation, and Lela was determined to get one.

~ ~ ~

Kricorian and Viscar took turns with navigation duties while the two warriors on board the transport helped prepare it for receiving refugees. Everyone was still surprised that Meega had insisted on going with them. She arrived in the reception bay just as the doors to the transport were about to close.

"Do you have any idea where we're going?" Viscar asked her.

Meega moved remarkably well in her lavender heels and tight matching flight suit. "I certainly do."

"She probably heard there were warriors on board," Kricorian called from up front.

"Kricorian, you know me so well, you wench," Meega said with a laugh. "Actually, I'm going along so I can see firsthand what these Corlon dregs will need in a few weeks. I'm treating this like a business trip where I can assess their needs for possible future sales and marketing purposes."

"A business trip," Viscar said with a grunt. "They've got mass destruction there, you idiot. They'll need everything!"

"Not only that," Kricorian said over her shoulder from the navigator seat, "they won't *buy* things from you once they realize they need something. They'll just come and take it."

"You're such a cynical thing, Kricorian," Meega said. She settled into one of the reclining seats. "Someone wake me when we get there. I didn't get much sleep last night."

Command Suite

Lela found the princess outside the door to the command suite talking to Jaret.

"We're in constant touch with them," Lela heard Jaret say. "I'll let you know as soon as we hear something new." Jaret turned to go and greeted Lela as she was leaving.

"Who are we in constant touch with?" Lela asked the princess.

Tavia opened the door to the command suite and let her go in first. "We're still monitoring the activity on Corlon. I was wondering if you saw the children before they were taken to Ambrose."

"Yes," Lela said. "They've all made complete physical recoveries." She was still so angry that it was difficult to remain civil.

"Have a seat," Tavia said. "What can I do for you?"

Lela remained standing. She was a pacer by nature, and she found this to be a perfect opportunity to get some sort of control of her anger.

"I reviewed several documents associated with the Cirala Project. I guess my big question is why you were so insistent on my seeing them?" Before Tavia could answer, Lela was asking her other questions as well. She couldn't stop herself from carrying on as if a huge joke were being played on her.

"Please sit down, Lela."

"I don't want to sit down." Lela shot her a piercing look from across the room. She was hurt, and she wasn't sure she could stay there much longer.

"I know this has been a shock for you."

"A shock?" Lela said. "You have to know what's in that report. It insinuates that Alaric is a cyborg."

"Insinuates?" Tavia said. "Alaric *is* a cyborg. She's the prototype mentioned in the Cirala Project."

Lela felt tears sting her eyes.

"I don't know if you noticed it or not," Tavia said quietly, "but the word Cirala is actually Alaric's name spelled backward. My mother's idea."

Lela was so upset that she was shaking. "There's no way Alaric can be a cyborg. I've touched her, I've healed her . . . I've kissed her."

"I know," Tavia whispered. She sat down at the table and

rubbed her forehead with her fingers. "But it's true, Lela. Please sit down so we can talk about this."

"I'm afraid you don't understand," Lela said. "There's no way this can be true. I've made love to her, Tavia. I've seen her laugh and —"

"Please sit down," Tavia said again tiredly. "I know this is a shock, but I didn't know any other way to tell you. I need your help. You're the only one I can trust with this. Don't you see that?"

Lela pulled a chair out away from the table and plopped down in it, exhausted. "There's no way she's a cyborg," Lela said again. "It's not possible."

Chapter Twenty-four

Corlon Air Space

Kricorian had nothing but confidence in Alaric's ability to get them in and out of Corlon safely. They had gotten word that the same rendezvous point would be used to pick up the new group of refugees, which consisted of three women and seven children — luckily none with serious injuries. Kricorian surmised that her navigational duties would be much easier now that they knew where they were going!

Having spent a good part of the trip thinking about Jaret and how upset she had been, Kricorian knew that having an Amtec warrior for a lover would eventually fill her life with many terrifying good-byes like the one they had just experienced. Kricorian imagined that Jaret had second thoughts about being with her now and putting them both through such things again. There was a reason warriors stayed together and remained single.

"Here we go," Alaric said.

Kricorian looked up to see the huge gaping hole where the Corlon perimeter should be. It was burning around the edges and needed mending as soon as possible. Without immediate attention, the entire perimeter would be destroyed and leave them vulnerable from every part of the galaxy.

"The hole is twice as big as it was last night," Alaric said. "And nothing's being done about it."

As they entered Corlon proper, Kricorian could see glowing ruins in the distance. Parts of Corlon were still on fire, while the rest of it was reduced to smoldering rubble. Kricorian watched as Alaric entered coordinates and the transport took a gradual turn to the right toward the foothills. Eventually they reached a small valley in the rugged terrain with plenty of room to land.

The warriors opened the transport door, and within seconds Kricorian could smell the smoke that permeated Corlon's interior.

"We are so glad to see you!" came a hoarse, unfamiliar voice from the back. It was one of the three women they were there to pick up. "We need help carrying the children. We sedated them just before you got here. We need to hurry. Star Fighters are in the area."

Kricorian left her seat and went to help get the children on board. She saw a woman dressed in black hug a warrior in gratitude for coming back for them.

"Let's go," Kricorian said to Meega as Meega sat filing a lavender fingernail. "You can help us get the children in here."

"Did you see how dirty these people are?"

Kricorian leaned into her and said, "If you don't help us get these people on board, I'll make sure we leave your butt here. Do you understand me? Now get out there and help!"

Meega led the way out the door and walked with ease over jagged rocks to where one woman held a sleeping child. Meega took the child in her arms and strolled just as gracefully back to the transport.

"This dirt better not stain my outfit, Kricorian," Meega warned as they passed each other. Kricorian was already going back for another child.

"I saw the full trunk of clothes you brought with you," Kricorian said over her shoulder. "I'm sure there's more where that one came from."

Kricorian took another limp, sleeping child from one of the women and asked if that was everyone.

"Yes," the woman said. She had smudges on her face and clothes, and her eyes were wide with fear.

"Let's go then," Kricorian said. "We need to get out of here."

The woman clutched the child she was carrying and went ahead of Kricorian. Two warriors jumped down from the transport and helped get the children on board. Kricorian heard shouting behind her, and suddenly saw both Amtec warriors in hand-to-hand combat with six raggedy Star Fighters. Alaric brushed past her and hopped to the ground. Kricorian's heart was pounding as she watched the scene unfold. Two more Star Fighters came storming from behind a boulder, then one by one they fell to the ground writhing in pain from the stun guns Alaric and the warriors had. Within seconds all eight Star Fighters had been taken care of and Alaric and the other two warriors were climbing back on board again. There was congestion there in the doorway, with people still holding children and waiting to put them into a seat. Kricorian watched in awe as Meega carefully set a sleeping little girl down then marched to the door and stuck her head out to see what was going on. Before the warriors could get everyone out of the way and close the door, a grungy Star Fighter lunged for the opening. Meega gave him a stiff kick, and he fell to the ground with a thud.

"I knew these heels would come in handy," she said as she dusted herself off and returned to her seat.

The warriors closed and locked the door. Banging, cursing, and shouting from the outside began almost immediately. The Star Fighters wanted in, and the pounding continued until Alaric got the transport in the air again.

They got each child in a reclining seat and strapped in. Kricorian felt much better once they were in the air and on their way. She walked up front and gave Alaric a pat on the shoulder. Viscar was now sitting in the navigator seat.

"What was all that punching and tripping and kicking that went on out there?" Kricorian asked. "You had stun guns. Why weren't you using them right away?"

"It's good to practice on live ones occasionally," Alaric said. "Everyone take a seat and hang on. We're not out of here yet."

The woman who had hugged the warrior when they had first arrived moved up front and told Alaric and Viscar that there was no power available to generate any type of missile attack but that there were a few spidercrafts that still had fuel.

"My name is Spence, by the way," the woman said as she took a seat in the front row close to Viscar. "I can't begin to thank all of you enough for doing this."

Kricorian glanced across the aisle and smiled when she saw Meega moving the soft, blond hair out of the eyes of a sleeping little girl. Kricorian then saw the other woman who had been the last of the refugees to get on the transport. The woman was staring at her while she tightened the straps on another sleeping child beside her.

"Here they come," Alaric said.

Normally, a huge transport against the smaller, more mobile spidercraft would make the transport nothing more than a giant target, but with Alaric as its pilot, Kricorian knew they had the advantage.

Still in the Corlon foothills, the transport now seemed to be hovering in place.

"Two down," Alaric said as she touched the mouthpiece on her helmet. To everyone else on the transport, Alaric explained that ten Amtec warriors had arrived in spidercrafts and had already shot down two of Corlon's pilots. "We're not moving until it's safe," she said.

Suddenly they lurched forward, and then Kricorian heard an explosion behind them. The transport was building up speed again, and Kricorian heard Viscar say, "Forget that idea!"

Star Fighters were aiming their spidercrafts directly at them now, and Alaric was doing her best to dodge them. She was able to use the foothills to her advantage and had sent two Star Fighters into the side of a small mountain with nothing more than speed adjustments that kept her passengers lurching and jerking. From her window Kricorian could see Star Fighters standing on boulders with angry, dirty faces and charred clothes. They shook their fists and threw rocks and clubs at the transport. Kricorian was afraid now and didn't want to think about their fate in the event that Alaric couldn't get them out of here.

"Six down," Viscar announced.

"And here they come," Alaric said.

Kricorian braced herself for the impact and could feel her heart pounding in her chest. She noticed something out of the corner of her eye and then looked out her window again. Alaric had them above the foothills, and Amtec warriors in their spidercrafts in an escort formation now surrounded the transport. Everyone who was awake in the cabin began to cheer. Minutes later they were through the gaping hole that had at one time been Corlon's perimeter.

Kricorian leaned back in her seat and took a deep breath. She was giddy with nervous energy but happy that they had succeeded at their mission. Kricorian looked up and saw the same woman across the aisle staring at her again.

"I heard someone call you Kricorian," the woman said. A tear scampered down her cheek, making an eerie trail through a thin layer of dirt. "Are you from K Sector?" she asked in a quiet voice.

"Yes," Kricorian said. "I'm from K Sector."

"Kricorian," the woman whispered. "It's me, Romney."

Kricorian suddenly saw the resemblance to Meridith, but she was too stunned to move.

"They told me you were dead," Romney said.

Kricorian scrambled over the child she was sitting next to and took Romney in her arms, hugging her, not wanting to let go.

"Romney," she whispered. Kricorian clung to her as if someone might try to take her away again.

"There was an explosion where you were supposed to be," Kricorian said into Romney's ear. Romney was holding her just as tightly. "No one survived the blast."

"They told me you were dead," Romney said again. Kricorian stepped back to get a better look at her. Both were smiling through their tears.

"You look like your mother."

Romney blinked back more tears. "Do I?"

Kricorian took her by the hand and led her to the back of the transport where they could talk without an audience.

Command Suite

Lela and Tavia continued to sit across the table from each other in silence. Lela felt numb. Everything she had ever known about women was now in question. Cyborgs didn't feel passion and didn't respond to someone else's passion the way Alaric had. It was impossible.

"Tell me what you're thinking, Lela."

The urge to pace was no longer the emergency it had once been, but Lela was confused about what she had heard so far and what she was feeling.

"I'm still thinking that it's impossible."

Tavia leaned back in her chair and drummed her fingers on the table. "Everything you've ever heard about cyborgs has to be forgotten for the moment. This is a whole different type of technology. If you read the report, then you know that already, so let me tell you what I know." Tavia then told the story of how Alaric came into her life.

"In the beginning, Alaric was to be a companion for me. She was my first lover and has remained my only lover for many years now."

Their eyes met, and Lela again was surprised at how numb she felt.

"My mother thought it was important that I not be promiscuous with the Amtec women or the warriors that I'd someday be leading. I'm the Amtec princess. My personal life has to remain unblemished. There are a different set of rules and higher standards for Amtec royalty. My mother drilled that into me at a very early age. She was right, of course, but it was a lonely existence for me."

Lela was pale as she listened. "Alaric is your lover now?"

Tavia offered a weak smile. "Not since I came back from K Sector. Anyway, my mother worked on creating Alaric for me. She knew how lonely I was because she remembered how lonely she had been when she was my age. She went through the same things and had the same feelings. My mother wanted my life to be different. It might seem strange to have one's mother choose her daughter's lover, but it was the perfect solution to a difficult situation. I was able to get on with my studies and my training with Alaric by my side. I was happy, and no one ever questioned what we did or how we came to be. My mother helped make my life easier than it would have been. She gave me something very special. She gave me Alaric." Tavia smiled. "I'd never had such an incredible gift. Alaric is intelligent and perceptive. She can also be compassionate when it's appropriate to be." Tavia sat up straight in her chair and put her elbows on the table. "And the most amazing thing about all of this is that Alaric doesn't know any of it. I'm the only one who's known about it all these years. Now I'm telling you."

"Alaric doesn't *know*?" Lela said.

Tavia shook her head. "She doesn't know." She stopped for a moment and held her breath. With a weak smile she said, "At least she's never told me that she knows. There have been times when I've seen her confusion about where she came from. Her earliest memories are of my mother and me. She questioned me about that once, but we never discussed it again."

"What did you tell her?"

"My mother had a story ready for me. Something about Alaric arriving with a small group of women. She only asked that once, but Alaric is extremely intelligent. It's very possible that she knows more about all this than either of us do, but it's never been discussed with her, so I go on the assumption that she doesn't know."

"Tell me why you think it's important that we keep this a secret from her. It's her life, after all."

Tavia nodded. "My mother explained it to me this way: If this technology were to get into the wrong hands, we would eventually be faced with having to defend ourselves against entire armies of intelligent and powerful cyborgs. Can you imagine such a thing? That was never my mother's intention. She designed a toy for me . . . a playmate . . . a bodyguard . . . a lover . . . a friend."

Lela nodded. "I understand."

"I also can't even begin to explain to you what her presence has meant to the Amtec people. Alaric worked her way up through the ranks of the Amtec Army. She didn't get there because she was my lover. She did all that on her own. She's truly a superb being, Lela."

"But what is she? I mean really?"

Tavia smiled. "She's Alaric. It's as simple as that. She's everything an Amtec warrior hopes to be someday. She's respected and lusted after. She's loved and admired. She has the strength of seven men and the intelligence of a hundred. She has the capacity to achieve, as well as give, multiple orgasms, and she can run faster than a spidercraft can fly. There's nothing else like her. She's Alaric."

Lela remembered being trapped in the tunnel at K Sector and how Alaric had found her so easily. She had to have a tracking system in her programming. Lela remembered the dead Star Fighters she had seen in the tunnel with their necks twisted in the most horrifying of ways.

"Tell me what you're thinking now," Tavia said.

Lela took a deep breath. "I didn't know Alaric was your lover."

"I know you didn't, and there's no need to apologize for that. I encouraged Alaric to spend time with you." More finger drumming on the table. "I wanted you to see her in many different ways before we had this conversation. It seemed important at the time that you know what she was capable of." Tavia smiled again. "You're the only one I can tell these things to, Lela. It's also imperative that no one else know about what we've discussed."

"I understand." Lela sat there in a daze. "I have so many questions that I don't even know where to start."

"Maybe the files on the Cirala Project will make more sense to you now," Tavia said.

"I'm sure they will. I see why only one was made even though this is something that could possibly change all our lives for the better."

"It could also change things for the worse. I'm sure neither one of us wants to take that chance."

"I agree."

Tavia seemed to be studying her closely. "You can't tell anyone else about this."

"I know." Lela sat forward in her chair and put her hands on the table. "There's something I want you to understand, though. As a scientist and a researcher, this is a discovery of a lifetime. People in my profession work their entire lives in hopes of being a part of something like this. However, I respect you. I respect your mother's work. And I respect Alaric's right to privacy above all else right now. This isn't easy for me, but I do agree with your decision to keep this information a secret."

"Thank you."

Corlon Air Space

Kricorian and Romney sat close together in the back of the transport and held hands.

"They told me you were dead," Romney kept saying over and over again.

Kricorian held her and stroked her short black hair. Its smoky scent was a clear reminder of where they had just come from.

"Tell me what happened," Kricorian said. "How many of our children were taken that day?"

Romney sniffed and closed her eyes. "There were four of us," she said quietly. "Star Fighters found our hiding place and gagged us and tied us up. It seemed like days later before they released us from the mobilecraft. I remember staying in one position for so long that I couldn't straighten up or walk well when they let me out." Romney's expression hardened as she remembered that time in her life. "There are parts of it that I don't recall. Whatever abuse followed my capture . . . has been erased from my memory. There was a small group of women whose sole purpose on Corlon was to rescue children from Exidor. I spent my life underground, hiding from him and his followers. Exidor would give Star Fighters extra privileges for every child they could bring him. That was the main reason for the raids back then. They were searching for children. Now their priorities have changed. Lidium is what drives them now." She looked up at Kricorian. "Not everyone who lives on Corlon is bad, Kricorian. It's just that the bad people are in charge."

Kricorian nodded and kissed the side of her head. Romney's reference to Star Fighters looking for lidium made the hair on the back of Kricorian's neck stand up.

"They told me you were dead," Romney said. "They bragged about leaving no survivors after the raid."

"Your mother died in the raid," Kricorian said. "Lela was with her and —"

"Lela," Romney said with a choked sob. "You'll never know how much I've cried over losing all of you." She finally let go of Kricorian's hand and dabbed her nose on her dirty sleeve. "At least they didn't die alone. They had each other."

Kricorian took Romney's face in her hands and looked into her eyes with a tearful smile. "Lela is very much alive, Rom. We're taking you to her right now."

Romney closed her eyes and let the tears go. Kricorian held her tightly again and cried right along with her.

Command Suite

Lela didn't want to leave or be alone right then. She sat with the princess in a comfortable silence, deep in thought about what had already been discussed. Finally Lela spoke up.

"You mentioned earlier that you needed my help with something."

Tavia shrugged. "Alaric's been around here a long time. About fifteen years or so, and she hasn't aged a day. She looks the same now as she did then. I've heard comments lately

222

about it. They've been in the form of compliments about how good Alaric looks for her age. It seems that something needs to be done to make her look more her age and less... less... appealing."

"And how do you suggest we do that?" Lela asked. "Put some gray in her hair while she's sleeping?" She shook her head in frustration. "Does she even sleep?"

Tavia smiled. "She sleeps. In that sense, she's like a normal person."

A ripple of jealousy moved through Lela's body, and a visual of Tavia and Alaric in bed together planted itself in her head. To Lela's surprise, her jealousy was directed at Tavia's having a lover instead of Alaric's having one.

"Maybe you could give her some wrinkles," Tavia suggested. "Or something."

"I understand the problem," Lela said. "Let me think about it."

Tavia smiled at her again. "And while you're thinking about it, would you like to go to Ambrose with me and see how our visiting Corlon children are doing?"

Needing a change of scenery in the worst way, Lela said yes.

Chapter Twenty-five

Ambrose

Lela hadn't thought much about how she would feel going back to Ambrose again. Memories of the time she had spent with Alaric by the lake made her more sad than anything else. She felt as though she had lost Alaric; the person Lela had thought she knew was now a stranger to her again.

"If we don't at least stop to see the Amtec children, I'll be in trouble," Tavia said.

"We wouldn't want that."

As soon as they landed and got out of the spidercraft, giggling, excited little girls surrounded them. Lela was surprised to see Tavia get on the ground with them and roll around in the grass. They were on top of her, hugging, kissing, and squealing as Tavia tickled them and gave her share of hugs in return.

"We like when you come to visit, Princess!" Lela heard one of the children say.

"I like it too," Tavia said. "I was supposed to be working today."

"What is it you do all day, Princess?" someone asked as they tried to help Tavia stand up.

This made Lela laugh. "Yes, Princess. What is it you do all day?"

Tavia cut her eyes in Lela's direction but didn't answer the question. "Everyone give me another hug. I'll be back soon to spend more time with you. We just came by to say hello."

One of the counselors came out and told the children to go back inside. Then she informed Tavia that a Corlon child was missing.

"Get in," Tavia said to Lela. "Any idea where she is?"

"No," the counselor said. "She bolted out the door and started running."

Tavia had them in the air and flying low a few seconds later. The scanner in the spidercraft picked up the child's movements quickly, and they headed toward the trees near the lake. Lela kept looking out her small window, trying to see the bright red uniform all the children wore. It wasn't long before the princess spotted her.

"How fast can you run?" Tavia asked as she set the spidercraft down.

"Depends on who's chasing me."

They were both out of the spidercraft and racing toward the red blur dashing through the trees. Lela was amused at how fast Tavia was as she ran around in front of them and scooped the child up in her arms, sending them both tumbling to the ground.

"Easy now," Tavia said as she held the young girl close to her. "Where are you going?"

The child was gasping for air and attempting to pound her

fists against Tavia's face and chest. But Tavia had a good hold on her and was trying to calm her down with soothing words.

"She's terrified," Lela said. "I'm going back to the spidercraft and let you two work this out, okay?"

"You're leaving me here alone with her?"

"You can manage. A fearless warrior like you against a little girl? She'll calm down faster if just one of us talks to her. If she gets away again or if she hurts you, just yell and I'll be back." Over her shoulder as she was leaving, Lela said, "Oh, and by the way, Princess. You run like you've done this before. Good job."

Intergalactic Corridor

Kricorian had an arm around Romney's waist as they sat there together in the back of the transport. She didn't want to let go of her. Romney motioned one of the other women over and held out her hand when the woman got closer.

Romney explained that Spence was her partner and that Disto, the other woman with them, was a friend. Once Spence heard who Kricorian was, she gave them both a long hug.

"I've held her many nights as she cried herself to sleep over losing her family," Spence said.

"You're all coming home to K Sector with us," Kricorian said. "You'll be safe there this time."

Ambrose

Lela waved the two counselors over to the spidercraft as soon as she spotted them. About fifty yards away, Tavia and the youngster were still sitting together at the edge of the trees.

"The princess is talking to her," Lela said. "Does anyone know what happened?"

"She was upset about being inside," the taller of the two said. "Apparently she hasn't been in a building for a while. She feels more comfortable out here."

"And the next thing we knew she was missing," the other counselor said.

All three looked up when they saw the princess and the little girl walking toward them. The youngster clung to Tavia's hand and held her head up high.

"We're going for a ride in the spidercraft," Tavia announced. She lifted the child up and set her inside the spidercraft, then put Lela's helmet on her small head.

"You're coming back for me, right?" Lela asked.

Tavia gave her a grin. "Sure I am."

Amtec Reception Bay

Kricorian was glad to be back at the palace again. The door to the transport was opened, and everyone helped get the sleeping children unstrapped and out of their seats. Each child was handed to a warrior who, in turn, carried her to the infirmary. Romney and Spence seemed anxious having so many strangers around, but Kricorian assured them both that they were all safe now. She went on to explain how healers would check the children and then psychologists would be available if needed.

"I'm worried about the children waking up and seeing all these people in uniform," Romney said to Kricorian. "It's unnerving even for me."

Kricorian looked around and saw several warriors helping with the children.

"People in uniform are bad where we come from," Spence explained.

"I understand," Kricorian said. "I'll talk to Alaric about this. Please don't worry. In the meantime, let me show you where the children are being taken. Then we'll see about getting you some food, clean clothes and proper rest."

As a healer led them away, Kricorian turned to her friends who had been on the transport with her. She gave Alaric and Viscar impulsive hugs.

"An excellent job as always, Alaric," Kricorian said. "And thank you, too, my quirky friend," she said as she gave Meega a big hug as well.

"It's wonderful to see you so happy," Viscar said.

"All of you helped me find my other daughter," Kricorian told them in a voice that broke with emotion. "I don't know how I'll ever be able to thank you."

Meega nudged her in the ribs with an elbow and said, "Can you get me a date with Lela? That'll be thanks enough for me."

Ambrose

While waiting for the princess to return for her, Lela made herself comfortable. The grass was soft as she ran her hands over it; the breeze on her face was relaxing. The lake was close by, but Lela didn't want to go anywhere near it. Her time there with Alaric had turned into a confusing mixture of dull emotion. She felt betrayed for reasons she didn't completely understand. The Alaric that Lela thought she had known had never even existed! Adjusting to this new information would take time.

Lela moved over to lean back against a tree. She loved smelling the fresh air at Ambrose and imagined this to be the perfect place to live as a child. She knew that the Corlon children would eventually learn to like it if they stayed there, and one day they would grow into healthy adults. Lela chuckled as she thought of the princess getting mobbed by the

Amtec children. She had noticed that they were much less formal with Tavia than they had been with Alaric. Lela couldn't imagine Alaric with a dozen little girls piled on top of her, although the squealing that Lela had heard during both visits was nearly the same.

She looked up and saw the spidercraft land in a small grassy area close by. Lela smiled and stood up.

"See? I knew you'd come back for me."

Tavia took off her helmet and set it inside the spidercraft. "I couldn't very well leave you here."

"How did it go?" Lela asked. "Did she like the spidercraft ride?"

Tavia smiled. "She did. You should have seen her face light up when I took her back. The other Corlon children saw her get out of the spidercraft with that huge helmet on, and she was suddenly the center of attention."

"You made new little friends today?"

"I hope so. The next time I come, I'll know all the new children's names."

They began walking back to the spidercraft, but Lela wasn't in a hurry to leave.

"Someone sent word that Kricorian is looking for you," Tavia said as she handed Lela a helmet. "I need to get you back."

Lela wanted to stay there and walk and talk and laugh with this woman. *It must be Ambrose,* Lela thought as she got in the spidercraft. *Each time I come here I feel like I'm falling in love.*

Amtec Palace

Kricorian spoke to Alaric about the children's fear of uniforms, and Alaric assured her that she would take care of the problem. Kricorian had also requested that someone find Lela for her, but so far there was no sign of her. Kricorian was eager to have both of her daughters with her again, and she was finding it hard to let Romney out of her sight. Kricorian arranged to get all three of the women clean and into new clothes. She assured them that the sleeping Corlon children were in good hands, but Kricorian understood their need to have at least one of them be with the children at all times. Food was brought to the infirmary, and while Romney and her friends were eating, the children began to wake up.

Just as Kricorian was about to see if she could find Lela on her own, one of the Amtec women came in to deliver a message from Jaret. With the infirmary now off limits to all warriors by order of the commander, Jaret wasn't allowed in there. The message stated that Jaret wanted to see Kricorian out in the hallway.

"I found Lela and the princess at Ambrose," Jaret said. "They'll be here soon."

"Thank you," Kricorian said with relief.

"I'm sorry about what happened earlier," Jaret said. She turned to leave, but Kricorian caught her by the arm.

"Come here," Kricorian said and led her farther down the hallway. She saw one of the doors that blended so easily into the gold ornamental decor in the main hall. Kricorian opened it only to find a room full of Amtec women having a meeting. Closing the door quickly, she mumbled, "Well, it worked for Lela."

She spotted another door on the opposite side of the hallway and went to open up that one. The room was empty, and Kricorian went inside and pulled Jaret in there with her.

"I don't like us arguing," Kricorian said. She kissed Jaret hard and felt so relieved when Jaret kissed her back.

"I don't like it either," Jaret whispered. Their foreheads touched and Kricorian knew things would be all right again. "It scared me seeing you leave that way," Jaret said, "and a warrior seldom admits to being scared of anything."

Kricorian ran her fingers through the front of Jaret's hair.

"There's nothing wrong with being afraid." She smiled and loved touching her this way. "There's someone I want you to meet. Do you have something you can put over that uniform?"

As soon as she was in the spidercraft again, it crossed Lela's mind that Ambrose really was a magical place for her. She didn't want to leave, and she was already thinking of a way to go back again. *It's not just Ambrose that I like so much. It's being here with someone I'm attracted to that makes the difference.* She briefly wondered if things with Alaric would have gone so far if they had been somewhere else that day. Wistfully, Lela looked out the window.

As if reading her mind, Tavia said, "I need to start spending more time here again."

"How often do you usually visit them?"

"About three times a week. If the children had their way, I'd have a bunk right next to theirs."

"Would that be so bad?"

Tavia laughed. "No."

They were back at the palace quickly; the princess set the spidercraft down, and took off her helmet.

"Tell me what you're thinking," Tavia said.

Lela took off her helmet as well and gave her hair a shake with her fingers.

"I liked seeing you with the children today. They adore you."

"Would you have dinner with me tonight?"

Lela laughed. "Sure. I have to eat anyway." She glanced at Tavia, and their eyes met. Lela had an uncontrollable urge to touch her hair.

Just as Lela decided that she wanted to kiss her instead, the princess leaned toward her also. The moment their lips touched, Lela knew it was more than just a simple kiss. They pulled away from each other, and Lela kept her eyes closed in hopes of prolonging the wonderful feeling she was experiencing.

"I've wanted to do that all day," Tavia whispered.

"So have I," Lela admitted. *If she doesn't kiss me again right now, I'll —*

A light tap on the window made them both jump. Tavia opened up the spidercraft to see what they wanted.

"The commander is back from Corlon," the young warrior said after a snappy salute. "They've sent me to bring both of you to the infirmary right away."

Chapter Twenty-six

Amtec Infirmary

Kricorian was alternating between happiness at having Romney back in their lives again, and sadness and anger at having lost her in the first place. It was hard for Kricorian to let Romney out of her sight, and she tried not to think about the terrible things that had happened to her after she had been taken away by Star Fighters. The one thing that Kricorian kept remembering was the help that would be available for all of them once they were settled again at K Sector. That made Kricorian even more determined to get home as quickly as possible.

The children were finally awake, bathed, clothed, and fed. They were a timid group huddled together in their red jumpsuits while staying close to the three Corlon women. The Amtec women who were there to help were kind, and Kricorian made a mental note to thank Alaric again for making this as easy as possible for everyone.

"When can we see the other children?" Romney asked.

"I'll find out for you," Kricorian said. Just then she saw Lela and the princess come in.

"That's her," Romney whispered. She stood up and reached for Kricorian's hand. "That's my Lela."

"Wait here," Kricorian said. She met Lela halfway and gave her a fierce hug.

"What's the mater? Are you okay?"

Without letting go of her, Kricorian calmly whispered, "We went after more Corlon children, and one of the women we brought back with them is Romney."

Lela's face turned pale, and she became almost limp in Kricorian's arms.

"Romney's alive and is waiting to see you."

Lela grabbed Kricorian and searched her face as if looking for some hint that this was a joke.

"She's alive and she's here."

Lela looked over Kricorian's shoulder and scanned the room. She saw a woman who resembled her mother, and Lela let go of Kricorian's uniform and walked toward the back of the room.

Romney walked toward Lela at the same time. They were in each other's arms quickly, hugging, squeezing, and sharing tears. Then Lela held Romney's face and whispered, "It's really you!"

Romney smiled and sniffed again. "You're all grown up." She hugged Lela once more and held her for a long time. "They told me all of you were dead."

"Have you been at Corlon all this time?"

"Yes," Romney said.

"Why didn't you try to contact us?"

"They told me you were *dead*!"

Lela hugged her again.

"Come," Romney said finally. "Let's sit down." She waved Kricorian over, and the three of them went to the back of the room. Lela never once let go of her sister's hand as they made their way toward a corner in the infirmary.

"I still can't believe it," Lela said. "It's really you. How could you have been alive all this time and we not know?"

Romney smiled sadly. "I've spent the last fifteen years at Corlon underground. I was one of the lucky ones. Most of what happened to me when I got there I don't remember."

"It must've been horrible," Lela whispered. "Horrible." She leaned her head against her sister's. "You had to have been so scared." Lela began to cry.

"I was. I'm just grateful that I don't remember much about those first few days. A group of women eventually took me away and hid me. I stayed with them for several years until they were discovered and killed by Exidor's regime. By then I was one of the older ones, so I made it my life's work to help save other children who had also been taken from their families."

Lela squeezed her hand and hugged her again.

"I'm sure I was raped and beaten and passed from one Star Fighter to the next when I first got there. Several good psychologists that were part of the underground worked with all the children that had been captured. Our stories are all basically the same. There's no reason to think mine was any different. But all memories of that time have been erased through hypnotic therapy. The psychologists worked with us until we were all free of the demons. We couldn't have coped with the terrible things that were done to us had we been forced to live with those memories."

Romney sniffed and squeezed Lela's hand. "But I still had all the memories of my family before the raid. We would tell each other happy stories about our lost loved ones. It made us stronger." Sitting in the middle between Lela and Kricorian, she leaned her head against Lela's again. All three of them were quiet before Romney said, "Now tell me about you two. I want to hear everything."

The princess immediately arranged to have the infirmary converted into an area large enough to accommodate all the Corlon children, including the ones who had been staying at Ambrose, and the three Corlon women. There was also a moratorium declared on all uniforms, which made things more interesting at the palace. Lavender tunics and gray pants temporarily replaced the usual dark blue uniform of a warrior. The new splash of color seemed to lift everyone's spirits.

With input from Spence and Disto, several warriors moved most of the beds out of the infirmary and piled blankets in the middle of the floor. The princess sent for the other Corlon children at Ambrose and the two psychologists who had been working with them. Twenty minutes later all the children were together again.

"What else can we do for you?" Tavia asked. She could see that Spence was too grateful for what had already been done for them to ask for anything more. Tavia gave her a reassuring smile. "We want you to be comfortable while you're here. I'm also hoping that some of you might even decide to live here once you have a chance to think about your options, but there's no hurry in making any decision."

"You've literally saved our lives," Spence said.

"Welcome to the Amtec palace," Tavia said. "My people have been instructed to make sure you have everything you need. Don't be afraid to ask if you can't find something."

Spence thanked her again and returned to one of the

groups of children sitting on the blankets in the middle of the floor. Tavia could see Lela, Kricorian, and Romney alone near the back, with Lela and Romney talking. Tavia left them alone once she was satisfied that everyone was comfortable. On her way to the communications center, she kept in mind that there were still pirates to worry about.

Amtec Communications Center

Jaret briefed the princess and Alaric on what more they had learned since the last refugees had arrived. There were no more signals coming from Corlon, so it was determined that the Corlon women in the palace now had been the ones responsible for sending the only signals they had received since Corlon had been attacked.

"The most important question for the moment," Jaret said, "is who's doing all of this raiding? We keep calling them pirates, but what exactly does that mean? Where are they from? Where are they now? Where do they sleep and live?" Jaret tried to keep her voice calm. "And how do they know so much about what we do and when we do it?"

These questions went on for quite a while as they tried to figure out the hows and the whys of it all.

"We also have delegates who need to get home safely after the summit ends," Alaric said. "Another agenda item might be a good idea for tomorrow. I suggest the four sectors begin patrolling the corridor on a regular, full-time basis until we can find out where the pirates are coming from. Eventually we'll see or hear something."

They had talked about those and several other issues for quite some time; the princess felt confident about being prepared for whatever would happen next. It was late and she was tired. On her way back to the command suite, she toyed with the idea of stopping by the infirmary and checking on the group from Corlon, but decided against it. Most of them would have already settled in for the night. Tavia decided to see them in the morning before the summit began.

Once in her room, she took off her boots and switched on a scanner out of habit. Tavia turned it off again when she heard a knock on her door. She went to answer it and was surprised to find Lela there. Tavia had expected her to still be spending time with her sister.

Lela came in and leaned back against the door. She reached for Tavia's hand and brushed it against her cheek. Tavia closed her eyes and felt the warm rush of excitement as Lela turned her hand over and then lightly kissed the palm. Lacing their fingers together, Lela leaned closer and kissed Tavia's mouth with the same tender curiosity and a gentle, easy exploration of her lips.

Tavia felt lethargic and weak from her touch. Lela tugged at the soft fleshy center of Tavia's lower lip and then gently sucked at the corner where both lips met. As Tavia trembled with desire, she took Lela into her arms and kissed her deeply. It was a kiss filled with passion and longing . . . a kiss that made Tavia's heart pound and her body ache from wanting her. Tavia had no idea how long they stayed that way nuzzling, kissing, and holding each other. The softness of Lela's mouth made Tavia want even more of her, and the little sighing noises that Lela made each time Tavia's lips touched her throat and neck sent tiny ripples of pleasure through Tavia's already throbbing body. Lela was an intoxicating woman, and for Tavia to have her in her arms this way was everything that she had dreamed it would be.

"I want to make love with you," Lela whispered, her voice low and husky. Her hands moved to Tavia's breasts as their kisses again merged into one long, deep swirling exchange of passion. Tavia felt overwhelmed with sensation and pulled Lela even closer to her.

"Please," Lela whispered. "I need to touch you."

Tavia managed to get them into her bedroom without

losing any of the momentum or intensity. Lela urged her down on the bed and kissed her again. Tavia was immediately ready to show Lela how much she wanted her, and she sucked Lela's tongue into her mouth. Tavia loved the way Lela touched her through her clothes, all the while continuing to make those small sighs of pleasure. Lela began taking Tavia's clothes off in a less than subtle way, and in return Tavia wanted to feel Lela's soft, warm skin next to hers as well.

With a steady persistence that never once got in the way of their slow, deep kisses, Lela took the last of their clothing and tossed it on the floor. Gazing down at Tavia's naked body, Lela smiled as she took in the sight of her.

"I've never wanted anyone the way I want you right now," Lela said quietly.

Tavia found it nearly impossible to believe that Lela could be saying such things to her. These were the things she herself had wanted to say. The very feelings she had been having for what seemed like forever.

Lela gently brushed soft brown hair away from Tavia's eyes and took a nipple into her mouth. With a wet fingertip, she circled Tavia's other nipple while she continued to suck and lick the first. Lela took her time, and occasionally she gave Tavia's other breast the same amount of attention.

Again and again they went back to kissing and letting their hands wander as their bodies introduced themselves to each other. Finally, Lela moved one hand down Tavia's belly and inched farther and farther until she cupped her possessively between the legs. Tavia's breathing changed, and she knew she would come quickly if Lela kept this up. But ever so slowly, as if reading her mind, Lela opened her with her fingers and kissed Tavia's hot, trembling body.

"You're beautiful," Lela said as she licked Tavia's breast again and urged her legs open with a hand. "And I didn't expect you to be such a good kisser."

Tavia was beyond words now. Her body was doing enough talking in the way it quivered in Lela's hands.

Lela moved down and kissed the inside of Tavia's thighs and kissed all around the edge of her dark triangle. She brushed her cheek against Tavia's pubic hair and ran her fingers through it. Lela never stopped kissing Tavia's body. Tavia was so aroused that she thought she might be delirious. Tavia opened her legs farther and reached down to touch Lela's head and sift her fingers through her hair.

Lela responded to that with a low moan of pleasure. She spread Tavia with her fingers, and her tongue finally found what it wanted. As Lela began licking with long, bold strokes, Tavia closed her eyes and gave herself over to the most exquisite sensation.

Lela couldn't imagine that they had gotten more than a few minutes of sleep, but she felt remarkably rested and happy when she woke up a while later. Her first conscious thought as Tavia kissed her nose and cheek was that they were very good together. Lela liked waking up with her, and from the way Tavia was once again touching her, she was making it clear that she felt the same way. Even though they had done little talking so far, Lela felt a connection with Tavia that she could neither explain nor deny. Tavia pulled her into her arms and kissed Lela gently on the lips. Lela felt her body responding again, and she marveled at how easily Tavia could make her ready.

"I didn't get a chance to tell you something earlier," Lela said. Turning over on her side so they could see each other better, Lela got comfortable and propped her head up with her hand. "You're such a nice person," she said simply. "I hadn't realized that until yesterday."

"What kind of person did you think I was before yesterday?" Tavia asked with a furrowed brow.

"They call you a princess. I expected you to be spoiled and selfish."

"Oh, I am," Tavia said as her hand caressed Lela's bare thigh. "I feel spoiled and selfish right now, as a matter of fact."

Lela laughed and kissed her quickly on the lips. "I have to go. I want to spend more time with Romney. She and Spence were using my room for a while earlier."

Tavia kissed her and gave her a hug. "I'll find you later."

The next morning Kricorian wasn't surprised to find Lela's bed empty, and she went to the infirmary to see how everyone was doing. Lela and Romney were in a corner talking.

"Good morning," Romney said as she gave Kricorian a kiss on the cheek. They walked around children sleeping on pallets in the middle of the room. "Do you have time to talk before your meeting?"

"Good morning," Lela said to Kricorian. "I'm going to see about getting breakfast for everyone."

Kricorian and Romney went to a table in the corner of the infirmary and sat on top of it. Romney had questions about Ambrose and stated that the children who had been there liked it.

"Where did you find these children?" Kricorian asked. She was still amazed to see so many of them in one place. K Sector no longer had very many children. "How did they come to be with you?"

Romney lowered her voice. "These are Corlon children, but outcasts in Exidor's regime. Once it was discovered that they were all genetically predispositioned toward females, they were selected to be destroyed. There was a woman like us who helped get them safely to the foothills one at a time over a two-year period. Spence, Disto, and I kept them hidden there."

"How long had you lived in the foothills?"

"I was taken there not long after I arrived at Corlon. The group of women I mentioned earlier took several of us there.

We were loved and cared for by women. Once I was old enough to try to escape from Corlon, I realized that other children needed me, so I stayed and carried on with their work."

"Would it have been dangerous to escape?"

"Nothing worthwhile goes without a certain amount of danger." Romney paused and watched the children play and tumble on the blankets. "There were many more who couldn't be saved. It makes my heart ache when I think about them."

"There's only so much you could have done." Kricorian felt a lump in her throat and swallowed slowly. "I'm so happy to have you back."

Romney put her head on Kricorian's shoulder. "I'm very glad to be back."

They continued watching the children play, feeling comfortable in their silence.

"How did some of the children get injured?" Kricorian asked.

"There was a cave-in when a Star Fighter's spidercraft crashed into the area we were living. We had to dig most of them out, and we finally called for help when we saw how badly they were hurt. Luckily the Amtecs picked up our signal and responded." Romney stared at the children as they continued playing on the blankets. "You see how they stay together?" Romney asked. "Have you also noticed that there are twenty-two of them and yet they're still relatively quiet?"

Kricorian was embarrassed to admit that she *hadn't* noticed that before.

"They need a place to run and play and learn how to be kids again," Romney said. "That's why I'm asking you about Ambrose."

Just then Kricorian saw Lela return; Kricorian waved her over.

"Lela is the expert on Ambrose," Kricorian said. "She's been there twice now."

~ ~ ~

During breakfast Lela answered Romney's questions, and Kricorian began to see what was happening. Romney's only concern was for what was best for the children. Her own personal needs were never discussed or even hinted at.

"Are you thinking about staying here?" Kricorian finally asked her.

"The princess and the Amtecs are nice people," Romney said.

"K Sector has nice people. Don't let Ambrose be the determining factor in where you chose to live." Kricorian had never even been to Ambrose, and already she hated it. "K Sector is our home. We can make it your home again too, Romney. It's safer now than it's ever been." She looked around Romney and glared at Lela. "If it's a lake and grass and trees that'll keep children happy, K Sector has the meadow. We can make that the primary place for you to live if you want to stay together."

Romney lowered her eyes and crossed her arms over her chest. Kricorian remembered how Meridith used to sit that way when she had something difficult to say. Kricorian realized then how closely her daughters resembled each other. They both looked like Meridith, only Lela had a reddish tint to her hair.

"Well, what is it?" Kricorian asked. "I know that look."

"K Sector," Romney said. "It has lidium. The raiding will intensify now that it's known how valuable it is." She shook her head and shuddered. "I want the children in a safe place."

"K Sector is safe," Kricorian said. She told Romney about the plans to have an abundance of lidium available at Tracon. She then explained how the lidium deposits were located away from the meadow. "K Sector will be as safe as anywhere else. Maybe even safer since we have a new force field and a greater understanding of what lidium can and can't do."

Romney didn't say anything.

"I feel safe there now," Lela said. "I've been through three raids, but I've also seen the new features that are in place there."

Relieved at having Lela's support in this, Kricorian added, "We'll do whatever it takes to make all of you feel safe there. It's your home, Romney. You belong there with us."

Chapter Twenty-seven

Kricorian was walking a lot faster than usual, which was a sure sign for Lela that she was upset. Saying anything to her now would only make matters worse, but Lela didn't want to go to the summit meeting with so much anxiety in the air. She needed to know why Kricorian was so angry. She caught up with her and matched her stride down the hallway leading to the command suite.

"Talk to me, Kricorian. What are you thinking about?"

"Star Fighters. Lidium. Losing fifteen years with my daughter. *Ambrose!*" she said, practically spitting the word out. "I can't lose either one of you again, Lela. You're the only family I have."

"You aren't losing anyone, Kricorian, but there's a lot

more to consider here than what any of us wants." Lela was grateful to finally have a slower pace. "It's not just me, you, and Romney now. Romney comes with a partner, a friend, and twenty-two children that she feels responsible for. She needs to do what's best for them and not what's best for us."

"K Sector is best for all of us. I'll make sure of that."

By the time they got to the command suite, they were clouded in silence again. Lela knew that once Kricorian was able to calm down a little it would be easier to talk to her. Lela believed that they needed to support Romney in whatever decision she made.

"There you are," Viscar said to Kricorian as soon as they arrived. "We were wondering if your other daughter or one of her friends would be interested in representing Corlon for the summit?"

Lela looked across the room and saw the princess looking back at her. Lela's heart skipped a beat when she saw the smile on Tavia's lips and the longing in her eyes. It would be an interesting meeting today, and Lela reasoned that sitting next to her wouldn't be as easy as it had been the day before.

"Let's get started," Keda said.

"What are the chances of getting this thing wrapped up today?" Meega asked. "I've got work to do and a business to run."

"We all have real lives somewhere else," Keda said, "but we've got a job to do here first."

A message was sent to Romney asking if one or two of them would be interested in representing Corlon, but a message declining the invitation was returned. In addition, two more agenda items were added, which made Meega even testier.

"What's the matter with you today, Meega? Did you have to sleep alone last night?" Viscar asked.

They worked through the agenda and took care of many things, but discussing the lidium issue was proving to be interesting. Kricorian confirmed that K Sector could extract it with some help from the Amtecs. Viscar volunteered Alpha Sector's services to deliver the lidium to Tracon. Then Meega confirmed that she could store it and make distribution easy for anyone who wanted it at no cost. Further discussions came up on why K Sector didn't just extract it, store it, and then sell it from there. Why were all the other sectors getting involved? After all, should just anyone be handling such a dangerous mineral?

"K Sector doesn't want all that traffic," Kricorian said, "and Tracon needs all the traffic it can get. If you come to K Sector for lidium, there's a good chance that's all I'll have for you. But if you go to Tracon to get lidium, there's a saloon, a square full of merchants, and a casino that could benefit from your business. It makes sense for everyone to share in the responsibility, especially if there's no cost involved for the customer."

All but Keda were in agreement with that reasoning. Then Kricorian brought up how she wanted the Amtecs to help. Jaret's name was mentioned, and Kricorian officially requested that Jaret be reassigned to K Sector and put in charge of the lidium project.

"No one else knows lidium the way Jaret does," Kricorian said. "We can't overharvest, and we can't neglect the deposits that are currently rejuvenating themselves."

"Lieutenant Jaret has duties here," Alaric said.

This turned into a heated discussion between Alaric and Kricorian, with Lela finally asking if they could all take a break. There had been moments when Lela had actually forgotten what she knew about Alaric. As the princess had promised, the Cirala Project had indeed captured Lela's attention.

"I agree that we need a break," Keda said.

As everyone was getting up, Lela leaned over to Tavia and

asked if she could speak to her privately. One at a time they went to Tavia's bedroom.

"First things first," Lela said, and then kissed her.

"It's been hard for me to keep my hands off of you out there," Tavia said while nuzzling Lela's neck.

"I have a proposition for you," Lela whispered. She tilted her head back so Tavia's lips could continue exploring her throat. "You transfer Jaret to K Sector, and I'll come here and do my research."

Tavia put her hands on Lela's shoulders. "Alaric says we need Jaret here."

"We need Jaret at K Sector, too."

"Is that the only way you'll come here?" Tavia asked. "Is that the only reason you can think of to *want* to be here?"

Lela didn't like where the conversation was going. "Forget I said anything." She backed away and opened the door. No one had even noticed they'd been gone.

Back out in the command suite, the other delegates had broken into three groups as they stood sampling the refreshments that had been set out. They were all discussing the same thing, so Lela joined the group that Alaric was in and pointedly asked her if Jaret was absolutely indispensable.

"Can't you promote someone else to take her place here?" Lela asked. "You have no one else qualified to do what she does?"

"Forget it, Lela," Kricorian said. She was angry again, and Lela was unaccustomed to seeing her this way. "I have a better idea."

Keda announced that the break was over, and they all returned to the table. The meeting was called back to order, and Kricorian stated that K Sector would keep its lidium and not harvest any of it. They could all find another source if they needed some.

Lela shook her head in disbelief. *That's certainly going to make Romney want to stay there!*

248

"Now let's move on to the next item," Kricorian said. "I agree with Meega. We should try to get finished today."

"I'm not agreeing to any of that," Viscar said, giving Kricorian a meaningful look. "We'll all need lidium eventually and probably a lot more often than we have in the past."

"The majority of it belongs to K Sector," Kricorian reminded her. "We either all share in the responsibility of making it available, or it stays where it is at and no one gets any."

"Lieutenant Jaret is the only one capable of handling it properly?" Sporae asked.

"K Sector is officially withdrawing its previous offer," Kricorian said.

Lela bit her lip to keep from smiling. *She's bluffing! Excellent idea, Kricorian!*

"I say we vote on that," Viscar said. "We vote on whether or not K Sector has to share its lidium supply."

Kricorian and Lela were the only two who voted against the motion. Then Lela asked for a vote on whether Lieutenant Jaret should be sent to K Sector to head the lidium project. The princess gave her a curious look, but the two Amtecs came up losers on that vote.

"What just happened?" Meega asked. "Am I getting lidium or not?"

"You are," Viscar said, "and Alpha Sector will be delivering it to you after Jaret gets it out of the ground for us."

"That's what I thought, but I wasn't sure," Meega said. "Then I have another question. If we make lidium available to everyone, is there a limit to how much is given to each person? What if someone comes in and wants most of what I have in stock?"

"Jaret can work out the details of distribution," Viscar said.

All the other agenda items moved along much more easily, the only snag being the corridor patrol that Alaric had suggested. Tracon had no forces available to help with such a patrol, but a compromise was reached. Tracon agreed to provide a place for the patrols to start and end their various shifts.

"Is everyone happy now?" Keda asked.

"No," the others said in unison. To everyone's surprise, light laughter broke out around the table.

"Compromise, people," Keda said. "We all lost something, and we all gained something. The summit is officially adjourned, and I think we should all congratulate each other and ourselves. Let me also suggest that we do it again this time next year."

Everyone stood up; a few shook hands while others hugged.

"When are we leaving?" Lela asked Kricorian.

"As soon as I can make arrangements to borrow an Amtec transport to bring Romney and the others with us. Alaric," she called. "Can I speak with you for a moment?"

Lela left the command suite and headed for the infirmary to see her sister. She had gotten a clear indication earlier that Romney wasn't quite ready to decide where she wanted to live yet. Lela also wondered if part of the reason Kricorian was in such a hurry to get them all out of there was that she was afraid that Romney might want to stay at the palace.

"Lela!"

Slowing her pace, Lela turned to find the princess following her.

"Kricorian is making arrangements to leave now," Tavia said.

"I know."

"Is that where you're going? You can just leave this way?"

"A lot is involved in all of this."

"You can't leave," Tavia said quietly. "I'm in —"

250

"Come with me to see Romney." Lela held out her hand and urged Tavia to follow her.

"I can't believe you!" Alaric said. "You take my best officer and now you want one of my transports, too?"

"I'll bring it back," Kricorian said sheepishly. "I can't take a chance on leaving anyone here with you people. If word gets out at home about this place, I'll be the only one *left* on K Sector."

"Do you have any idea how hard it's going to be for me to find a replacement for Jaret?"

Kricorian looked at her with a knowing expression. *Yes, my friend,* she thought. *I know exactly how hard it would be.*

Lela and Tavia found Romney and the other two women in the back sitting on the table talking. The children had rearranged a few beds that had been pushed to one side of the room. They were in the process of draping blankets over them making a huge fortress. The noise level was considerably louder, which Lela attributed to the children feeling more comfortable with their new surroundings. Lela had to agree with Kricorian on one thing, though. They all needed to be somewhere safe and stable.

"Is the summit over?" Spence asked.

Lela nodded. "We should be leaving soon."

"It'll be good to be home again," Romney said. "Kricorian has strong opinions about us settling at the meadow. What do you think about that?" she asked Lela.

Lela told her that the meadow was a beautiful place. She looked around and smiled as she watched the children play.

The princess moved in front of her. "You're going back with them."

Lela nodded. "Kricorian needs me now."

"I need you too."

"I'll be back, Tavia."

"When?"

"I'm not sure. I'll have to see how it goes."

Kricorian came in with Alaric and Jaret behind her. She asked Romney if she wanted the children to be sedated before they left.

"No," Romney said. "They can enjoy the trip with the rest of us this time."

"Then is everyone ready?" Kricorian asked. Lela could see how anxious Kricorian was. "I have a transport waiting."

"Then let's go," Spence said. She and Disto went to get the children calmed down and lined up.

Lela looked for Tavia, but didn't see her anywhere. Everything seemed to be happening so quickly. They were actually leaving! She had to find Tavia and explain that she would definitely be back, but that she wasn't sure when.

"Where did the princess go?" Lela asked Jaret.

"She just walked out."

Once Lela and Kricorian were in the hallway and headed toward the reception bay, they met the other delegates going in the same direction. Viscar and Keda carried Sporae on the miniature throne one more time, while Meega had a warrior loaded down with enough luggage to last her a month. The Rufkin leader, however, seemed to be walking in his sleep.

Then Lela saw Tavia standing with Alaric near a transport. Together they were two of the most striking women she had ever seen. Imagining them as lovers made Lela's heart sink. *And here I am leaving them alone together.*

Lela watched Tavia laugh when Keda and Viscar set the little throne down. The princess helped Sporae get into Tracon's spidercraft, and she shook his hand. She stood there while Meega gave her a hug and the usual kiss on the lips. Lela didn't like seeing someone else kissing Tavia. She was indeed a mixture of unsurpassed emotion. Lela couldn't take her eyes off of Tavia as she shook hands with Viscar and Keda. Lela heard the princess offer them an Amtec escort all the way to Alpha Sector to help guarantee their safety.

"Are you going to stand there all day?" Kricorian asked Lela. "We've got twenty-two children to load on this thing before we're going anywhere."

"Can we all have a little less attitude from you?" Lela asked. "You're the only one around here getting what you want."

"What's that supposed to mean?"

"Forget it," Lela said. She picked up one of the younger little girls and gave her a hug before putting her in the transport. Tavia came over to help, as did Alaric and Jaret, and within minutes all the children were on board and getting strapped in.

Romney jumped down to once more thank Alaric for getting them out of Corlon safely, and she thanked the princess for her hospitality.

"Without your help," Romney said, "I would have never found my family again."

As she got back into the transport, Kricorian asked Alaric when K Sector would be getting the Amtecs' best officer.

"Immediately," Alaric said. "Lieutenant Jaret is ready to leave with you now."

The smile on Kricorian's face made Lela feel guilty for having barked at her earlier. *She deserves to be happy*, Lela reminded herself. As she looked up at Tavia, Lela thought sadly, *And so do I*.

"Lela," Alaric said, "it's been a pleasure, as always."

Lela nodded. She still had trouble with the concept of Alaric being a maintenance-free but brilliant machine. *Not to mention being very nice to look at*, she thought.

Jaret saluted both the commander and the princess before she and Kricorian got on the transport. Lela looked into

Tavia's eyes and saw tears. Lela didn't want to leave, but she knew she had to. Kricorian and Romney needed her now, and she had projects to tend to in her own lab.

"Good-bye, Lela," the princess said. She took Lela in her arms and kissed her.

"I'm coming back," Lela said. "You know that, don't you?"

"Sure you are." Tavia let go of her, turned, and walked away.

Alaric and Lela watched her leave, and Lela felt her heart breaking. She turned to get on the transport, and Alaric reached for her arm and stopped her.

"If you don't come back to her on your own," Alaric said, "then I'm coming to get you."

"I'll be back," Lela said, choking on tears that she hadn't realized were even there.

"She doesn't believe it."

"I love her, Alaric. I'm coming back." Lela got on the transport, and Disto helped her close the door securely. It wasn't until she was in her seat and the transport was beginning to move that she let herself cry.

Chapter Twenty-eight

K Sector

Their first night in the cubicle went smoother than Lela thought it would under the circumstances. There wasn't more than a few inches between each person asleep on the floor. Some of the children slept with their arms around each other in spoon fashion, while others lined up in a row. Lela slept in the middle of the room surrounded by the children on pallets, while Disto slept near the door with children all around her as well. Lela had insisted that Romney and Spence take her room so they could have time alone together, while Jaret and Kricorian slept in Kricorian's room. There was no place to walk in the common area, but everyone was too tired to complain.

Lela stretched out in the darkness on the hard floor and kept remembering her night with Tavia. Lela knew what she had to do in order to get back to the palace, and she intended to get things moving in the right direction first thing in the morning. Putting a plan together, she hoped to speak with Romney and get some idea about the type of temporary accommodations that would work best for them until something more permanent could be built. Lela had some resources available to her at the lab, and now was the time to use them.

" 'Scuse me, ma'am," Lela heard a little voice say. " 'Scuse me. Are you awake?"

Lela opened her eyes and saw four children in front of her on their stomachs with their faces propped up with their hands.

"Sure I'm awake," Lela said sleepily. "Who's hungry?"

"We are," about ten of them said at the same time.

"Yeah? So am I." Lela stretched and sat up, all the while wondering what there was to eat. She and Kricorian weren't good at keeping the place stocked with provisions, and it had been nice not having to eat their own cooking over the past few days while they were away at the palace. Someone opened the front door, and Lela saw Kricorian and Jaret come in with breakfast for everyone.

Once they were all fed, Disto, Spence, and Kricorian took the kids outside so they could work off some energy. Lela and Romney sat down at the table and spent a few minutes savoring the quiet.

After a moment, Lela said, "It feels good to have you home again."

"K Sector isn't too much different than I remember, and it feels good to *be* home again."

"What do you see happening now?"

"It's important to all of us that we keep the children together for a while," Romney said. "In a safe place where they can adjust to being free and being themselves."

"Then let me make a suggestion," Lela said.

Romney smiled. "Please do." She reached across the table and held Lela's hands. "It's so strange to see you all grown up. I've always pictured you as the little girl I remembered."

"It's just as strange for me," Lela said.

"Tell me your suggestion."

"We'll take a trip out to the meadow and talk to Ab and Nooley," Lela said. "I'm sure you remember them. It's important that we get their blessing and their cooperation first, but from what I remember, they like children and it'll be a good thing for them as well as for you. Do you want to go to the meadow immediately in some sort of temporary housing until a more permanent place can be built for you? Or would you rather that we make arrangements to find a place for you here, closer to us and the Command Post?"

"Let me talk that over with Spence and Disto. I can give you an answer soon."

Lela squeezed Romney's hand. "Welcome home."

Lela was a little upset at Kricorian's unwillingness to get Romney and the others settled somewhere. When Lela asked her if she expected all of them to live in their tiny cubicle together, Kricorian didn't answer right away.

"You do!" Lela said in exasperation and surprise.

"I just want us to be a family," Kricorian said.

"We *are* a family, but that doesn't mean we all have to live together."

"Your mother would have wanted us to stay together," Kricorian said carefully. "Can't you see that?"

Lela could tell that Kricorian was close to tears. "Listen to me," Lela said gently. She reached for her and took her in her arms. "My mother would have wanted you to take care of us, and you *did* take care of one of us. I think I turned out great," she said with a teasing smile, "and that's all because of you. If Romney hadn't been taken away, you would have been there for her, too."

Kricorian hugged her fiercely, so Lela kept talking.

"We're still a family, and we can be a family and not live together. We can have separate lives and still be part of each other."

Kricorian let go of her. "I know you're right. It's just that I have you both back now. I feel responsible for you. And you have to admit that you don't make good personal decisions sometimes, Lela. You still need me."

Lela chuckled. "That's one thing I can't argue about. But it's my life and I need to make my own mistakes. Just as Romney needs to live her life too."

"You're telling me that you've both grown up?"

"Something like that."

"Well, I don't like it."

"Well, that's too bad." They both laughed.

Lela, Kricorian, and Romney went to the meadow to see their old friends, Nooley and Ab. The women were as excited about seeing Romney again as they were about the possibility of soon having children nearby.

"It's lonely here sometimes," Ab admitted. "We're getting older, and I would like the idea of having people closer to us."

While they were there, Kricorian told everyone what she had learned late the night before. Alaric had sent a message saying that with help from Alpha Sector, the pirates had been located and that steps were being taken to capture them.

"Where have they been hiding all this time?" Romney asked.

"Bravo Sector," Kricorian said. "The survivors who were rebuilding the space station there were imprisoned by the pirates quite a while ago. They're also more organized than we thought. Any message traffic we've received from Bravo Sector over the past several months has actually come from the pirates."

There was silence before Ab asked who exactly the pirates were and where they had originally come from.

"Alaric says they are renegade Star Fighters," Kricorian said. "Exidor's followers who turned out to be greedier than he was. Exidor's earlier claims that the raids were being done by pirates, or troublemakers from outside our galaxy, were his way of hiding the truth about his own army being out of control. It seems as though the same renegade Star Fighters attacked Corlon, their own sector, and did an enormous amount of damage. They took Corlon's lidium supply, only to discover that it was weak and useless. They had hopes of getting Bravo Sector fully operational again." Kricorian took a deep breath. "Pirates have been trying for weeks to find a way into our perimeter so they could get as much lidium as possible. It was just an amazing bit of luck for them that our force field failed while they were in our area."

"How did Alaric get all this information?" Lela asked.

"One of the Star Fighters that the Amtecs captured during our last raid finally talked. Two were taken to Tracon, remember?"

"What's happening to Corlon?" Romney asked.

"There's still a revolution going on. It'll be hard to get information without sending in outside help."

Romney nodded. "There were many Star Fighters who were loyal to no one. They worked for whoever could pay them the most. It was always easy to bribe them and get whatever was needed. I hope one of them doesn't come to power."

"What's the current situation at Bravo Sector?" Lela asked.

"Alpha Sector has the pirates under surveillance," Kricorian said. "Apparently they sleep and eat and live in the only part of Bravo Sector that's been renovated. Their lidium levels are so low that there's no force field. Very little power is left. The space station was reduced to a shell after the last attack several years ago."

"Are the real inhabitants of Bravo Sector still alive?" Lela asked.

"Alaric thinks some of them are. Bravo Sector had people who worked with lidium. They should have been spared, but it's hard to say. I can't imagine that pirates would ask about someone's occupation before they killed them." Kricorian shook her head. "The Amtecs have asked us to provide ten pilots to help contain Bravo Sector's perimeter while warriors go in and round up the Star Fighters."

"Are we sending ten pilots?" Lela asked.

Kricorian nodded. "I asked for volunteers late last night and they left right away. We're waiting now to hear how things went."

There was too little information for Lela to feel good yet, but there was a sense of optimism in the air that gave her hope. She knew instinctively that Alaric was leading the attempt to capture the pirates.

"Does Jaret know what's going on?" Lela asked.

"She knows," Kricorian said, "and of course she wanted to be one of the pilots to go, but I reminded her that lidium had to be her main focus right now. That's the reason so many people have died lately. We can't neglect it again. She eventually agreed with me. She's at Security Central now, waiting for word from Alaric on how things are going. We should hear something soon. Alpha Sector is still monitoring Corlon for any signals, but there's been nothing to report. There's also been some discussion about offering to help with Corlon and Bravo Sector's reconstruction. Alpha Sector and the Amtecs are willing to send people in to evaluate the situation once it's safe to go in again. So as far as Corlon goes, now that Exidor is gone, there might be a way to make some progress with them if someone reasonable takes over."

"Someone just as bad or even worse than Exidor will rise to power," Romney said. "There were too many like him for it not to happen."

"Corlon needs some women in charge," Ab said. Chuckles went around the table as everyone agreed.

After a moment, Nooley pushed her chair away from the table and stood up. "While you're all here we might as well see if there's something suitable out there for Romney and the children. There's plenty of room for everyone."

A place near the trees and not far from the lake was selected for Romney's permanent quarters. It was decided that the temporary housing would be constructed in an area not too far away. The excitement and enthusiasm for the location as well as for the overall vision for what Kricorian and Romney had in mind was incredibly contagious. Nooley and Ab became just as caught up in the planning stages as everyone else had. After viewing a few potential sites, they all returned to the cabin just as Jaret arrived in a spidercraft with news from Alaric.

"Well?" Kricorian said. "Did we lose anyone?"

Jaret was beaming. "K Sector's pilots are helping transport the prisoners to Tracon. Fifteen Star Fighters were captured and another twenty were killed during the Amtec raid."

Relief was instantaneous. Kricorian hugged everyone who was close enough to reach.

"The Amtecs have healers on the way to tend to the survivors at Bravo Sector. About thirty of them were found hiding in a sealed section of a lab." Jaret reached for Kricorian's hand.

"Is it safe to assume that all the renegade Star Fighters

have been found and dealt with?" Lela asked as they headed back toward Ab and Nooley's cabin. She and Romney had their arms around each other's waists as they walked.

"The commander is confident that those causing the problems have been taken care of," Jaret said. "It should be safe to travel again."

A few days later, Lela made arrangements to have the temporary shelter brought to the meadow and erected. Jaret proved to be helpful with getting things set up and finished in a timely manner. The temporary quarters were like a huge, portable insulated warehouse with several individual rooms and a big common area in the middle. Once the work inside was completed, Kricorian delivered a large crate of food, toys, and new clothing.

"Meega sent this," Kricorian said with a smile. "She promised that more was on the way."

"Those red Amtec uniforms for the kids are a good idea," Lela pointed out as she helped Kricorian open the crate.

"They make them look like little convicts," Kricorian said.

"But if they get lost in the woods, it'll be easier to find them if they're wearing red."

Kricorian nodded. "But in the event that we're ever raided again," she whispered, "it'll also make it easier for Star Fighters to find them too."

It was Lela's turn to nod. "Good point."

Finally, Romney and her group were settled, and, to Lela's surprise, Kricorian and Jaret spent their free time, including nights, with them. They had their own room and commuted to work at the Command Post every morning. Lela had dinner with them a few times a week and then went home to her empty cubicle. Kricorian urged her to move out to the meadow with them, but Lela liked being close to the lab and preferred visiting the children instead of living with them. She saw Kricorian and Jaret several times during the day going in and out of the Security Command Post or visiting at the lab for various reasons. Lela also liked the fact that they both still seemed very happy.

One evening after work, Lela went to the meadow for dinner and met two psychologists. Lela knew them both to be excellent in their field, but was surprised to hear that they would now be living with Romney's group. Lela was finally able to get Kricorian alone and ask her what exactly was going on.

"You wouldn't believe the number of women who want to help with the children," Kricorian said.

"So I see." They walked near the lake; it was already beginning to get dark. "Has anyone considered letting some of these women adopt a few of the children?"

"Romney wants to keep them all together."

"The purpose of that being?"

Kricorian shrugged. "Because Romney wants to keep them all together. That's the only purpose I care about right now."

"How long do you and Jaret intend to stay here with them?"

"How long?" Kricorian said. "I don't know. I haven't thought about it."

"So this could be a permanent thing? You and Jaret living here?"

"Why are you asking me all these questions?"

"You seem happy, Kricorian. You and Jaret. Romney and Spence. The kids and the women volunteering to help with them."

"That's true. We are."

"But not all of us are happy."

Kricorian stopped walking. She asked, "What is it you want me to say, Lela?"

Tears welled up in Lela's eyes. She sniffed and put her arms around Kricorian and pulled her close.

"I need for you to tell me it's all right for me to go back to the palace," she whispered. "I can't go there if you really think you need me here."

They let go of each other and began walking again. "How long will you stay?"

"It's not so far that we can't visit each other."

Kricorian nodded. She was crying too. "You won't be coming back here to live." When Lela didn't say anything, Kricorian whispered, "I'll miss you, little one."

Fresh tears rolled down Lela's cheeks. For everything good in her life, there was always a heavy price to pay.

Lela had a sense of urgency about her now. She worked late in the lab every night trying to get her old projects to a place where someone else could take them over, and she was working to finish two new ones before she left.

The first of her new projects was tried out on a small group of the children. It proved to be a success, and Lela hoped that the Amtec four-year-olds would like it just as well. Her second project wasn't quite so easy to test, but the preliminaries were promising.

Lela met with Kricorian in her office at the Command Post and told her she would be leaving soon.

"We still have the Amtec transport you promised to get back to them," Lela reminded her.

"You're right! I forgot all about it."

Lela sat on the corner of Kricorian's desk the same way she had since she was tall enough to reach it.

"When are you leaving?" Kricorian asked.

"In the morning."

Kricorian sighed. Lela knew that if anything else was said, they would both start to cry again.

264

Lela woke early. She had said good-bye to her coworkers the day before and had spent a nice evening with Romney and the others at the meadow. Lela promised to return for a visit soon, and Romney seemed to understand more than anyone else Lela's need to do this.

The morning air was crisp as she made her way to the loading dock where the Amtec transport was sitting. She was pleasantly surprised to find Kricorian waiting for her.

"We said good-bye last night," Lela said. Already she could feel tears threatening.

"I can't let you leave without holding you one more time," Kricorian said. She hugged her tightly.

"I'll be back to see you in a few weeks," Lela managed to say with a sniff. "Take care of yourself."

"You, too."

Kricorian helped her open the transport's door, and Lela pitched her bag inside.

"Guess what I did last night before I went to bed?" Lela asked. She smiled and said, "I remembered that it was my turn to clean the purifier."

Lela heard Kricorian's quiet chuckle as the door to the transport closed.

Amtec Air Space

Lela had met the new patrols in the Intergalactic Corridor earlier and was glad to have them there. She felt safer and enjoyed the company as they talked to each other and helped pass the time. Once Lela was finally into Amtec air space after having asked for clearance to enter, it was only a few more seconds before she had an official Amtec escort to the palace. Lela heard Alaric's voice flow into her helmet welcoming her back.

"Tell me this isn't just a visit," Alaric said. "She hasn't been the same since you left."

"Neither have I."

Lela set the transport down in the Amtec reception bay like she'd been doing it all her life, and then she took off her helmet. Two warriors opened the door from the outside, and Lela jumped down, then reached back in for her bag. She turned around to find the princess there, her eyes glistening with tears as she searched Lela's face.

"You're really here," Tavia whispered. She took Lela in her arms and buried her face in her neck.

"Someone had to bring the transport back," Lela whispered in her ear as she kissed the side of Tavia's head. "And I've got these chewy, nutritious, tasty treats shaped like little Rufkins that four-year-olds seem to just love to eat."

Tavia kissed her, and Lela melted deeper into her arms. She didn't get a chance to tell her about the new shampoo that would help dull Alaric's hair, or her idea about giving Alaric a different kind of uniform . . . something less majestic and a bit more matronly. Or the cream that would promote tiny wrinkles at the corners of Alaric's eyes once they found a way to get her to use it. But Lela never got to say any of that her first few hours back at the palace. The princess had other plans for her.